VEIL OF LIGHT & SHADOW

K.L. PERLEY

To the reader who needs a little nudge into the realm of possibility.

WHISPERING GLEN
RIVERHOLM
RAVEN'S RIDGE
ELDERSMOOR
LARKSPIRE
SILVERVEIL
MOUNTAINS
NORTHERN SHADOWS
SILVERVEIL

VEIL OF LIGHT & SHADOW

K.L. PERLEY

Prologue

The sentinel tossed and turned in his sleep. He wrestled with the silken sheets of his bed, his movements frantic and uncontrolled. Sweat clung to his dark hair, matting it to his forehead as he struggled against the oppressiveness of the night. Despite the autumn air drifting through the open window, its chilly caress brought little relief from his fevered dream.

He traversed through an unfamiliar wood, a place thick with the musty scent of damp earth so potent it coated his tongue. But his body was not his own. The coolness of the group kissed his belly as he glided along the forest floor.

His head swung in a rhythmic motion as his tongue, dark and agile, flickered in and out, tasting the stale air. His serpentine senses homed in on a shadowy figure that beckoned him.

Slithering to the base of the figure's form, he hesitated before ascending the leg of a woman. The rise and fall of her chest held him spellbound. A deep yearning surged within him to nestle against the comforting cadence of her heartbeat. Though the details of her face blurred, her sky-blue eyes pierced through the haze, locking onto his in a shared trance.

Their connection abruptly shattered. But not before the woman's gaze sparked with a flicker of acknowledgment.

Jolted awake, the sentinel gasped for air, his mind clawing back to consciousness. He lay amid the chaos of rumpled sheets, his body bare. An unsettled energy filled the room.

Something profound was stirring, and he knew, with a sense of inevitability, that come morning, his world would never be the same.

Chapter I

Sweat refracted the light from the midday sun as it dripped down Aurora's forehead. She was huffing when she dropped her pack to the ground, disrupting the quietude of her surroundings. She brushed away the wispy curl creeping along her dampened brow and bent over, drawing in a deep breath of forest air as she braced her hands on her knees.

Camryn had found a small clearing in the woods, just large enough to fit their tent and kindle a campfire. Though it was afternoon, the soil was still damp from the morning rain, and Aurora's boots sunk into the earth with a subtle squelch. The sun drew higher in the autumn sky, brushing the top of lush trees, and casting a kaleidoscope of luminous patterns on the forest floor.

September was drawing to a close, but a surprising heat lingered in the air. Aurora's disdain for camping and aversion to long hikes left her unprepared for the unexpected warmth. She wasn't the type of person who ventured miles into the wilderness to embrace the elements for days on end.

Yet here she was. The reason behind this trek into the wild was Camryn—her best friend and recently acquired roommate. She was grappling with the aftermath of the heart-wrenching breakup with her boyfriend of three years, and Aurora was there to offer her support.

In contrast to Aurora's more reserved demeanor, Camryn was the essence of spontaneity. She could embark on a new adventure at the drop of a hat, always eager for the thrill of the unknown.

The warm air penetrated her pores, and Aurora's face twisted into a scowl as she contemplated the lackluster chapters of her own love life. She was nearing thirty, and her most enduring relationship had barely surpassed the six-month mark. She shook her head at the memory of how it had taken her too long to summon the courage to part ways with the un-remarkable man who, with each intimate encounter, emitted grunts reminiscent of a farm animal. Aurora had given him the moniker "Grunter" in her phone before blocking him from her life. Casual hookups had been few and far between since.

A week before their trip, she returned home from work one evening when Camryn ambushed her, bubbling with excitement. She pored over the elaborate plans she had concocted — venturing into the desolate wilderness and spending a weekend traversing along the river. Camryn envisioned this as a soul-reviving escapade, immersing herself in the open air and the thrill of adventure. Aurora secretly longed for a well-planned retreat to a cozy, rustic cottage with the modern luxuries of electricity and running water, indulging in her preferred pastimes of reading, and watching B-rated movies.

Setting aside her personal preferences, Aurora agreed to the excursion. Camryn had been Aurora's best friend since grade school, and they'd seen each other through their darkest times. Aurora was confident that Camryn would make the trip an unforgettable experience. She was the spark in their duo, drawing people to her like the warmth of the sun on a chilly fall day.

Aurora had always admired Camryn's air of confidence. Even among the picturesque beauty of the landscape, she was a striking figure with raven hair cascading like a waterfall of midnight silk down her back. Her eyes, dark and intense, held a spark of unquenchable fire, reflecting a spirit as wild and untamed. Her gaze was penetrating, displaying a willpower that refused to bow or break.

She was a flame in human form, burning bright and fierce, illuminating everything around her with spirited essence.

And if Camryn was the flame, Aurora was the serenity of a spring rain.

She stood in gentle contrast, a portrait of subtlety. Her golden-ash curls framed her face like soft, sunlit waves, cascading in a tumble that danced with each movement. Golden threads wove through her hair, catching the light in a captivating halo.

Her tranquil blue eyes were like an undisturbed ocean. They reflected a world of internal thought and careful consideration. There was a calmness to her gaze that suggested a mind always weighing and measuring the world with a gentle but discerning eye.

Aurora's features were delicate and well-balanced. Her cheeks, fair and flushed, gave her a youthful appearance. Her lips—often pursed in thought—spoke of her reserved and contemplative nature. Her presence was like a calming breeze, soothing and gentle, a stark contrast to Camryn's fiery energy.

Together, they were a study in contrasts—the fiery and the serene, the bold and the cautious—but each complemented the other in a delicate balance.

"This is perfect." Camryn beamed, her hands on her hips as she surveyed the land. "Rory, help me set up the tent, and then we can eat before we explore."

Aurora stifled a groan, but a smile crept across her face as she witnessed her friend's happiness. For weeks, Camryn had languished on Aurora's couch, sorting through the material remnants of her heart's devastation. Aurora had watched her friend become a shadow of herself, going through the motions of daily life. But in this moment, as Camryn radiated cheerfulness and inspiration, the impending two days of primitive camping faded into the background.

"You're the boss. Just give me the orders," Aurora said with playful obedience.

Camryn's smile widened, and she unfolded the tarp to place beneath the tent. The crinkling of plastic cut through the organic melodies of the forest. With a *whoosh*, she tossed it into the air, holding two corners as the free end descended toward the forest floor. Aurora caught the opposite side, and in a coordinated effort, Camryn tossed her the metal stakes to secure them in place.

The aroma of the damp ground assaulted Aurora as she crouched. The sweet, musty smell triggered a pang of nausea. Her legs screamed as she bolted upright, forcing the air from her lungs to dispel the lingering scent.

Despite her nausea, Aurora's stomach growled. She threw Camryn a glance. "What exquisite culinary masterpiece have you packed for our lunch?" she asked. The sarcasm dripped from her tongue as she braced herself for the inevitable mishmash of the camping provisions—none of which promised to be satisfying or appealing.

Camryn expected her friend's dismay at the hodgepodge of trail mix, bread, and almond butter stowed in her backpack. To offset Aurora's disappointment, Camryn had packed a jar of fresh strawberries, knowing they were her friend's favorite. It was a simple gesture of gratitude for agreeing to her wild-haired camping adventure.

With a subtle huff, Camryn settled onto the tarp, pulling the food pack to her lap. She unzipped it and delved into the contents with eager anticipation. "Well, I know it won't satisfy your refined palate, but I got these just for you." She beamed up at Aurora, presenting the jar filled with bright red berries in her outstretched hand.

Aurora's stomach unleashed a low rumble at the sight of the fresh fruit. The three-mile hike to camp had caught up with her. She took a seat next to her friend and grabbed the jar without hesitation. She twisted off the lid, the sweet, delicious scent flooding her senses and chasing away any lingering bout of queasiness. "Thank you," she said with a smile. The gesture had lightened her mood, and she readied herself for the rest of the food stock.

"You're most welcome," Camryn said. "I thought it would pair nicely with the granola and almond milk." From her backpack, she produced a chilled thermos, camping mugs, and spoons, offering Aurora a set. Camryn watched her friend fill her mug, generously crowning it with a handful of berries. "After we settle in a bit, I thought we'd trek down to the river to capture the sunset," Camryn said, her mind buzzing with ideas.

Aurora flinched, thinking of her throbbing feet. She yearned to be cocooned within the warmth of her sleeping bag, hibernating like a bear until it was time to go home. She suppressed her fatigue and mustered a smile. "Sounds perfect," she said.

As they fell into companionable post-meal silence, Camryn sprang up with eagerness. She ventured down a hill for a brief nature call, leaving Aurora to seek solace in the shelter of their tent. As she settled on top of her sleeping bag, she removed her boots, sighing in relief. She rubbed her toes, grateful she didn't feel any evidence of festering blisters.

When Camryn had proposed this escapade, Aurora was happy to rediscover a pair of hiking boots she had purchased on a whim years ago. They had long rested in their box at the back of her closet, a sad symbol of failed aspirations to be more adventurous like her friend. She pulled the boots from her closet a mere week ago when Camryn warned of the imperative need to break them in to avoid painful blisters.

Haunted by the prospect of navigating woodland trails with bloodied and aching feet, Aurora took a proactive approach. The hiking boots became omnipresent in her daily life—seen in the aisles of the grocery store, the silence of the library, and the small marketing agency where she worked. As the night before their departure unfolded, even a casual outing for drinks saw Aurora adorned in the hefty footwear.

Sighing, Aurora eased back against the coolness of her sleeping bag's waterproof fabric. She sank into the gentle breeze that filtered through the mesh windows like a lullaby, soothing her into a tranquil sleep.

When Aurora stirred, there was a distinct chill in the air. With groggy eyes, she untangled herself from the confines of the tent, stepping into the shifting kaleidoscope of the forest. She discovered Camryn perched on a log beside a modest fire.

"Hello, sleepyhead." Camryn's radiant smile matched the flickering flames.

"How long was I sleeping?" Aurora asked, her throat parched.

"About four hours, give or take," Camryn said. "You were out like a light. Didn't even twitch when I was hacking firewood." She gestured to a compact camping ax, its blade embedded in the ground beside her. The chopped wood, though no heftier than Aurora's arms, showcased Camryn's impressive skill.

"Sorry. I hope you weren't bored," Aurora said, contemplating the immense sense of isolation she would feel alone in the wilderness, devoid of modern comforts and conversation.

"Bored? This is my *sanctuary*," Camryn said, extending her arms out wide. "I've scouted the perfect path to the river and found an amazing perch for watching the sunset." Her excitement was palpable, and her eagerness hummed in the crisp forest air. Camryn's zest for finding joy in the simple things struck a chord in Aurora's tarnished heart, reminding her why she loved her friend so much.

Camryn motioned to a nearby stump, inviting Aurora to sit.

Aurora's stomach growled in protest. Camryn glanced at her, a knowing smile playing on her lips. "Hungry much?" she said, her own stomach chiming in agreement.

Aurora chuckled, rubbing her belly. "I could devour a feast right now."

If there was one thing about Aurora, she didn't shy away from food. She'd always had more curves than Camryn's slim form. Aurora enjoyed indulging in delicious food and exploring different cultures through their authentic cuisine. She had prepared her mind for the departure from her usual fulfilling meals for the trip, but not her stomach. She flashed a teasing smirk at her friend. "Are you planning on a dinner menu of foraged acorns and forbidden berries?"

Camryn took the jab in stride and shook her head. "You'd only be so lucky." She reached around to grab the food pack behind her, pulling out a pair of red apples, two protein bars, and a package of turkey jerky. She handed Aurora one of the packaged bars, and the two of them sat in silence while they unwrapped and chewed the first few bites.

Camryn's gaze drifted into the wooded landscape, her thoughts carried away by the untamed beauty around them. "It's like living in a different world, isn't it?" she asked.

With the turn of the seasons, the forest was transforming. The leaves had started to adorn the trees in vibrant shades of amber, russet, and gold. Each leaf danced in the light, creating a canopy that flickered like flames against the crisp, blue sky.

Beneath this fiery crown, the forest floor was a mosaic of fallen foliage, a soft carpet that cushioned every footstep and whispered secrets of the wood with each gentle breeze. The air was cool and fragrant, filled with the earthy scent of damp soil and decaying leaves, mingling with the faint, sweet aroma of distant wood smoke.

Sunlight filtered through the branches, casting dappled shadows that played upon the ground and the gnarled trunks of ancient trees. These stoic sentinels of the forest stood as silent witnesses to the passage of time, their branches outstretched as if in respect to the seasonal transformation.

Aurora shivered. "You're telling me."

"Doesn't it make you wonder what your life would be like if you lived in a different time or place?" Camryn asked, still captivated by the panoramic view. The question lingered in the air, blending with the scent of pine and the distant murmur of the river.

Aurora's thoughts wandered into the realm of hypothetical, and her anxiety rippled beneath the surface. The carefully crafted contours of her life blurred as she entertained existing beyond the boundaries of her own making. *What would her life look like in a different time or place?* The idea unsettled her. But the question drew her into the exploration of alternative possibilities.

Camryn's voice became a muted murmur, as if Aurora had slipped beneath calm waters. She found herself lost in the depths of contemplation.

She surrendered her vision to the canvas of her mind, where she found herself at the base of a mountain. Its obsidian peak soared into the sky, shimmering in the sunlight. Deep green hills descended into a dense forest behind her. A quaint cottage stood before her, its structure constructed from weathered logs. A thatched roof sheltered the home, and a steady wisp of smoke ascended from a robust stone chimney.

In this mental image, Aurora was draped in a silvery-white wool cloak. A smile graced her lips as she contemplated this alternate self, a stark departure from her familiar identity.

She watched the door of the cottage swing open, revealing the warm glow within. A tall, imposing figure emerged, casting a shadow on the sun-kissed porch. Aurora's heart quickened at the sight, and a glint of passion ignited in her eyes. A man with dark boots crossed the threshold, stepping into the dappled sunlight that painted the covered porch's edge.

Aurora's gaze ascended to the robust silhouette, tracing the contours of powerful leather-clad legs and a white linen shirt that offered a glimpse of a sculpted chest. A gentle breeze danced, molding the thin fabric to his muscled arms. Hands bearing the mark of weathered experience emerged from the sleeves, settling against his thighs. As her eyes followed the line of his torso, a glint of metal seized her attention, revealing a sword sheathed at his hip.

Intrigued, Aurora's attention returned to the man's face, where dark brown locks caressed a jawline carved with precision. Just as her eyes explored his face, a sudden jolt shattered the illusion, snapping her back to reality.

Her eyes flew open, and the ambient sounds of the forest rushed back with a swift and unyielding force.

Camryn's brown eyes widened in alarm as they locked onto her friend. "Rory ... don't panic, but a snake is slithering at your feet." Keeping her body stiff as stone, her eyes darted to the ground.

Aurora's mind sluggishly processed Camryn's words. The realization of the situation slowly seeped into her consciousness. Leaning forward, she peered over her knees. Coiled atop her nearly new boots was a snake, as dark as the night. Its robust head glided up along her shin, fixing its gaze on hers. The creature's tongue flickered in and out of its mouth, a hiss accompanying its unsettling presence.

Aurora's chest tightened with panic, an expanding balloon of fear. But the snake's golden amber eyes held her in a trance, stealing her focus.

"Rory," Camryn's urgent voice echoed through Aurora's mind. Thinking about her friend, paralyzed by fear, Camryn scanned the ground for a makeshift weapon. Her fingers closed around a long branch, untouched by the fire. Raising it above her head, she targeted the serpent, determined to intervene.

In a sudden burst, Aurora's right hand shot out from her side, intercepting the descending branch just before it could strike. The spell broke, and she turned her head to see Camryn's startled face.

Her gaze returned to the snake, and Aurora watched as it lowered its head, slithering away into the brush. A sigh of relief escaped her lungs, and she withdrew her hand from the branch still held in Camryn's outstretched arms. The branch fell to the ground with a soft thud.

"Holy shit. What just happened?" Camryn's eyes scanned her friend's face, seeking answers.

Aurora shrugged, uncertainty lingering in her expression. "I don't know. I just had this strange feeling that it didn't want to hurt me, and I couldn't let you bludgeon it to death and risk breaking my foot in the process." She thought of the slithering snake drawn to the warmth of her body. Its scales, smooth and cool, glided across the bare skin of her legs, feeling like a deliberate kiss. The sensation was both chilling and intimate, as if the creature were examining her.

Camryn huffed. "Well, all I could imagine was me dragging your ass through the woods, bleeding to death from a snake bite."

Aurora chuckled. The absurdity of the situation struck her, and she couldn't fathom why her own reaction wasn't one of complete panic and terror. Snakes and creepy crawly creatures usually sent shivers down her spine. But something peculiar had occurred. A distraction, an unexpected calm silenced her fight-or-flight instincts. *Was it the gnawing hunger playing tricks on her mind? Or maybe there was a hallucinatory mushroom nearby, releasing its spores into the air that infiltrated her nervous system?* The situation left her both perplexed yet strangely composed.

Aurora retrieved her uneaten apple from the ground. She dusted it off and took a bite, breaking the lingering tension with a satisfying crunch. Camryn retrieved the bag of jerky from the leaf-strewn ground, both friends finishing their meals in silence after the flurry of commotion.

With the comfort of food settling in their stomachs, Camryn suggested it was time to embark on the short hike down to the river. Aurora welcomed the idea, as the vivid imagery of her alternate reality had consumed the previous hour, interjected with sudden bursts of the snake winding its way up her leg. A change of scenery seemed like the perfect remedy for her preoccupied mind.

Camryn led the way down a narrow trail through trees that stretched toward the fading canvas of a powder-blue sky. Aurora listened in silence as Camryn enthusiastically chattered about future hiking adventures and made a mental note to decline any future invitations. She followed her friend in silence, the sound of rushing water drowning out Camryn's voice.

As they emerged from the trees, a vast limestone ledge spread before them. From their perch, they had a panoramic view of the muddy river below, flowing with purpose some 20 feet away. The water, propelled by a steady current, continued its journey downriver. Aurora's gaze followed the fluid path until the fiery sun, perched just above the water's horizon, blinded her. Despite her internal reservations, she couldn't deny Camryn's choice of location—the view was spectacular.

Aurora marveled at the scenery, the sheer beauty leaving her speechless.

Camryn, noticing her friend's reaction, beamed with pride. "It's breathtaking, isn't it?" She removed her backpack, placing it a safe distance from the edge, and settled down beside it. Aurora folded her legs beneath her and joined Camryn, captivated by the tranquil beauty laid out before them.

Camryn unzipped her backpack and pulled out two plastic champagne flutes. Placing them on the uneven stone surface, she retrieved a small bottle of prosecco, tiny beads of condensation dripping down the chilled container. She peeled off the foil and twisted the wire from the bottle's top. With the gentle nudge of her thumbs, the cork surrendered to her expert touch with a soft *pop*. Bubbles danced in the liquid as Camryn poured the sparkling drink into both glasses, offering one to Aurora.

Raising her glass, Camryn beamed at her friend. "To new adventures and fresh beginnings," she said.

Aurora offered a smile, raising her glass to meet Camryn's with an unsatisfying clack of cheap plastic. "Cheers."

As they sipped the champagne, the crisp fizz of bubbles sent a delightful tickle coursing through Aurora's body. She allowed herself to relish the sensation, closing her eyes. A gentle breeze caressed her neck, and her wispy golden curls swirled along her face. In the quietude, the world around her buzzed with life. When she opened her eyes, a blazing orange sun descended closer to the water, casting a fiery reflection upon the river, reminiscent of flames dancing atop gasoline.

Somehow, Aurora knew that change was on the horizon. Normally, the prospect of something disrupting her equilibrium would cause her to panic. But an undercurrent of exhilaration coursed through her veins, warming her faster than the waning sun. She found herself drawn to the unseen force that beckoned her. Despite her practical nature, curiosity propelled her forward.

As they both watched the sun nestle closer to the horizon, Camryn rose and said they should return to camp before the trail became too dark to navigate. Aurora's mind still buzzed with the lingering effects of whatever had transcended her on that rocky ledge. She was prepared to retreat and take whatever small comfort their tent offered. It had been a day, and she believed that some rest would rejuvenate her mind and body.

They arrived back at camp just as the darkness enveloped their surroundings, prompting Camryn to switch on her headlamp. The combined effects of prosecco and water intake caught up with Aurora, and Camryn guided her to the designated restroom area. Her friend led her a short distance away and handed over an additional headlamp upon reaching the spot.

To Aurora's mortification, Camryn placed a plastic bag in her hand, containing a small cut of cloth. Camryn explained it was for Aurora to use for drying herself and then rinsing with clean water, to be hung up to dry upon returning to camp.

Camryn headed back toward the tent, ensuring her friend knew the way back. Aurora returned a few minutes later and found her friend already nestled inside her sleeping bag, the darkness falling around the camp like a velvet blanket.

As the temperature plummeted, Aurora was grateful for her foresight in packing a sweatshirt and sweatpants for the night. She pulled the tent's zipper closed and quickly layered on her clothing. She tugged the dark sweatshirt over her snug black tank top. Aurora slid off her khaki shorts and pulled on her sweatpants. She kept her socks on for an extra layer of warmth as she nestled into her sleeping bag, facing her friend.

Aurora was on the verge of wishing Camryn a good night when her friend shifted next to her.

"Dammit. Now I have to pee," Camryn said. With an exasperated groan, she cast aside the covers, illuminating the tent with her headlamp. Aurora watched her friend move with intent to the tent's entrance. Camryn tugged on her boots and stepped through the zippered opening. "I'll be right back," she said over her shoulder. Her voice faded into the darkness as she disappeared, closing the zipper behind her.

Aurora stilled in the encroaching darkness, the profound quiet of the wilderness intensifying her sense of solitude. Without her friend's comforting presence, the unfamiliar surroundings became more palpable.

An uneasy tension settled within her. Aurora redirected her focus to the nocturnal symphony of nature. Distant crickets hummed a soft melody, and a gentle breeze stirred the leaves overhead.

Anxiety clawed at her, and Aurora groped in the darkness beside her, searching for her headlamp. Her fingers located the reassuring device, and she clicked it on, securing it onto her head. As the beam cut through the shadows, her heart quickened. An unspoken fear lingered in the vast unknown of the wilderness—an eerie void that heightened her discomfort.

In the hushed night, Aurora strained to hear the slightest sign of Camryn's return. But the rhythmic thudding of her heartbeat reverberated through her, creating a deafening pulse that muffled external sounds. The minutes stretched, and the unsettling silence persisted, surpassing the expected duration of Camryn's absence.

Aurora sat upright, fingers trembling, as she reached for her boots and slipped them on. She grasped the tent's zipper, hesitating before pulling it open. The fabric parted, unveiling the darkness outside. The feeble glow of her headlamp cast a limited radius of light. Only a fraction of the surrounding clearing shone, while the rest remained veiled in shadows, twisting and contorting among the trees and underbrush.

"Camryn?" Aurora's voice emerged in a mere whisper, as if afraid to disturb the silent night. The softness of her initial call hung in the air, dissipating into the darkness. She understood delicacy was pointless and regained her composure. Her next utterance cut through the stillness of the night.

"Camryn?!" Her voice bore more weight, echoing with a hint of desperation, a plea for reassurance in the quiet unknown.

The lack of response heightened her unease, and vulnerability spurred her into action. Determined to find Camryn, she followed the path, illuminated by her trembling headlamp, its weak beam dancing over gnarled roots.

As she ventured deeper into the ink-black forest, Aurora clung to the hope of spotting the reassuring glow of Camryn's headlamp. The terrain sloped beneath her feet, and the air was thick with uncertainty. She pressed on, each step marked by the rustle of fallen leaves and the occasional snap of a twig. The designated bathroom spot must have been farther than her memory served.

Aurora steadied herself with a grasp on thin, prickly branches, the forest path revealing itself in fits and starts. She counted her steps until she reached 100 before stopping. She should have reached Camryn by now. Panicking, she scanned the darkness, realizing that the only companions were the silent trees shrouded in the night.

In a desperate attempt to improve her vision, Aurora clicked off her headlamp and plunged herself into a consuming darkness. As her veil of sight dimmed, her other senses stepped forward to fill the void. The symphony of unfamiliar sounds—rustling leaves and distant animal calls—engulfed her ears. A subtle aroma of damp earth and wet foliage surrounded her, intensifying the sensory experience.

Breathing in the inky blackness, Aurora strained her eyes to find any trace of light. Then, like a beacon in the dark, a soft white glow emerged in the distance. A surge of hope raced through her.

"Camryn!" Her unrestrained voice reverberated through the silent woods.

Desperation fueled Aurora's sprint toward the distant light, her urgency to reunite with Camryn overpowering any hesitation. But the cruel terrain had other plans. Without warning, the ground vanished beneath her, hurtling her into a chaotic descent. In the disorienting free fall, the once-visible light slipped away.

Limbs flailed in a wild ballet, boots colliding with an unyielding surface. The impact sent Aurora sprawling forward. The abrupt shift in momentum propelled her into a dizzying somersault, her body careening through the untamed wilderness. Twigs, rocks, and leaves became frenzied companions in her endless tumble.

Every inch of Aurora's body collided with the unforgiving ground, and her mind braced for the inevitable fatal blow. This couldn't be the new beginning she had envisioned. Consumed by anger at herself for succumbing to the allure of uncertainty, Aurora's violent descent abruptly halted, and she landed with a furious thud on solid stone.

The icy surface seeped through her battered body, chilling her to the core. In the aftermath of her fall, Aurora envisioned death as an imminent companion. She was keenly aware of the stinging scratches on her skin through her tattered sweats, and each limb throbbed in pain.

Sprawled on her back, she gazed up at the bright white moon hanging low in the clear night sky. Despite the circumstances, she couldn't deny that it offered a serene view of her solitary final moments in the unforgiving wilderness.

She closed her eyes, attempting to quiet the swirling chaos in her mind, and a gentle sound reached her ears—the soft trickle of water nearby. Aurora cautiously turned her head and opened her eyes to behold a small stream flowing just beyond her feet. A warm and wet sensation crept toward her brow, prompting her to touch her forehead. When she withdrew her hand, the deep red hue on her fingertips and the metallic tang of fresh blood assaulted her senses.

The sight of her blood sent her head spinning once more, and she was grateful she was already lying down. Determined to divert her thoughts from the unsettling sight, she refocused on Camryn. She must have heard the intensity of her fall. A shiver ran down Aurora's spine at the prospect of her friend discovering her battered body. She swallowed hard, contemplating the disturbing scene that might await her friend.

Aurora's hand returned to her head, confirming the inevitable—the loss of her headlamp during her chaotic descent. Eager to gain a better understanding of her surroundings, she took a deep breath and clenched her teeth, bracing herself as she shifted onto her elbows.

Her strained breathing and the throbbing ache in her torso suggested several bruised ribs. Gazing across the glistening stream that flowed at her feet, she saw a rocky ledge on the opposite side, ascending to rolling hills. The moonlight highlighted fields of grass swaying softly in the breeze, creating a serene backdrop to her unexpected predicament.

Nothing in Aurora's surroundings offered a hint of familiarity. Unease settled over her like a heavy fog, and she yearned for the sight of her friend rushing down the hill.

Pain coursed through her body, and she held her breath, summoning all her strength to sit upright. Panting, she prepared herself for the challenge of standing. Inhaling deeply, she forced her trembling body onto its feet, muscles and bones protesting. Tears streamed down her dirt-streaked face as she turned to inspect the landscape she had tumbled down.

Her eyes beheld a 50-foot ravine of jagged rocks and twisted saplings. The forest at the ravine's summit stood as a wall of thick trees, their branches grasping at the darkened sky. A desperate gaze scanned the tree line for any sign of Camryn, but the familiar silhouette was absent. Something was amiss.

"*CAMRYN!*" Her voice erupted from deep within, tearing through her lungs. The anguish stretched her chest and sent searing pain coursing along her ribs. Aurora vibrated in agony, and not just from the physical toll. But from the fear and unsettling revelation that she was no longer in the familiar wilderness where she and Camryn had set up camp less than 12 hours ago.

Her desperate scream echoed through the ravine. Overwhelmed by the profound understanding that she was in unfamiliar territory, Aurora collapsed against the cool stone. She lay there, her breaths coming in ragged gasps, grappling with the crushing weight of isolation. Or so she thought.

CHAPTER 2

Aurora's sobs ceased late into the night, her chest aching deep within her bones. When she had no tears left, she closed her eyes after one last glimpse of the full, brilliant moon.

Despite the warmth heating her face and the light peeking through her lids, Aurora willed her eyes to stay closed. To shut out the reality they'd reveal when she let them open. But the sound of water trickling over stone and birds chirping from their perch in a nearby tree nudged her further awake. She lay on her back in the open air, the pain of her battered body roaring to life, reminding her she hadn't just awoken from a nightmare. She was returning to it with her consciousness.

She blinked back tears. Her throat burned with thirst, and she scooted a few feet to the edge of the stream. She dipped her hand into the icy water, bringing it to her cracked lips, and swallowing it down by the handful.

Aurora became more coherent with every frigid sip. She splashed her face, rubbing the dried blood and dirt from her forehead. She pushed back from the stream and lifted her face to the sun. The rays penetrated her skin and ignited her cells, warming and waking her body little by little.

She relished the sun's warmth before her stomach growled with hunger. She imagined what Camryn would say of her never-ending appetite. Aurora tried to remember the last thing she ate. *Was it the dry protein bar Camryn had handed to her before the trance with the snake?* Aurora was uncertain of how many hours had passed since then.

A dull ache twisted in her stomach. She didn't know where she was or what food she would find. But she had a critical choice to make. She could stay where she was and hope someone would find her soon, or she could go looking for help and food.

Her entire body hurt, and the steep incline of the ravine kept her from traversing back up from where she had fallen. She looked at the gentle hill beyond the stream, rising to fields across the ravine. Fear threatened to root her to the ground as she clung to the hope Camryn would come racing down after her.

Aurora closed her eyes as if shutting off her sense of sight would direct her mind's eye to the correct course. She took a deep breath and a gentle brush tickled the back of her hand. She opened her eyes to find a large yellow and black butterfly resting on her hand. Several seconds passed as she watched its wings open and close before it took flight, lifting skyward toward the rising sun.

Maybe the winged insect knew something she didn't. Or maybe she was delirious from hunger. But Aurora took it as a sign. A life preserver from the gods. She turned and hobbled along the uneven ground downriver in the direction of the butterfly, letting the sun warm her with every step.

Her legs ached and strained beneath her, and the heat of the sun bore down on her more severely in the cloudless sky. Aurora noticed the widening of the stream. She stopped for a break and watched the sparkle of the flowing river, eyeing other movements beneath the surface. She stepped closer to the water's edge and saw silver scales shimmering in the sunlight. Several fish about the length of her forearm swam together in the river. Her stomach clenched with hunger at the sight.

Aurora cared little for fishing and never had much luck with a fishing pole, but her stomach reminded her of the prospect of food. Without the luxury of equipment, she scanned the riverbank to see if she could find a stick to use as a spear.

She approached the rocky shore, and her eyes caught sight of a branch, long since fallen and lying among the stones. With a purposeful stride, she picked it up and tested its heft, gauging its suitability. One end of the branch bore jagged ridges, evidence of its violent separation from its mother tree. Aurora scoured the waterline with a keen eye, hunting for the perfect tool to sharpen her weapon—a jagged rock. She plucked a promising candidate from the ground, its weight familiar and reassuring in her hand.

She perched herself on a large boulder and positioned the branch with the jagged end against the stone's surface. Determination etched across her features, she wielded a sharp edge of the rock as her improvised chisel. With each forceful strike, the rock collided with the wood, the sound echoing through the quiet wilderness.

Aurora persisted, her efforts amplifying with each impact. The violent blow of the rock on the branch rang out in the secluded space. Nature bore witness to her relentless pursuit.

Amidst the repetitive thuds, a distinct snap echoed through the air, signaling a breakthrough. Aurora paused and examined the branch. A lingering splinter clung to its end. With a calculated tug, she pulled the thin wood away, revealing an imperfect point at the tip of the branch. A proud smile split her cracked lips.

Empowered by her makeshift weapon, Aurora limped toward the water. The oblivious school of fish continued its undisturbed dance in the river's current. With an unwavering focus, she selected a solitary fish at the center of the group, preparing to unleash her primitive hunting skills.

Positioned about three feet away from her target, Aurora gauged the distance with a keen eye. She channeled her energy and retracted her arm, the spear poised for action.

In a swift and calculated motion, she propelled the sharp end of the stick into the water. The sudden movement shifted her weight, and she found herself precariously balanced on the uneven rocks beneath her feet.

Aurora tightened her grip, clasping both hands atop the branch. To regain equilibrium, she shifted her weight back. The rocks beneath her feet became treacherous terrain, and for a fleeting moment, she thought the river might claim her. Aurora wrestled for control, restoring her stability and dispelling the imminent threat of a watery plunge.

Her effort lacked all traces of grace, a clumsy disturbance that sent the fish scattering in different directions. Aurora lowered her gaze to the stick submerged in the water, but the ripples distorted the view of her makeshift spear. With cautious anticipation, she withdrew the sharpened end from the water's grasp, hoping to discover a successful catch. Her heart dropped when the realization hit—what she thought might be a successful capture turned out to be nothing more than a clinging clump of river mud.

Despite Aurora's lack of affinity for the outdoors, her stubborn nature reared its head. The idea of leaving the river without a fish was unacceptable. She staggered back to the boulder, frustrated tears threatening to spill out.

She tugged off her boots, now molded to the contours of her feet. She peeled off the thick wool socks that shielded her toes and placed them beside her on the rock. Her bloodied knees glistened in the sunlight as she rolled up her sweatpants—a patchwork of holes and random slits. She slowly rose to her feet and moved toward the water, acutely aware of each step.

The chilly water nipped at her toes. Step by step, she plunged further into the stream, noticing the fish had returned to their unbothered state. She took one more careful step and halted. Her gaze fixated on a particular fish, its tail methodically moving to maintain its position while others swam around it.

As Aurora concentrated on the fish, the world blurred around her. She could almost hear the gentle swish of the fish's tail beneath the water. She kept her attention on the aquatic creature mere inches from her ankles.

Her surroundings froze, and a delicate tickle traced the back of her neck. It was as if an elastic had snapped, and her arm descended with the wooden spear, cutting through the water in eerie silence. Her eyes remained locked on the target, witnessing the sharp edge of wood penetrate the silvery scales.

Aurora lifted the end of the branch from the water and observed the fish that had moments ago been peacefully swimming in the river, now wriggling on the pointed wood. Her initial reaction was one of horror, contemplating the violent end she had brought to the fish's life. But the sentiment didn't last long, as her need shifted to pure survival when her stomach churned with hunger.

She limped back to her boulder and retrieved the jagged rock that helped craft the spear.

"I'm sorry," she whispered, as she looked into the fish's round, glittery eyes, before bringing the rock down at the base of its skull, putting an end to its thrashing.

Aurora lingered in thought, uncertain of her next move. She'd never been one for raw sushi, always leaning toward the comfort of fried rolls. She drooled at the thought of a Las Vegas roll dipped in soy sauce. This was a far cry from that.

She surveyed her surroundings and spotted an embankment a few yards from the river, leading to a thin tree line beyond. The thought crossed her mind—*Could she gather wood and start a fire to cook the fish?* But the growls emanating from her stomach reminded her of the urgency of her hunger.

Aurora looked at her fresh catch before employing the sharp edge of the rock to slice it open. Peeling back the skin revealed bright white flesh. Without a second thought, she picked a small chunk from the bone and placed it in her mouth. She swallowed quickly, her primal instincts took over, devouring the fish within a matter of minutes.

Though far from satiated, Aurora acknowledged she was no longer in the grip of starvation. She closed her eyes as she allowed her stomach to settle. She basked in the sun's warmth.

A forceful huff near where she sat interrupted her brief solace.

Her eyes snapped open, and her head swiveled to witness a black bear padding toward the river. The creature positioned itself about ten yards to her left, moving in a diagonal path.

Aurora's breath hitched, and she found herself caught in a tense stillness. The unwritten rule echoed in her mind—*never run from a bear.* Her options were a cruel joke: remain still, hoping the bear would amble past, or summon the strength to appear larger and louder, an intimidating act meant to ward it off. Even standing was a challenge, leaving her unable to transform into anything more formidable than the bear approaching her with unsettling ease.

The bear paused at the edge of the water in the very spot Aurora had occupied just minutes earlier in her quest for food. She realized the hungry creature likely lurked nearby when she speared the fish, recognizing the tantalizing scent of blood in the stream. A wave of horror swept over her as she looked down, discovering a delicate trail of the fish's blood still clinging to the rock's surface below. The remnants of her recent catch rested at Aurora's feet.

The bear's snout dipped toward the rocks, and Aurora caught the distinct sound of it snuffling the earth. Fused to the ground like granite, she watched in tense silence as the bear lifted its head, directing its snout straight toward her. A lump formed in her throat, and fear gripped her. She dreaded the unsettling possibility that her recently consumed meal might make an unwelcome return journey.

Her heart thundered in her chest, the rapid beats pulsating in her ears. The bear swayed its head in a deliberate rhythm toward Aurora. Each impact of its powerful limbs against the earth caused its black fur to ripple, catching glimmers of sunlight. The bear's menacing claws, several inches long, held a threat that made Aurora shudder at the mere contemplation of their touch. Tears welled in her eyes, and the overwhelming realization that this might be her fateful end gripped her once more.

In the heart of the unfamiliar wilderness, a journey meant for adventure and camaraderie now unfolded into a solitary struggle against the imminent threat of a bear mauling. Thoughts of her friend echoed in the silence as the unsettling notion of a tragic end clawed at her consciousness. In that precarious moment, she couldn't help but ponder the fate that awaited her—alone and far from anyone who knew her. Questions loomed in her mind—*Would she ever be found? Would her absence become a haunting mystery, a tale of a vanished life without closure for those left behind?*

Five feet away, the bear's mighty presence pressed upon her. Its warm breath brushed against her exposed legs. As tears spilled over her eyelids, a cacophony of primal sounds erupted—both animal and man entwined in a thunderous symphony. The unmistakable clopping of hooves echoed along the water bank, adding an unexpected layer of urgency to the already tense encounter with the imposing bear.

Above the thundering hooves of the racing horse, an even mightier roar resounded—a deep, booming voice.

"YAH! YAH!"

Aurora and the bear swiveled their heads in unison, drawn to a cascade of spraying water and the imposing silhouette of a figure astride a dark horse, swiftly closing the distance between them. The bear, squaring its body to face the oncoming rider, unleashed a sharp roar. The stranger, undeterred, pressed forward, causing the bear to retreat step by step.

As the figure advanced, closing the gap with the retreating bear, a sword materialized from the space beside the horse's left flank. The sleek metal, catching the sun's rays, cast a sharp glare into Aurora's sky-blue eyes, prompting her to shut them against the blinding light.

The thunderous symphony of galloping hooves and the commanding voice of the approaching man roared through her. When she dared to open her eyes, the scene had shifted—the bear, spurred by the imposing presence, sprinted away from the river, vanishing into the shelter of the woods.

Aurora, perched on the boulder, grappled with the shock of the chaos that unfolded in less than a minute. She realized she had been holding her breath, and as she released a pent-up rush of air, a dull ache settled in her chest.

She looked at the man, who had halted his horse at the woodland's edge, ensuring the bear's retreat. With his back to her, Aurora seized the moment to study her mysterious savior. Dark boots and pants flanked each side of the robust horse, while a sweeping black cloak cascaded from the man's shoulders. His deep brown hair, touched by slight waves, dusted the nape of his neck.

Once the man saw no lingering threat, he directed his horse toward Aurora with a subtle nudge of his heel. As he approached, she eyed the captivating details of his features. Each contour of his masculine face was sculpted with precision. A sharp jawline held a hint of stubble. His lips were softly sloped, and deep, golden eyes emitted a warmth underscored by authority.

His long lashes cast fleeting shadows over high cheekbones. A nose, ever so slightly bent, hinted at the tales of adventure that had sculpted his character. In the aura of his presence, time itself paused, allowing the world to recede into a distant backdrop, leaving only the magnetic appeal of his captivating features in focus.

An uncanny sense of familiarity tugged at Aurora in the presence of the enigmatic stranger. He halted his horse before her, his gaze never wavering from hers. The sun, positioned above him, cast a halo around his head. It was then that Aurora noticed her gaping mouth. A hot flush traveled from her stomach to her face, painting her cheeks with a blush.

"Are you injured?" echoed the man's robust voice.

Aurora sat speechless, her eyes locked onto the towering figure astride his horse. With no words escaping her, the man surveyed their surroundings with visible concern before refocusing on Aurora's face.

"Are you hurt?" he asked again. His voice, now tinged with urgency, jolted her out of the initial shock, prompting her to shake off disbelief.

"Not really, no," she muttered.

The man glanced down at Aurora's tattered pants and the scratches and bruises that were visible on her bare skin before returning his gaze to her face.

A fresh wave of embarrassment cascaded over Aurora, the realization settling in that her spoken assurance didn't align with the visible truth of her physical appearance. "I, I mean, yes, I am a little hurt. But it's not because of the bear."

A look of curious concern spread across his face, and the man swung his leg over the rear of his horse, dismounting with ease. Aurora couldn't help but be startled at his swiftness. He took a few measured steps until he stood an arm's length away. Even without the elevation of his horse, Aurora saw his height was imposing, surpassing six feet by a few inches.

"How did you get here?" he asked, noticing her tattered clothes and hiking boots that were placed at the base of the boulder she was sitting on. His eyes scanned their surroundings before he returned his gaze to her, awaiting her reply.

Aurora struggled to pinpoint the origin of the distinctive cadence in his authoritative voice.

"I was camping with my friend, and she left to use the bathroom, and then she never returned to camp. I went looking for her and I lost my way in the dark. Then I slipped down a ravine and landed by the river a little way back." Her voice rushed out like a flowing faucet.

"And then this morning, I was so hungry, so I followed the water in search of food and caught a fish, and then the bear came, and you showed up just in time to save me from being mauled to death." She paused, taking a breath to steady herself.

"I just want to go home." The words spilled out in a torrent like a dam had burst open. Tears welled in Aurora's eyes as she released everything she had been holding onto. She looked up at the man, cheeks reddening for her emotional outburst.

The man's concerned look remained, but his eyes and voice softened. "What is your name?" he asked.

"Aurora. My name's Aurora," she stammered.

A glimmer of compassion broke through his lingering suspicion. "Aurora, it's a pleasure to meet you. My name is Soren, and I would like to help you. I know a place with warm food and someone to tend to your injuries.

When you're settled, we can talk about how you ended up here and how to get you back home. Will you come with me?"

Aurora's eyes flickered to his outstretched hand, her gaze lingering on his face for a moment. Though his eyes maintained a softness, the tightness of his jaw hinted at a persistent concern.

"Where am I?" she asked. Her eyes scanned the man's unusual attire and noted his undistinguishable accent with suspicion.

The man took a deep breath, and his focus narrowed. "You're in Silverveil, which I'm guessing is a long way from your home. I'm happy to explain everything to you once you're cared for."

Aurora considered the weight of the events of the last several hours and looked at the man's waiting hand, raising her own to grasp it. The back of his hand bore the marks of weathered experiences, but the touch of his fingers and palm radiated a comforting warmth and softness.

She wondered if she had slipped into a coma when she fell down the ravine and her mind was playing a cinematic fantasy while she healed. But there was something about the man's face that comforted her, and she couldn't detect any harmful intentions in his amber eyes.

She sighed. "Okay," she said, her chest sinking with exhaustion.

The man's lips curved into a gentle smile. "That's good."

In a single, fluid motion, he drew Aurora toward him. He slipped his other arm under the back of her knees from the top of the boulder, scooping her to his chest.

"Oh!" was all that could escape Aurora's lips.

With Aurora in his arms, he took purposeful strides toward his horse. He lifted her effortlessly to the horse's back. She turned to see Soren collecting her discarded socks and boots from the rock and securing them in a satchel attached to his horse.

He gestured for Aurora to edge forward, and she shifted, wrapping her arms around the warm neck of the horse. In response to her touch, the horse nickered.

"Aurora, meet Ash. The bravest horse in the land, though wary of new company. Don't worry, though, by the time we reach the village, he will be wrapped around your finger." Soren smiled, shifting his gaze from his horse to Aurora.

She returned a nervous smile, still clinging to Ash's neck. The memory of the last time she rode a horse surfaced in her mind—she was fifteen when her dad dragged her and her sister to the Grand Canyon, embarking on a daunting ride atop a mule to the bottom of the canyon. It was a journey fraught with fear. As she clung to Ash, Aurora silently hoped they wouldn't traverse any steep ridges, conjuring memories of the anxiety-laden experience.

With graceful ease, Soren mounted the horse. Though his body didn't touch hers, Aurora straightened at the warmth of him on her back. A shiver coursed through her. Witnessing her reaction, Soren unclasped the thick, black cloak from his back and delicately draped it around Aurora's shoulders.

"Thank you," she murmured. Pulling on the fabric, she wrapped it snugly around her body. The scent of open air, earth, and smoke wafted from the cloak, but intertwined within was a sweet whisper of jasmine that clung delicately to the fibers.

Silent as the rolling hills around them, Soren reached around each side of Aurora's body, taking hold of the horse's reins. A tingling sensation ran up her spine from the proximity. His presence was like a warm blanket in the cool air, comforting and intimate. With a subtle nudge from his boot, the horse trotted into a leisurely walk.

Nestled in front of Soren, Aurora found herself in a dizzying sense of security and exhilaration. The rhythm of the horse's gait was soothing, a gentle rocking in perfect harmony with the tranquil scene around them. She could feel the steady heartbeat of the horse beneath her, a comforting, constant pulse that matched the quiet beauty of their surroundings.

But she didn't know what to make of her situation. It went against all logic. She had never heard of Silverveil before, though she wasn't too familiar with the area Camryn had chosen for their camping excursion. It was like Soren knew that Aurora had somehow traveled far from home with a simple tumble through the forest.

Though uncertain of where Soren was taking her in his medieval-looking clothes on horseback, Aurora watched the landscape unfold. She tried to note certain landmarks of the area in case things went south and she needed to escape from the stranger. The trees stood tall, their leaves whispering secrets she couldn't hear in the gentle breeze. The air flowed with the subtle sounds of life—a distant bird call, the rustle of small creatures in the underbrush.

Questions swirled in her exhausted mind, but Aurora felt a growing sense of peace with every stride of the powerful horse beneath her. The worries and fears that had clouded her mind were distant now. She turned her head to glance up at Soren, his features softened by the golden light of the sun, and gratitude for this stranger moved through her. He'd found her. Saved her.

The horse's hooves drummed a soft rhythm on the ground, a poetic cadence in the quiet expanse. Each step echoed the uncharted possibilities of Aurora's journey, reflecting her courage to venture beyond the familiar and into the heart of the unknown.

Chapter 3

The rhythmic sway of the horse's gait cradled Aurora into a peaceful rest, prompting Soren to secure his hold around her waist to prevent any chance of her slipping off. As the sun made its descent toward the western horizon, the light hit the rooftops of a nearby village.

Soren slowed his horse to a halt outside the doorstep of a cottage on the village's outskirts. Delicate plumes of smoke drifted from the stone chimney, carrying with them the soothing fragrance of burning herbs.

With a gentle hand securing the small of Aurora's back, Soren dismounted Ash, cradling Aurora's limp form against his chest. They approached the cottage, and Soren tapped his boot against the thick wooden door. He took a breath as a latch clicked, and a small cutout swung open. Curious green eyes regarded Soren and his slumbering companion, initial scrutiny softening into understanding. The hatch slammed shut and with the mechanical turn of metal, the door swung open.

In the doorway stood a stout woman, her round rosy face framing inquisitive emerald eyes. Fiery red curls twisted into a low bun, while an apron sat atop her billowing skirts.

"Oh my. What have we here?" The woman's voice carried the same melodic accent as Soren's.

"I found her this morning along the river, about to be eaten by a bear," he huffed. "She has some injuries I was hoping you could tend to and perhaps provide a new set of clothes." Soren gently laid Aurora down on the small bed nestled in the corner of the cottage. His eyes filled with concern as he looked at her.

"Of course, dear," the woman said as she assessed Aurora.

"Thank you, Clara," Soren said. His expression remained weary as he pulled out a wooden chair from the kitchen table not far from the bed. His eyes remained focused on the peacefully slumbering Aurora.

The woman immersed herself in the task at hand. She gathered fresh cloth and tiny bottles from her shelves lined with various vials and dried herbs. With a kettle of water in tow, she poured a gentle stream into a small bowl. Clara approached the still-sleeping Aurora, placing her array of supplies on a small table by the bedside. Submerging the cloth into the warm water, she dabbed away the dirt and dried blood from Aurora's legs with a healer's practiced touch.

As Clara's nimble fingers worked, Aurora stirred. She lifted her eyes to see the curvy woman tending to her wounds. Clara turned her gaze toward her patient, an air of gentle concern in her eyes.

"Well, hello there, love. I'm sorry to have disturbed you, but I wanted to treat your injuries straight away." Clara's soft and comforting melodic voice enveloped Aurora.

As Aurora scanned the unfamiliar cottage, she turned her head to spot Soren sitting at the table in the kitchen area. The sight of him put her at a surprised ease.

Clara followed Aurora's gaze to Soren, then shifted back to her patient. "Yes, Soren brought you here, to my home, so I could care for you," she said. "I am the healer of the village. Not to worry, you're safe now." She offered Aurora a reassuring smile.

Dizzied by the surreal scene unfolding before her, Aurora settled back onto a lumpy pillow, her head spinning with disorienting thoughts. *Did I die in the fall, and my spirit was now enduring some peculiar fantasy?* Her rational mind grappled with the odd circumstances.

Clara chuckled softly at Aurora's unspoken thoughts. "No, you are not dead. You are in Riverholm and are very fortunate that Soren found you when he did. Starvation and bears are only the beginning of the troubles you could encounter here." Her words hung in the air, painting a mysterious world in Aurora's mind.

Aurora's eyes flashed to Clara, bewilderment etched across her face. She took in the woman's appearance—her curvy, stout figure. The way she moved exuded a quiet confidence as if she drew her strength from the earth itself. Her skin had a warm, earthy tone that complemented her fiery red hair. Her eyes were a striking shade of green.

Aurora's gaze fell on ears that tapered to fine points, peeking out from the woman's hair. *What the hell is going on? I've lost my damn mind.*

Clara's lips, full and expressive, curved into a knowing smile. "I can assure you, your mind is not lost, even though your body may be," she said to Aurora's shocked face. "We call it The Listening, and very few are fortunate enough to hear the thoughts of others." Soren's gaze stayed indifferent, but he nodded in agreement.

Aurora couldn't help but wonder if he also had the same ability to delve into the mind, her cheeks warming at the memory of her first thoughts when she first met him by the river.

Clara's laughter rang out before she continued, "No, Soren does not share my gift. He has his own blessings." The woman gave Aurora a cheerful wink, and she marveled at the golden flecks that danced in Clara's emerald eyes.

The air in the quaint cottage was charged with otherworldly energy, leaving Aurora to wrestle with the realization that she was amidst individuals not like herself. She looked down at her cleaned skin and healing wounds. "Thank you," she whispered, unsure of how to proceed with that information.

She licked her lips, her throat burning with thirst. Clara filled a small glass with water and brought it to Aurora's mouth, supporting her head as she sipped. The water was refreshing, with a subtle hint of sweetness that quenched Aurora's parched throat.

"My name is Clara," the woman said, as Aurora drank.

Aurora gulped down the last of the water. "I'm Aurora," she said, wiping her lips with the back of her hand.

"Pleasure to meet you," Clara said. "What a beautiful name. A bright, breathtaking light." Her warm smile cast a glow of hospitality over the humble cottage.

Aurora blushed. She'd never been fond of her name. As a child, she struggled to find pencils or keychains with 'Aurora' on them, leaving her wishing her parents had named her something more common, like Ashley or Rachel. "You can also call me Rory. It's a nickname most of my friends and family use," Aurora said, feeling a sudden twinge of sadness thinking of the people she cared for.

"Ah, a name that is nice as well, yet I don't see it as fitting for such a beautiful woman with golden locks." Clara gently touched Aurora's matted hair.

Aurora glanced over at Soren, confused by Clara's comment. "Rory has ties to the color red and is typically a male's name in our lands," he explained.

Aurora blushed. She had never considered the meaning behind the nickname. Camryn started calling her Rory back in grade school, and she had always seen it as a shorter alternative to Aurora.

"Rory may be fitting after all," Clara said, her keen observation catching the hint of embarrassment in Aurora's flushed cheeks.

Aurora cleared her throat and shifted her gaze from Soren back to the healer. Clara returned her attention to Aurora's battered body, warmth and empathy in her eyes.

"We should finish cleaning you up and get you dressed in a fresh set of clothes," Clara said, her eyes turning to Soren.

Aurora met Soren's amber gaze.

"The gentleman will take his leave, of course." Clara's stern voice echoed through the one-room cottage. Soren held Aurora's gaze for a moment longer before rising from the table.

"Of course. I will be just outside," he said, making his way toward the door.

"I could use a fresh bucket of water from the well. You can fetch some while you wait," Clara said. Her voice, though soft, carried an air of authority as she shifted from host to healer.

Soren turned back toward Clara, his eyes briefly meeting Aurora's before he lifted a wooden bucket from the floor next to the fireplace. With a silent nod, he strode from the cabin.

"He's a quiet one," Clara said. "But beneath his hard exterior, there is a gentle soul who loves the land and the people he protects." Clara's voice softened. She reached for Aurora's free hand and placed her other behind Aurora's back. "Up you go." She pulled gently, guiding Aurora into a sitting position with practiced care.

Clara repositioned Aurora's legs until they dangled over the edge of the bed. With a reassuring hold on Aurora's hand, she guided her into a standing position. She paused, allowing Aurora to find her balance. In a seamless motion, Clara bent down and pulled at Aurora's tattered sweatpants, guiding them to her ankles. Aurora stepped out of them and Clara retrieved the discarded garment, inspecting it with mild curiosity before shifting her gaze back to Aurora. She then reached for the threadbare sweatshirt that hung loosely on Aurora's body. She lifted the hem of the garment over Aurora's head and dropped it on the bed.

Aurora stood clad in a pair of black bikini-cut underwear and a ribbed tank top that was cropped just above her navel. She shifted on her feet as she waited for Clara's next instruction, a subtle awkwardness lingering in the air.

Clara moved around to Aurora's back and reached for the hem of Aurora's torn tank top. "Arms up," she demanded.

Aurora lifted her arms without protest, only her ribs groaning from the movement. She sucked in a breath. With a gentle pull, Clara pulled Aurora's top over her head, peeling the black fabric from Aurora's body. She shivered as the air kissed her bare skin.

Clara strode to another area of the room. The whisper of fabric moving against the floor was the only sound drifting across the cottage. Moments later, she reappeared, careful to approach without intruding upon Aurora's exposed state. She held open a gown, its neck opening wide. She guided the dress over Aurora's sculpted legs, lifting it with a fluid motion over her curved backside. The fabric whispered upward, caressing Aurora's skin in its ascent. Aurora slid her arms through the sleeves, the soft fabric of the gown cascading down to kiss the floor.

Clara surveyed her handiwork. The fabric, delicate and cool, accentuated the lines of Aurora's form as it pooled softly at her feet. The gown clung to every contour of her body, leaving little to the imagination.

Aurora couldn't contain the whirlwind of questions churning in her mind, and her words spilled forth. "Who *are* you people?" she asked. The question hung in the air. She added, her voice now a hesitant murmur, "I mean, I'm clearly not in the same place that I came from. And you and Soren are ... are different." Her eyes flickered to the narrow points of Clara's ears that poked through her red hair.

In response, Clara's eyes mirrored a thoughtful contemplation. After several moments, Clara sighed and met Aurora's gaze. "Yes, you certainly are far from home," she said. "This is the realm of Silverveil, as it has been since the Mother above cast down a bead of magic, willing it into existence." The rosy-faced woman chuckled. "And as for Soren and me, well, we are fae, just one of many types of beings that live in these lands."

"Fae … like fairies?" Aurora asked. She couldn't believe the words coming out of her mouth.

Clara laughed. "More or less, though not precisely as mortal storybooks may have portrayed."

Aurora's curiosity bubbled to the surface like a long-suppressed spring—overriding all semblance of logic. "So, you have powers … or magic? Isn't that what fae means?"

Her mind drifted back to the countless evenings she had spent isolated at home with a book, the smell of aged paper and ink enveloping her as she pored over stories. In those pages, she had journeyed through fantasy realms, her heart dancing alongside tales of the fae—beings of a world parallel to her own, yet so vastly different.

She remembered the depictions of these ethereal creatures, each story painting them in a light both mesmerizing and cautionary. The fae were beings of great power and mystery, guardians of ancient magic that flowed through their veins like the lifeblood of the earth itself. They were the whisper in the wind, the flicker in the flame—entities bound to the natural world in ways no human could fully understand.

Aurora's mind swirled with images of moonlit dances under starry skies, of fae with wings flitting through the night. She recalled tales of them wielding magic that could bend the very fabric of reality, creating illusions so vivid they could ensnare the senses, leaving one lost between worlds.

Aurora found herself at the threshold of myth and reality. The stories she once used to escape to now blurred what was real with fantasy. With her heart caught between wonder and disbelief, Aurora stood on the cusp of an adventure that seemed to have leaped straight from the pages of her beloved books.

A light flickered in Clara's eyes as she beheld Aurora's vision of the fae. "To be fae means our existence entwines with magic, and each of us wields its gifts uniquely. I am blessed with the ability to hear the words that dance within others' minds, along with the gift to mend injuries and banish sickness," Clara said.

"And Soren?" Aurora whispered.

"Soren's power lies in his connection to the land and the elements of our realm, and he is a fierce protector of all the beings who make up our world." Clara's gaze pierced Aurora's as she spoke. Aurora absorbed Clara's words, a shiver coursing through her. "And, unfortunately, no wings for either of us." A mischievous grin played on her lips.

Aurora stood speechless in her fresh gown, a slight shudder vibrating her body. Clara retrieved a thick bundle of material from a trunk at the foot of the bed. Aurora watched, relieved as Clara returned with a heavy woolen garment. She slid a grey sweater over Aurora's head and guided her arms through the fabric, pulling it over her torso. The thick sweater fell below her waist, caressing her backside.

Satisfied, Clara helped Aurora settle at the table when a single knock echoed at the door.

"May I come in?" Soren asked.

Clara winked at Aurora. "Yes, we are decent."

Soren opened the door and strode across the threshold, a full bucket of water sloshing in his right hand. His shirt sleeves pushed to his elbows, revealed forearms a shade or two paler than his sun-kissed face. Taut muscles flexed beneath the skin, exposing bulging veins that stretched the length of his arms. He placed the bucket next to the hearth and stepped back, his intense gaze appraising Aurora's new look. She couldn't help but glance down as the warmth of his eyes scanned the length of her body. He huffed with satisfaction at the improvement in her attire.

Aurora shifted nervously and watched Clara bark instructions. She directed Soren to boil a pot of water over the flame while she fetched various herbs and spices from her cupboards. Aurora squirmed in her seat like an uninvited outsider. Her fingers trembled as she unfastened the hair tie that held her curls captive. A few strands escaped and draped across her face, but most of her hair remained in a tangled mass, matted together with dirt and dried blood.

Before Aurora could feel embarrassed about the sorry state of her locks, Clara reappeared behind her seat, cradling a small pitcher of warm oil and a brush crafted from wood and dried horsehair. She tilted Aurora's head back. Aurora closed her eyes as Clara poured the soothing liquid onto the crown of her scalp, letting it seep into her hair. With each careful stroke of the brush, Clara methodically detangled the knots, and Aurora could feel the weight of the day gradually dissipate from her body.

Soren, too, couldn't help but notice Aurora's transformation. Her face, once marked by caution and worry, had softened. While he had initially sensed her vulnerability by the river, it was under the soft glow of Clara's candlelit home that he felt as though he were truly seeing her for the first time.

Bathed in the gentle radiance reminiscent of the sun's first light, Aurora exuded a celestial allure that captured his gaze. Her eyes, fixed on the wooden beams above her, were blue like a serene summer sky. Long lashes brushed against her cheeks like heavenly wisps, each freckle like stardust scattered across her complexion.

Aurora sensed a watchful presence and turned to meet Soren's gaze. This time, it was the typically stoic man who experienced a sudden rush of embarrassment. He promptly diverted his attention to fiddling with bottles on the table. A soft smile graced Aurora's lips as she reveled in the closest thing she expected to a spa treatment, shutting her eyes in bliss.

With her hair now freshly detangled, Clara rinsed away the oil using water infused with the soothing fragrance of lavender. The scent had a hypnotic effect on Aurora, and she sat by the fire to let her hair dry. Clara, satisfied with the progress of her broth simmering over the flame, efficiently cleared the table. She then instructed Soren to retrieve three bowls and spoons from her cupboards.

Aurora watched the two moving about the cottage. The whimsical beauty of the scene captivated her. Despite the questions swirling in her mind about the place she found herself in, a sense of tranquility enveloped her. She belonged to this moment and time—a feeling both surreal and strangely comforting.

A large wooden table dominated the central space, scarred with years of use. On the wall nearest the bed and kitchen stood a modest fireplace. The glow cast a gentle light that danced across the room and warmed the small space. Nearby, a wooden shelf held an assortment of curious items—crystals, a well-thumbed grimoire, and a small cauldron.

In Clara's humble home, time moved differently, as if in tune with the natural rhythms of the earth and the forest, sparking a shift in equilibrium that Aurora couldn't ignore.

The trio gathered around the table. They sat in silence for several minutes, savoring the hearty broth Clara had prepared. A loaf of bread garnished the center of the table, its irregular shape adding to the charm of Aurora's presumed delusion. Letting her stomach roar louder than her skepticism, Aurora tore off a sizable portion of the bread, relishing the warmth of each bite as she dipped it into the rich broth.

Aurora was renewed with every morsel. She turned her attention to Clara, her curiosity burning through her skin. "How did I get here? How can I be in my world one moment and another in the next?" Her gaze shifted to Soren, who furrowed his brows in contemplation.

"You tumbled through a rift in the veil that separates our worlds," Soren said.

"Veil? ... Like a portal?" Aurora asked. "How is that possible?" She was aware of the look of disbelief on her face.

Soren's potent gaze lingered on Aurora's astonished expression. "The formation of tears remains a mystery," he said. "We don't know how, why, or when it happens. Only the powers above can answer that."

So, this must have happened before.

"Do people fall into your world often?" Aurora couldn't hold back the assuming tone in her voice.

Soren chuckled a low rumble that sent a tingling sensation down Aurora's spine. "It's not every day that the veil swallows people and spits them out here, but it happens more than we'd like. We call them 'travelers.' Records of travelers to our land date back hundreds of years." His amber eyes flickered with further knowledge.

Aurora's head swirled. *Hundreds of years?* She thought of how many people had just up and vanished from her world over time, never to be seen again. Maybe this is where they went, unbeknownst to anyone on their side of the veil.

"What happened to them?" Aurora asked, her curiosity demanding answers.

Soren's eyes turned dark, and Clara's face fell solemn. "I have not known a traveler to return to their realm," Soren said. "But that doesn't mean it isn't possible. I will do everything I can to get you back home safely. Tomorrow, we will visit my friend who can counsel me on the best route to return you home." His voice held an air of concern.

Aurora's heart sputtered as she lingered over his words, and terror laced her voice as she whispered, "Did they die?" Her blue eyes pleaded with Soren, searching for reassurance. His gaze held hers, unable to speak.

Clara, sensing the dark turn the conversation was taking, answered, "Ah, well, that is a tale for another time, my dear. You've had quite the day. Not to worry yourself. Soren and I will do everything in our power to see you safely return home. And no one is more knowledgeable about the rifts in the veil than Thorn. You should rest so that you can seek your answers tomorrow with a clear mind."

Aurora wanted to continue the discussion, to demand answers for what she was learning was an impossible way to get home. But she saw the sympathy in Soren's eyes, and the thought of pressing further made her sick to her stomach.

Soren rose from his chair. "She may have the bed at my home if she wishes," he said. He glanced down at Aurora, trying to hide her trembling body under her crossed arms.

Clara waved her hand dismissively across her face and responded, "Nonsense. You're a generous lad, Soren, but that dusty old place of yours is not fit for a lady recovering from injury. I have an extra mat I can unroll for myself. She needs a comfortable bed to rest her bones." Clara smiled at Aurora and then began to clear away the dishes from the table.

Aurora, wanting to busy herself to take her mind off her predicament, attempted to rise from the table to offer help. However, the pain in her ribs still throbbed, and her head spun with the abrupt movement. As she reached for the back of her chair to steady herself, she missed it by an inch. Sensing herself tilting toward the floor, a wave of a familiar scent—jasmine and smokey earth—wafted over her, accompanied by a warm grip around her elbows. Her back cradled softly against a broad, sturdy chest, and a warm breath, touched by a hint of sweetness, brushed her cheek.

"Whoa, easy now," Soren said. "I've got you." His deep voice was a gentle rumble that vibrated through the air. A spark ran down Aurora's spine, sending bursts of electricity to every blood vessel in her body.

Her breath hitched, and she murmured, "Thank you. I'm okay."

They stood there frozen in time, two bodies molded together before Soren helped Aurora into a standing position. He ensured she was steady before he lowered his warm hands from her body. As he turned to face her, his tall frame towered over her.

The sudden rush of blood to her cheeks painted them a rosy hue, casting a glow that brightened her entire face. Her blue eyes locked onto his.

Soren knew, in that moment, that if anyone could make it back through the veil, it was her. He would see to it.

He clung to the moment before exhaling, eyeing Clara emptying their used dishes into a bucket of water. "Very well. I will return first thing in the morning. Clara, you know where to find me if you need anything." He paused to look at Aurora, a promise blazing in his eyes. "Good night, Aurora. Sleep well."

The sound of her name rolling so hypnotically off his tongue made her catch her breath once again. "Good night, Soren ... and thank you." She offered him a shy smile, holding his gaze until he offered a respectful bow to the women and swiftly exited through the door of the cottage. Aurora's eyes lingered on the threshold until she heard Clara rustle behind her.

Her flustered reaction to Soren's hands on her body made her think she had actually lost her mind. She was falling deeper into the crafted illusion. She thought sleep would be good. Perhaps falling asleep in this reality would wake her up in her familiar one.

With Clara's help, Aurora hobbled to the only bed. Her host unrolled a thick mat next to the fire and settled in with a heavy blanket and lumpy pillow.

The soft glow of the fireplace dwindled, and before she knew it, Aurora heard the gentle cadence of Clara's soft snores. The familiar sound brought her comfort, grateful to not be alone in the eerie silence of the night.

The rhythm of Clara's breathing provided a comforting backdrop, and Aurora shut her eyes. Attempting to quiet her mind proved futile as images of Soren rode the currents of her thoughts. *His dark-brown hair fell to his chin and accentuated his jawline, drawing her attention.*

In her mental replay of the day's events, his entrance unfolded in slow motion. *The sun cast a spotlight on his breathtaking features and bronzed skin. Golden eyes ablaze with fury and focus locked onto hers, a rigid jawline and determined lips further etching his presence into her memory. As he passed on his horse, he briefly turned to meet her gaze before redirecting his attention to the ferocious threat that menaced her.*

Aurora's pulse quickened, her thoughts leaping forward to when Soren had acted with swift gentleness, catching her before she plummeted to the floor. The warmth of his hands and the proximity of his body ignited a heat deep within her stomach. His scent enveloped her senses. The mere utterance of her name by him was like a guttural roar. The intoxication of breathing him in left her mind swirling in a heady dizziness.

Her breath came in uneven gasps as a barrage of vivid mental images played through her mind. The onslaught left her grappling to comprehend the unprecedented intensity of her reactions to the man she had just met.

This wasn't the familiar territory of her carefully curated world back home; it was a place where she felt an unsettling lack of control. The unfamiliar surroundings unleashed a newfound liberation, and her body responded in ways she couldn't entirely fathom. The objectifying glimpses of Soren were merely the first ripples in this strange tide of sensations.

Nestled in a bed in the corner of a cottage straight out of one of her storybooks, Aurora slept—mostly hoping that when she woke, she would be in the comfort of her own bed. But she allowed a tiny part of her brain to tumble down the rabbit hole of what would happen if she followed this reverie. She'd opened the door—if only a crack.

Chapter 4

Aurora's eyes fluttered open to the sight of Clara moving with an elegant grace in the kitchen. The gentle morning light streamed through the window, bathing Clara's features in a warm, radiant light. Her auburn hair fell in a cascade of tight spirals down to her mid-back, each lock catching the light like a living ember weaving through the rustic ambiance of the cottage.

Clara's laughter echoed across the room, a melodic response that reminded Aurora that her thoughts were not private. "I hope I didn't wake you, dear," she said. Her voice, soft and comforting, drifted through the air.

Aurora shook her head, easing into a sitting position on the bed. "No, not at all."

"I assume you slept well? I didn't hear you stir," Clara asked with a knowing smile.

Aurora realized that the tantalizing images of Soren had swept her into a peaceful slumber. Her cheeks flushed with acknowledgment.

"I apologize," Clara said. "I try not to intrude into others' thoughts. But sometimes, the words just sing to me, like a distant song in search of a listening ear." She smiled softly at Aurora. "I will do my best to block them out while you're here."

Aurora smiled back with appreciation. She swung her legs over the side of the bed and touched her toes to the cool wooden planks beneath her feet.

Her golden curls cascaded over her shoulder and framed her face. She lifted her hands to run her fingers through the voluminous waves, wondering about Clara's magical touch.

"Oil of olives, burdock root, rosemary, and a touch of lavender." Clara's gentle voice echoed through the cottage as she handed a small bottle to Aurora, who accepted it with gratitude.

As the herbal elixir settled in her hands, Aurora's thoughts drifted to Camryn, whose absence was palpable. Such a potion would have captivated her. The very idea of it—the blend of rare herbs, the whispered incantations that might have been used in its creation, the ancient knowledge distilled into a single vial—would have sparked a light in Camryn's eyes, a light that Aurora missed more than she cared to admit.

Aurora set the vial on the bedside table and the weight of her friend's absence settled on her. She tried to keep the grief off her face as she thought about how terrified Camryn must be, unable to find her, having to return to civilization to seek help. A lump formed in her throat as she thought about causing her friends and family such heartache. She could only imagine the panic her mom would be experiencing by now.

A pressing physical need shifted her focus, as the consequence of diligent hydration announced its presence. Aurora's eyes swept over the quaint confines of the cottage, searching for any sign of a restroom.

Clara, clearly not sticking to her privacy pledge, asked, "Nature calls? There's a small outbuilding behind the cottage."

Aurora smiled and rose from the bed, stretching. She was pleasantly surprised that her battered body could move with little protest. She tested her steps, finding them steadier than expected as she navigated across creaking floorboards.

The cottage, charming in its rustic simplicity, had cooled in the morning air, prompting Aurora to wrap a thick woolen cloak around her shoulders.

She approached the front door and pulled it open, stepping from the muted light of the cottage into the brilliance of the morning. The sun, already bold and bright, enveloped her in its glow, overwhelming her vision. She lifted her hand to shield her eyes and stepped forward, embracing the promise of a new day.

As Aurora's eyes adjusted to the brightness, her hand traced the outline of the cottage, her fingertips guiding her around its exterior walls to the back. The small shanty designated for nature's call awaited her, nestled in the edge of the tree line. As she moved toward the awaiting restroom, a captivating sight in her peripheral vision made her pause.

Soren, a silhouette of strength and purpose, stood with an ax raised high above his head, the muscles in his arms tensing. The resounding thwack echoed through the air as the ax met the unyielding resistance of a thick log. His discarded cloak lay crumpled at his feet. Clothed in dark pants and sturdy knee-high boots, he had left his linen shirt unbuttoned, revealing a glimpse of his sculpted chest.

Aurora found herself entranced by the spectacle—the rise and fall of Soren's chest, the play of sunlight on his bronzed skin, and the sheer strength emanating from him as he split wood. It was a vision that etched itself into her consciousness, an unintended display of power and grace in the quiet morning air.

A gentle breeze wafted by, coaxing loose strands of his hair to flutter and adhere to his face. As beads of sweat formed on his skin, shimmering like tiny jewels, Aurora found herself mesmerized by the exhibition unfolding before her. Her hand drifted to her chest, where her heartbeat pulsed in sync with the rhythmic thuds of the ax as it met the wood with a determined force.

Soren, amid his wood-splitting endeavor, caught sight of Aurora. His surprise mirrored hers, and he halted his motions to acknowledge her.

"Good morning, Miss Aurora," he said, his tone a mixture of genuine surprise and something else.

A blush crept up her cheeks. "Good morning, Soren. I was just looking for the ... um, um," she hesitated, embarrassed to express her urgent need to relieve her full bladder.

Soren's gaze shifted from Aurora to the outhouse, and she thought she detected a subtle hint of a smile crossing his lips, an unspoken acknowledgment of a very human necessity.

"Of course. I was just cutting some wood for Clara, as she demanded," Soren said, lifting several chopped logs with ease. With purposeful strides, he moved toward Aurora, his presence engulfing her in that familiar scent. His gaze rested upon her. "I shall see you inside."

As he brushed past her, Aurora caught another trace of the earthy and intoxicating scent that clung to him. She nodded before turning her attention to the small outhouse nearby. While the restroom situation wasn't luxurious, it was a step above what Aurora had experienced in the woods with Camryn. Grateful for the relative privacy, she stepped inside, closing the door behind her with a sigh of relief.

***

The cabin welcomed Aurora back with the enticing aroma of fresh bread and cooked eggs. Soren sat hunched over the table, engrossed in his breakfast, while Clara hummed a cheerful tune. Soren's attention drifted from his meal as Aurora entered, her presence lighting the room. He turned to watch her in the doorway, captivated by the cascade of golden curls framing her face.

Soren glided from his chair and moved around the table, pulling out a chair for Aurora. She watched him, surprised and somewhat uncomfortable at his unprompted act of chivalry. It was a large departure from the typical manners of the men she knew back home, and her resolve as a strong, independent woman.

She approached him, her movements slow as she considered him. But there was something touching about his act of courtesy, a silent acknowledgment of her presence and worth in his eyes. Aurora suppressed the urge to scoff, and her lips curved into a soft, genuine smile. "Thank you," she said.

As she took her seat, she couldn't help but feel a novel sense of being pampered. She found Soren's chivalry surprisingly endearing.

Soren's amber eyes remained fixed on Aurora. As she settled into the chair, the comforting aromas of the morning meal enveloped her, creating an ambiance of warmth and homeliness, and her heart twinged.

Aurora's stomach growled at the enticing scents of a hearty breakfast wafting from the table. Spread out on the roughly hewn wooden table lay an array of dishes, each more inviting than the last. The centerpiece was a large iron skillet, sizzling with thick slices of bacon, its edges crisped to a perfect golden brown. Next to it, a heavy, cast-iron pot bubbled with a hearty stew, a medley of root vegetables and tender chunks of meat simmering in a savory broth infused with herbs.

Eggs, cooked to perfection with their sunny yolks, offered a vivid splash of color. Freshly baked bread sat sliced on a board. A mug of peppermint tea rested next to Aurora's hand. Steam rose in gentle curls, carrying with it the comforting scent of home and hearth. Beside it, a dish of golden butter and a pot of dark, fragrant honey awaited.

Unaccustomed to such a lavish breakfast prepared for her, Aurora set aside her usual hesitation and indulged in the meal. Soren watched her with lighthearted amusement.

While Clara's lively voice filled the room, Aurora found it difficult to pay attention, her focus consumed by the delightful flavors of the food. It was only after she had polished off her plate that she glanced up to notice her hosts' smiling faces.

Aurora wiped her mouth with the back of her hand. She took a deep gulp of her warm peppermint tea, its steam carrying the crisp, revitalizing scent of the herb, accompanied by a subtle, grounding earthiness. Although she longed for a hot cup of coffee with a splash of almond milk, the tea was a novel comfort.

Gathering her thoughts, she turned to Soren with a question that had been lingering in her mind. "If you're fae, why don't you have pointy ears?"

Soren's eyes snapped to her, pausing mid-chew on a succulent piece of bacon. Clara nearly choked on her tea, barely preventing it from spraying across the table.

Aurora, surprised by their reactions, looked apprehensively at Soren, worried she might have offended him.

After a reflective pause, Soren said, "Some don't regard me as a true fae, even though both of my parents were pure-blooded, high-caliber fae." Aurora noticed a fleeting shadow of anger flicker in Soren's amber eyes.

Clara cleared her throat. "It's quite the enigma," she said. "When I took Soren in as a boy, he was the only one in the village missing the distinctive fae trait, and he faced mockery from the other children because of it. But hearing the stories of his parents, I can assure you he's every bit fae." Her eyes filled with a maternal warmth, hinting at a bond that transcended mere bloodlines. Aurora noted this detail in her mind. A question for another day.

Clara explained, "The theory is that his lack of pointed ears is simply a physical anomaly and has no bearing on his abilities."

Aurora's cheeks flushed. "I'm sorry ... I didn't mean to offend you," she said, her blue eyes filled with remorse.

Soren's amber eyes fell on her. His voice was soft, but reassuring. "It's no bother. No offense taken." He managed a strained smile before returning to his meal.

"Are there humans who live in this realm?" Aurora asked.

Soren met her gaze. "There used to be, centuries ago. They've since ... vanished." His voice was low.

"What do you mean? How does an entire species just vanish?" Her mind was processing the information faster than words could escape her lips. "Did they all just *die*?" She wasn't liking the odds of being a foreign human in these lands.

Soren's solemn expression did little to comfort Aurora. "The lore is that they were ... exterminated from our realm hundreds of years ago by a tyrant king who no longer resides in our realm." *Well, at least there was that silver lining.*

She was the lone mortal human in Silverveil, alien to the mysterious realm, and she was putting her faith in otherworldly beings to deliver her to a tear in the veil that would return her to her world. Fate certainly had a twisted sense of humor after Aurora had spent her life having tight control over its trajectory.

Something grim lingered in the air for the rest of breakfast. After the meal, Soren informed Aurora they would ride into the village to meet with Thorn, whom he said could help with Aurora's questions and help in returning her home.

Soren had brought a change of clothes for Aurora when he arrived this morning. Practical riding pants, leather boots that reached her knees, and a snug sweater. She was grateful to change out of the somewhat revealing nightgown Clara had clothed her in.

As they readied themselves to leave, Clara crafted an herbal tincture for Aurora, designed to further reduce the swelling of her bruised ribs. The effectiveness of the concoction surprised her. The subtle pain that had lingered this morning was now almost nonexistent. Sensible fae magic.

The air in the cottage buzzed with an undercurrent of anticipation and uneasiness. Clara, with thoughtful foresight, packed a collection of elixirs and a substantial number of nourishing provisions for their journey. Aurora felt a pang of melancholy at the thought of leaving the sanctuary of Clara's cottage. She looked at the compassionate fae woman who had provided her with such diligent care. Eased her fears with her innate warmness. Aurora wondered if that was part of her power as a fae healer. Soren stepped outside to tend to his horse, affording Aurora and Clara some privacy for their parting words.

Clara extended the bundle of supplies, wrapped in sturdy fabric, toward Aurora. The healer's kind eyes fell on her. There was a depth in Clara's gaze, a silent communication that reached deep into Aurora's soul. Aurora, in response, took the time to truly see Clara, her eyes tracing the features of the woman who had become her unexpected guardian. Clara, only slightly taller than Aurora, was a picture of nurturing strength. But what captivated Aurora the most was a soft, golden aura that enveloped Clara, hugging her form in a luminous display.

Aurora's attention focused on this extraordinary light, noticing how it pulsed under her gaze. Accompanying this visual marvel was a faint, melodious sound, reminiscent of the gentle melody of wind chimes in a soft breeze. It was a mesmerizing display that left an imprint on Aurora's mind, a lasting image of Clara's enchanting and radiant presence.

With the bundle of goods placed in Aurora's arms, Clara held up a long cloak. Aurora looked at the white fabric adorned with threads of gold that shimmered in the early morning light. It was beautiful.

Clara draped the garment around Aurora's shoulders. She secured it in the front with a delicate golden clasp crafted to resemble two twigs entwined. As Aurora touched the exquisite piece, she couldn't help but marvel at the craftsmanship. Despite the thickness of the cloak, it rested lightly on her back.

Overwhelmed by the thoughtful gesture, Aurora whispered, "Thank you. It's beautiful." Her eyes lingered on the shimmering cloak.

Clara, radiating with pride, said, "Well, I thought such a beautiful item befits a beautiful woman like yourself." Her smile was filled with admiration. "I can't predict where your journey will lead you, but this should offer you protection and warmth along the way."

Aurora's heart swelled with gratitude. "Thank you so much for everything. Your kindness has been ..." She had no words for the compassionate woman. "I'll ensure Soren returns this to you when I find my way back home."

Clara gave a gentle nod. She glided toward the door with a purposeful stride, signaling it was time to set forth on the next chapter of their adventure. In the doorway of the cabin, Aurora wrapped her arms around her new friend, sharing one last smile before stepping outside. Soren stood just beyond the entrance of the home, loading Ash with saddlebags.

"You take great care of her now and come home safe," Clara barked to Soren, her maternal tone full of concern.

With one hand holding Ash's reins and the other resting against the horse's shoulder, Soren turned toward the woman and nodded. "Of course," he said. The sunlight bathed his face, revealing the thinnest of lines around the corners of his eyes. Aurora tried to imagine how an unrestrained smile would brighten his impassive face.

She strode to where he stood next to the horse, finding him mesmerized by the shining cloak she wore on her back. His eyes shifted to Clara, who nodded.

Soren offered out his hand, which Aurora grasped without hesitation. She was impressed at how effortlessly he lifted her onto the horse, as if she were as light as a feather.

Once Aurora settled near the top of the horse's back, Soren leaped on, grabbing the reins and pressing his body lightly against Aurora's back. She stiffened in response, tingling as blood coursed under her skin. Aurora turned and gave Clara one last smile.

With a subtle nudge from Soren's boots, the horse began its stride forward. It wasn't long until Clara's cottage dipped below the horizon at their back, and before them, several others appeared. The first few cottages Aurora saw were much like Clara's—small, square buildings made from a mix of wood and stone. Cozy, like out of a storybook. Aurora chuckled at the absurdity of it all. It was as if she had inadvertently stumbled across the grounds of a Renaissance festival.

As they rode on, the structures became larger and taller—the trade buildings of the village. She heard the clang of metal on metal and smelled the fresh scent of worked leather. Just ahead, Aurora spotted a market, with farmers and shopkeepers lined up with their daily goods. People moved about, many of whom took no stock of Aurora or Soren riding through the town.

Children ran about in front of the horse's path, mothers chasing behind, scolding them. Aurora spied the distinct fae ears among the townspeople, and the children giggled and watched the riders go past. She gazed down at them, mesmerized by their ethereal beauty that stood out from her muted human features.

Before long, Soren guided Ash to a halt in front of a towering stone building. A wooden sign, carved with the image of a feathered pen crossing a compass, swayed over the door and hinted at the nature of the establishment.

Soren took the lead, ascending a brief series of steps to reach the entrance. As Aurora trailed behind him, the soft chime of a bell rang out overhead. Soren, tall and broad, had to dip his head to pass through the doorway.

Inside, Aurora glanced at rows upon rows of towering bookcases, carved from dark mahogany and adorned with intricate filigree. Stacks reached toward a vaulted ceiling painted with constellations that glimmered as if touched by starlight.

Sunlight filtered through stained glass windows, casting a kaleidoscope of colors upon the polished stone floors. The warm hues breathed life into the room and the stories preserved within.

In the heart of the library, a circular reading nook beckoned with plush velvet chairs and ornate wooden tables, inviting visitors to lose themselves in the pages of forgotten legends. In the center, a majestic crystal chandelier hung like a suspended galaxy, bathing the space in a soft glow.

An office occupied the back corner. The scent of parchment and ink filled the room, and the shelves were lined with endless scrolls. A large oak desk, polished to a lustrous sheen, dominated the center of the office. Parchments bearing sketches, notes, and inscriptions were strewn across it. An array of quills, inkwells, and vials of powdered pigments stood lined the desk.

In this haven of parchment and ink, the scribe's office bore witness to the beauty and power of words, witness to the enduring connection between the past, present, and the uncharted future.

Aurora stood in awe at the serenity and intrigue that surrounded her. She'd always been captivated by libraries and books, enchanted by the stories held within their pages. Lost in her delight, the sound of Soren's booming voice rattled her.

"Thorn, you old man. You've got company." Soren's face bore a seriousness, but a glimmer in his eyes hinted at mischief.

Aurora heard shuffling above her, and her gaze shifted to the ceiling. She followed the sound of footsteps to the top of a spiral staircase just beyond the crystal chandelier. Feet appeared on the stairs, snug in woolen grey boots. As the figure descended, a deep blue robe swayed with each step. Upon reaching the last curve of the staircase, the face that Aurora met was unexpected.

Not in fact old, the man's angular face possessed smooth alabaster skin that held an air of youth. His nose was long and pointed, a heavy brow overshadowing delicate, stormy grey eyes. Sleek silver locks were pulled into a half ponytail, the rest cascading down to his upper back. Aurora spied the telltale point of fae ears.

The man smiled in delight at the sight of Soren and spread his arms out wide. "Soren, you beautiful beast, so good to see you!" His scholarly voice was friendly and inviting. They hugged briefly, then studied one another. Aurora watched with interest as Thorn turned to meet her gaze. "And who is this radiant woman?" Thorn scanned Aurora, causing her cheeks to flush.

Soren stepped forward, introducing them, "Thorn, this is Aurora. Aurora, this is Thorn, an old friend and master cartographer." Soren watched Aurora, noting the flicker of red that brushed her cheeks.

"Hello. It's nice to meet you," she said. Her eyes wandered around the room. She felt caught in a dream. "You have a beautiful library."

"Why, thank you. You must appreciate the written word," Thorn said with a warm smile, his curiosity about his guest growing. "And I must say, that is a stunning cloak of protection you have. Clara's work, I presume?" Thorn looked to Soren for confirmation, who nodded. Aurora glanced down at the gleaming cloak with wonder while Thorn watched her.

Noticing the questions forming on his friend's face, Soren spoke. "Aurora is not from our world. She stumbled through a tear in the veil." Thorn's eyes widened with intrigue. "We'd like to talk to you about the rifts, and find a way to return Aurora home," Soren said, gauging Thorn's reaction to the gravity of the situation.

"Ah … Well then, follow me to my office, and I will get us some tea." The striking man eyed Soren and then Aurora before turning and leading them to his office.

Soren gestured for Aurora to follow Thorn, and she brushed past him, stirring a waft of rosemary and lavender under his nose. Soren closed his eyes, inhaling deeply, before trailing behind her.

Thorn stepped behind his ornate desk and took a seat. Aurora sat in a leather high-back chair on the opposite side of the desk. She looked to the chair on her left, expecting Soren to occupy it. Instead, she gazed up to see him standing against the wall, watching Thorn with his arms crossed.

A steaming cup of chamomile tea waited on a small round table between the chairs. Aurora wondered about its sudden presence, but then she remembered the magic these beings wielded.

"So, what does she know?" Thorn asked, nodding in Aurora's direction while keeping his eyes on Soren.

Aurora grew irritated. Even if she was an outsider, it didn't diminish her ability or her role in the discussion. Just as Soren was about to speak, she interjected, her voice carrying a mix of frustration and urgency. "I don't know much. One moment, I was lost in the darkness, searching for my friend during a camping trip. The next, I was at the bottom of a 50-foot ravine, battered and bleeding. Then, a bear showed up and when I'm convinced that the end is near, this man," Aurora said, gesturing toward Soren still brooding by the doorway, "arrives out of nowhere, whisking me away to a secluded cabin in the woods, where I receive some sort of miraculous healing by a fae woman. She told me this land is called Silverveil and mentioned others like me who've passed through the veil but never returned home." Her voice trailed off, a note of somberness seeping in as she recounted the reality of her situation.

Soren's eyebrows lifted in response to the outburst. Thorn's chin rested in his hands, which were clasped together in front of him, elbows resting atop his desk. His index fingers pointed toward the ceiling and rested against his thin lips.

"I am very sorry for the circumstances that brought you here," Thorn said. "It is most unfortunate and must be very frightening for you to have stumbled into our land. But I can assure you we will do our very best to get you back home as quickly as possible." His eyes softened as he spoke to Aurora, but they remained intentional.

"As Soren and Clara may have explained, we've learned over time that our world is connected to others through temporal rifts, small tears in the dimensional fabric of place and time. While we work hard to close any tears that we find, we can only control what happens on this side of the veil. Part of what I do is map the location of known rifts and relay the information to sentinels such as Soren to close the portal and survey the land for any unexpected intruders."

Aurora's expression remained cool as the man spoke of sentinels, but a muscle twinged between her thighs as she imagined Soren covered in dirt and sweat wielding his elongated sword through the air as he swung at intruding enemies. She imagined the look of satisfaction on his face as he thrust his powerful weapon into his opponent. Heat crept up from between her legs and radiated up her body. *What was happening to her?* Aurora hoped Thorn did not heed the call of The Listening as well. She sat in silence for a moment, studying Thorn's face for any hint of comprehension of her lusty vision. She breathed a sigh of relief when Thorn waited for her to speak first, his face cool as stone.

"While I don't understand everything that you just said, it seems the plan is to travel back to where I fell through the veil and go home, right?" She couldn't believe the words she was saying, but she looked to Thorn for confirmation.

"That would be a fair assumption, Miss Aurora. However, the rifts are unstable. What we know is that when someone passes through the veil into our realm, that tear closes. But when one closes, a new one opens in another part of our realm. The trouble is, we don't know exactly where." Thorn focused on Aurora with humbled sympathy. He knew the words were not what she wanted to hear, and he waited for her reaction.

Aurora sat in silence for a moment, processing the information. She was stuck in this strange world with strange beings and no easy way home. *How big was this place? How long would it take to find a new portal?* Her self-controlled demeanor was beginning to crack.

As she dwelled on the fact that she had zero control over what was happening in her life right now, she wept. Her tears fell silently at first, but as she watched the men's faces turn from concern to sympathy, sobs heaved from her. She hated her body for betraying her and showing such vulnerability. Her anger only fueled her sobs.

Soren disappeared for a moment and returned with a fresh glass of water. *He obviously didn't wield the gift of summoning objects out of thin air.* He placed the glass on the table beside Aurora and returned to his post by the wall. Thorn leaned forward and offered her a crisp white handkerchief. She took it, embarrassed by her show of emotion. She hushed her crying and took a drink of the cool water in front of her. Once she had regained her composure, Thorn continued.

"I know this isn't easy. Being in a foreign land. But this isn't the first time this has happened here, and though it may take some time, we will not stop until we deliver you back from where you came." Thorn eyed Soren, and Aurora knew there was more to what he was saying. "You have the finest sentinel in Silverveil at your protection and guidance, and he will ensure no harm befalls you." His smile didn't quite reach his eyes.

Aurora looked at her designated protector and saw a flash of pain in his eyes and a stern look of determination on his face. He looked at her, his voice soft. "Yes, of course. You are safe with me." His voice graveled.

No one had ever spoken those words to her in her life. Safety was something she created for herself, never able to rely on anyone else to ensure it for her. *Could she put her fate in someone else's hands—someone she had just met?*

Aurora was suddenly exhausted, and her head throbbed from the weight of her situation and what was to come. It was all too much. She had molded herself to be strong and independent, charting her own course, careful to consider all risks. And now she stood on the precipice of the unknown.

She rubbed at her temples. "Thank you. I appreciate all that you are doing for me. I'm just very overwhelmed right now."

"Why, yes, of course," Thorn said. "You are welcome to retreat to the library while Soren and I speak. Most of the tomes are in our ancient language, but you can enjoy the solace."

Aurora smiled with appreciation and rose from her chair. The thought of being surrounded by inanimate objects that couldn't speak words that terrorized her sounded like a haven. Thorn stood in respect, and Soren watched her leave the room. Once her hand reached the threshold, she looked behind her at Soren's watchful eyes. They stared at each other for a moment before Aurora disappeared into the stacks.

The library was hushed and reverent, but a palpable hum of magic hung in the air. Aurora wondered what ancient fae power lay hidden in the thick tomes. Books of all shapes and sizes filled the shelves. Some looked ancient, bound in leather with clasps of iron. Scrolls and manuscripts, some glowing faintly with enchantment beckoned Aurora, but she remained weary, afraid their magic would somehow harm her.

She walked deeper into the library, and she didn't remember the outside of the building being so wide. *Another illusion*, she thought. At the back of the library, she found a cozy nook under a stained-glass window created to look like stars under a midnight sky. The plush cushions called to her, and she nestled against their velvety softness.

She closed her eyes, the weight of her situation settling into her bones. She tried to clear her head and force out all the uncertainty and doubts. As she focused on her breathing to calm her mind, a melodic humming pierced her ears. Her eyes flashed open, afraid she wasn't alone. Afraid she'd find some mystical creature hiding between the stacks, watching her with curious eyes.

Aurora held her breath, straining to hear any rustle of movement. But it was just the soft humming that filled the space. She stood, enticed to find the source of the sound. Aurora moved through the labyrinth of shelves, her heart quickening with each step. The hum grew louder, more insistent, leading her to a secluded alcove. There, resting on a pedestal bathed in a shaft of light that pierced through a high window, was a book. It was thick and bound in leather that pulsed with a life of its own.

With a shaking hand, she lifted its cover. The pages whispered as they turned, revealing words written in a language she could not understand.

But it was the lithographs that captured her breath—beautifully detailed illustrations that told their own story.

Her fingers flipped to a page with an image of a woman, ethereal and radiant, her form glowing with an otherworldly light. She hovered above a dark mountain, her arms spread wide as if she was embracing or perhaps commanding the very forces of nature. Her eyes were closed, a serene expression on her face. Around her, the air was alive with swirling energy.

The woman in the illustration mesmerized Aurora. She exuded power and grace, a guardian spirit of the mountain, or a goddess from an age long forgotten. The image stirred something within Aurora, a feeling of connection. Of destiny, intertwining with the threads of ancient lore.

As she gazed at the picture, warmth spread through her fingertips where they touched the page. The hum she had followed now flowed within her, a harmonious blend with the silent song of the mystical woman in the lithograph. It was as though the book had chosen her, inviting her into its world.

Disturbed by the vibrating energy, Aurora slammed shut the cover and retreated to the comfort of the nook beneath the window. She pulled her knees to her chest and wrapped her arms around herself, hoping to shrink away from the mysterious pulse of this place.

Back in Thorn's office, Soren rested his palms atop the ancient wooden desk, his arms bracing his mighty form, and his brow furrowed in deep contemplation. Thorn sat in front of an intricately detailed map that covered the table's surface, his fingers tracing the lines that marked known portal locations.

"We have to find a new rift in the veil. Fast. She's vulnerable here," Soren said with concern.

Thorn nodded, unable to hide his sympathy. "I know," he said. He focused on the map. "I received reports of unusual energy fluctuations near Whispering Glen last night. That may be promising."

Soren's eyes tightened at the prospect of the journey ahead. Whispering Glen lay just south of the Silverveil Mountains and the Northern Shadows—formidable lands that were ruled by a dark, cursed lord and barren of any being outside of the darkest forces that dared to roam there. He knew it was only a matter of time before the lord learned of Aurora's presence and dispatched his cronies to take her.

Traveling to Whispering Glen meant traversing treacherous terrains, dealing with unpredictable energies, and facing potential threats from unknown creatures. It was a task he usually faced alone.

Thorn sensed Soren's hesitation and placed a firm hand on his shoulder. "Aurora is counting on you."

Soren nodded, acknowledging the truth in Thorn's words. Aurora's fate rested on his shoulders, and he couldn't afford to let doubt cloud his determination. The decision was made. They would head north to Whispering Glen, embarking on a journey in search of the portal that could reunite Aurora with her own world. Soren acknowledged the logic in Thorn's words, but he couldn't shake the weight of responsibility he felt for Aurora's safety. The unpredictable nature of interdimensional travel had brought her into their world, and now it was his duty to guide her back home.

Thorn continued, "I'll provide you with a map of the location, and we'll monitor any magical fluctuations along the way."

Soren appreciated Thorn's reassurance, but he couldn't ignore his inner turmoil. The day turned to night as they finalized their plans, the moon casting its silvery glow through the library's stained-glass windows. As the night deepened, their voices weaved through the air. Little did they know that, beneath the same starlit sky, something greater wove its own tapestry, entwining Aurora's destiny with the threads of Silverveil's reality.

In the quiet solitude of the library, Aurora stared at the intricate patterns of the ceiling. Sleep eluded her as thoughts of the impending journey and the mysteries of Silverveil swirled in her mind. As she listened to the hushed exchange of the men's voices down the hall, her eyes closed, and she drifted into a restless slumber.

After Thorn finished marking the map, he looked up and caught the somber expression on Soren's face. "Aurora may not be familiar with our world, but she is resilient," Thorn said.

Soren nodded. With the whisper of parchment, Thorn rolled up the map and Soren tucked it into a leather satchel, ready to embark on the journey at first light.

The night crept into the library's silent halls and hung on to the quiet hum of anticipation. Thorn retired to his bedchamber above the library, leaving Soren alone with his thoughts. As he pondered in silence, the weight of the journey ahead settled upon him. The responsibility of guiding Aurora through the perils of Silverveil weighed on his mind like a physical burden. He thought of the portals, the mysterious gateways that defied the laws of nature, and of Aurora, an outsider thrust into a world so alien to her own.

Soren walked through the library, the stacks of books offering a place of solace. The towering bookshelves were a sanctum of contemplation. Soren's thoughts drifted to the legends and tales he had grown up with, stories of heroes and adventurers who had faced insurmountable odds. He wondered if his story would be found within these walls one day. He hoped it would be a story of victory and not a cautionary tale.

He walked toward the back of the library, where he spied Aurora, curled up on the velvet cushions of the built-in nook. The moonlight filtering through the window above her cast shadows on her serene face. Soren paused at the sight of Aurora, and his heart caught in his chest. The scene struck him with an unexpected vulnerability that he seldom allowed himself to acknowledge.

As he neared her, he watched the gentle rise and fall of her chest. The moonlight played across her features, highlighting the soft contours of her face. Her hair shimmered beneath the moonlight.

In that quiet moment, a rush of emotions washed over Soren. Aurora appeared so delicate, so utterly human. There was an innocence he felt compelled to protect. It stirred a deep, primal urge within him to shield her from his world's harsh realities.

Soren's gaze lingered on her face, noticing the faint traces of a smile playing on her lips. He wondered what dreams danced in her mind; what secret fantasies played out behind her closed eyelids. *Was she dreaming of home?*

He took a silent step closer, careful not to disturb her. The urge to reach out, to brush away a stray lock of hair from her face was overwhelming. But he restrained himself, respecting the invisible boundary between them. In her sleep, she was untouchable—the being from another world where he dared not tread.

This vision of Aurora, so vulnerable and serene, etched itself in his memory. It was a reminder of her humanity—of everything he wasn't. As Soren stood there, watching over her in the moonlit quiet of the library, he realized just how much he feared the vulnerability that this charge unearthed within him.

The surrounding silence was both a comfort and a reminder of the solitude of his task. He knew that the decisions he made would not only shape his fate but also that of Aurora, whose trust in him was a heavy mantle to bear. Unable to tear himself away from Aurora's sleeping serenity, Soren settled onto the floor beneath where she slept. In the quiet of the library, with the night holding its breath around him, Soren steeled himself for the dawn.

Chapter 5

A figure loomed over Aurora, and a deep voice trickled down to her ears.

"It's time to go."

She blinked to focus on Soren's gaze. His golden eyes radiated, and he held out a hand to help her rise from the cushioned nook. She placed her hand in his warm grip and took in the brightened surroundings of the library.

"Did you rest well?" he asked, watching her as she stood, still gripping his hand.

She hadn't had a stirring dream or a darkened thought. "Yes. Very well, in fact."

Soren's lips curved into a faint smile, and he released her hand as she steadied herself. The first rays of dawn painted the sky beyond the window. Aurora could feel the air thick with anticipation, a sense of the unknown awaiting just beyond the door.

Soren turned and retreated toward the front of the library. There, he walked to a wardrobe by the door and retrieved her shimmering white cloak. He extended it to her, his eyes lingering on her face.

Aurora gripped the cloak and draped it around her shoulders, the material falling to her ankles. It held a comforting weight, and its warmth hugged her like a protective shield. Her fingers glided over the golden metal as she fastened the clasp, and she looked up at Soren. The crystal chandelier above him reflected the sunlight, casting rainbow splashes of color on his face.

Footsteps crossed the floor, and she turned to see Thorn. "Whispering Glen awaits," he said. "May the stars guide your journey, dear Aurora." His grey eyes settled on her. "It was a pleasure to meet you, and I wish you well in your life once you return home. Someday, this will all be a distant memory—an unbelievable tale to tell your children." His voice reflected a restrained delight.

Aurora fluttered with discomfort at the unexpected mention of children. The concept of motherhood had never found a place in the planned chapters of her life. Mostly because she'd never found a partner she'd deemed worthy enough to share them with. Despite the internal unease, she offered Thorn a gracious smile, appreciating the kindness of his words.

Aurora thanked him before she cast a glance at Soren, who stood beside her like a stone with an air of determination.

She watched Thorn and Soren share a few parting words as they stepped outside. She marveled at the camaraderie between the cartographer and stoic sentinel. A nod, ripe with unspoken understanding, sealed the brief encounter as Thorn slipped the bag from his shoulder to Soren's hand.

Soren, ever watchful, followed Aurora as they navigated toward the awaiting Ash, tied nearby. The world beyond the library's confines beckoned, and as Aurora cast one last glance at the dwelling, she knew that the tale unfolding before her would soon become woven into the fabric of her own life story.

Aurora approached Ash, standing with a regality that hinted at the years of adventures he'd shared with Soren. The horse's ebony coat glistened under the morning sunlight. Aurora reached out to stroke the velvety warmth of Ash's neck, a silent exchange of reassurance passing between them.

Soren's low and resonant voice cut through the morning air. "Thorn mapped the best route to find a rift to get you back home. It won't be an easy journey, but I trust you will manage just fine," he said.

Soren mounted Ash with a practiced grace and lowered a hand to Aurora. She threw a cross look at her travel companion.

"You certainly don't expect me to ride in your lap for this entire time? I'm perfectly capable of riding my own horse."

Soren grinned at Aurora's spirited declaration, appreciating the spark in her eyes. "No, Miss Aurora. I wouldn't deprive you of the joy of riding your own steed. We're making a brief stop to secure another companion for our journey."

Aurora, determined to assert her independence, confronted Soren. No longer content with being treated as a damsel in distress, she positioned herself by Ash's shoulder.

Aurora dismissed Soren's outstretched hand and reached for the reins, prepared to mount the horse unassisted. Turning her head, she discovered Soren watching her, a subtle amusement playing on his lips. Determination fueled her, and she huffed with frustration. She grappled with the challenge of hoisting herself onto the tall horse, aware of the amused gaze fixed upon her.

After a few awkward moments of huffing and shuffling, Aurora settled onto Ash's back, composing herself before turning her chin to glance at Soren.

"Ready?" he asked, holding her gaze.

She averted her eyes, offering no response, and tilted her chin toward the sky. Without another word, Soren secured the reins and wrapped his arms around Aurora's waist. He drew the reins toward her belly button, and his hands hovered just above her pelvis. A mixture of frustration and a subtle spark of excitement elicited a groan from Aurora. Unbothered by her reaction, Soren paid no mind, and the duo set forth on their journey.

As they approached a dense forest on the outskirts of town, the pair reached a small farm. Soren dismounted Ash first, once again extending his hand to Aurora. She ignored it, sliding down the horse's side to the ground. This time, Soren did not conceal his amusement.

Aurora trailed Soren toward the charming homestead, and a figure emerged from the rustic barn, sporting a grin that rivaled the brilliance of the sun itself. His eyes sparkled with mischievous light. With a flourish of his hand, he swept an unruly lock of red hair from his brow.

"Soren, my friend!" The man's gaze shifted from the sentinel to Aurora. "And who is this enchanting companion you've brought with you?"

Aurora's gaze met the cheerful man's eyes, and it was as if she had known him for lifetimes.

Soren introduced her with a subtle smile. "This is Aurora." His eyes shifted to her. "Aurora, meet Olin." He saw the interplay between his excitable friend and the burgeoning connection with Aurora.

With a theatrical bow, Olin's charm took center stage. "Ah, the luminous Aurora, gracing my humble home with her presence. Delighted to make your acquaintance, my dear." Laughter wafted through the air, carried by the breeze, as Olin's emerald eyes twinkled with delight.

Her thoughts flashed to Camryn. She knew her friend would love him. "It's nice to meet you, Olin," Aurora said.

Olin's amused gaze fixated on the tall, unflappable Soren. "Soren, you ol' brute. What is this lovely woman doing with you?" He playfully jabbed an elbow into Soren's ribs, eliciting a huff from the sentinel.

Soren shot his friend a stern look before responding. "She's an unexpected traveler who came through a rift a few days ago. We're embarking on a journey to Whispering Glen, hoping to find a new portal to send her home. That's the purpose of our visit. She needs a horse for the journey. Do you have one we could borrow?" His eyes met Aurora's before returning to Olin.

"Oh, I see," he said, eyeing Aurora. "Well, yes, of course. I'd be delighted to lend you a horse. Follow me to the stable. I believe I have just the one for Aurora." Olin's eyes sparkled with enthusiasm as he strode off toward his horses. His spirit was just as fiery as Camryn's, pulling Aurora into his orbit.

As she turned the corner of the stable, Aurora found Olin standing beside a light-grey horse with dark speckles. Olin stroked the horse's mane, whispering sweet words to the animal.

"This is Beacon, one of the finest horses I've ever owned," he said. "She's as sweet as a ripe melon in summer." Olin's face radiated with pride as he spoke of the horse, who chuffed in response.

"She's lovely," Aurora said as she approached the horse. She placed her hand on Beacon's shoulder, and the horse turned its head in acknowledgment. Aurora gazed into the dark, curious eyes of the horse. Her hand ran up and down its long muzzle. "You obviously take great care of her. I promise to do the same while she is with me," Aurora reassured Olin. He nodded with gratitude.

Aurora found Soren gazing at the grey sky atop the hill of Olin's farm. When she approached, he told her storms were rolling in—common this time of year in Silverveil. His face was grave as he told her they'd need to postpone their journey until the weather cleared. They wouldn't want to be caught in the storm in the open countryside.

Aurora's face fell as she absorbed being stuck in this strange world for longer, and she tried not to dwell on the panic that her friends and family must be feeling at home, unaware of what happened to her.

But fortunately, Olin's lively spirit brightened her own. He was a stark contrast to Soren, who calculated every movement and word in silence. Aurora welcomed Olin's company, especially considering that after this, she would be alone with Soren on their journey across the realm.

Olin's cottage was slightly larger than Clara's, having two bedrooms and separate living spaces. Although he was unmarried, with no particular lady currently captivating his interest, he had shared with Aurora how he hoped to fill his home with a wife and children someday. Aurora had smiled at the endearing thought and looked to weigh Soren's reaction. Her grin had diminished when she saw Soren's indifferent demeanor.

Around the dinner table, Aurora laughed as Olin retold animated stories of his youth and his experience as a farmer. She couldn't help but think how Camryn would love him. Someone to reignite the flame of her adventurous spirit. Aurora could tell Olin was the type of man who could stand behind his woman, lifting her up and cheering her on. Her heart ached for her friend, and for that intimate connection of having a partner—someone to share her world with.

The interaction between Olin and Soren captivated Aurora. But for all the warmth this friendship offered, she yearned for home. Soren had spoken of Whispering Glen, mentioning a trek of a few days' ride, and Aurora ached for the familiar. She longed to embark, to traverse the distance that lay between her and home. But it appeared Silverveil had charted a different course altogether.

The storms delayed them for nearly a week as they raged over Olin's farm. Aurora was grateful his house sat at the top of the hill for all the rain that was coming down. But the earth absorbed the water like a sponge. When one storm would cease, it wasn't long before another crack of thunder unleashed from the heavens once again.

Aurora was going stir-crazy. She had chewed her nails to nubs, and she was sure she wore a path in the weathered wood of Olin's extra bedroom she occupied.

Soren had settled into an oversized chair in the living area next to the fire, despite Olin's offers for him to take his bed. Aurora noticed how Olin easily brushed off Soren's stubbornness—a sign of their enduring friendship.

She saw a few grins cross Soren's face at his friend's playful stories and even heard a genuine chuckle escape his lips when Olin recalled the time when Ash was just a colt and had pulled Soren through the mud as the sentinel feverishly tried to tame him. Aurora had covered her face with her hands to hide the flush that crept up her cheeks at the image of Soren, dirty and angry.

The night before they left Olin's, Aurora thrashed in bed. A vivid nightmare held her in its clutches. She dreamed she was in complete darkness. A chill sent shockwaves of ice through her body as she struggled to see through the inky darkness. Only echoes of malicious laughter and screams filled her mind. As her heart beat faster and her eyes searched the void, a glistening pair of violet eyes appeared out of the darkness before her. Her breath hitched, and the creature leaped, its claws bared.

Aurora awoke screaming to find Soren sitting on the bed, his firm hands on her shoulders.

"Aurora," he said calmly. "It's just a dream. It's okay, you're here with me." His voice was a reassuring presence in her disoriented mind. Her terrified eyes looked at him and found solace. Although there was concern on his face, there was a softness that eased her fears.

She panted and swallowed, trying to catch her breath. Soren leaned forward to the nightstand beside the bed and retrieved a glass of water. Aurora grasped it, her fingertips brushing against his warm hands.

"Thank you," she said. He nodded in response.

"Do you want to talk about it?" Soren asked. Aurora's eyes widened in surprise at being asked by him to talk about anything. He typically preferred silence.

Aurora shook her head. She didn't want to relive the feeling of terror.

Soren stood to leave, and Aurora's heart skipped a beat. Since childhood, nightmares plagued her, and she hated being left alone in the darkness. After Camryn moved in with her, her friend often slept in bed with her after a bad dream, so Aurora wouldn't be alone.

Aurora tried to hold back the noise that escaped her lips, but she couldn't help it. She was overwhelmed with fear in an unfamiliar place. She'd take any semblance of comfort she could get. "Could you ... could you stay?" she asked. Aurora's gaze fell to her lap, embarrassed as a grown woman who was afraid of a nightmare.

Soren's brows lifted in surprise, but his gaze softened as he turned back toward her.

"Of course, if it will help you sleep," he said. His voice was low and soothing, and Aurora calmed at his answer.

"Thank you," she whispered.

His mighty form strode to the small, cushioned chair in the corner of the room. She stifled a laugh as he lowered himself into it, dwarfing the piece of furniture. Then her stomach twisted with guilt for asking him to sleep so uncomfortably. But she looked at the bed, which was barely big enough for her. There'd be no way they could share it, even if she got over being so close to him.

Soren slumped into the chair, stretching his legs across the bottom corner of the bed. Aurora scooted her legs over to make room for him—it was the least she could do.

She settled into bed, pulling the quilt to her chin. Aurora glanced at Soren, who looked at her.

"Good night, Aurora," he said. "Get some sleep. I'm hoping for us to depart tomorrow."

Her heart fluttered at the prospect. "Good night," she said. She clamped her eyes shut, feeling comforted by Soren's presence and renewed with the prospect of home.

Chapter 6

After a hearty breakfast of biscuits and bacon, Aurora stepped outside Olin's cottage, where she found Soren standing atop a hill, his gaze fixed on the horizon, dark locks rippling in the gentle breeze. Aurora ascended the slope, wrapping her cloak more tightly around her as a chilly breeze stirred from the ground. She stopped beside him and noticed a worried expression on his face.

"More storms are coming," Soren said. "We will want to get moving soon if we hope to make it to the next village before we are caught in bad weather."

Concern etched her face. "Where are we headed today?" she asked. Her thoughtful gaze met Soren's, who remained focused on the encroaching clouds.

"Larkspire. It's a trading post just before Raven's Ridge. We will lodge there for the night." His expression softened. He wondered whether he had been too stringent with Aurora, underestimating her abilities.

Aurora looked out across the vista. "I'm ready whenever you are," she said.

She mounted her gifted mode of transportation and said goodbye to her new acquaintance, feeling a twinge of sadness at the thought of parting ways so soon. She followed Soren, descending the rolling hill and venturing into the dense, enveloping forest that lay ahead.

As they trekked through the lush landscape, Aurora couldn't help but wish for more time with Olin. His free-spirited nature and unreserved banter with Soren provided a stark contrast to the sentinel's usual stoic demeanor. Despite their differences, it was clear they had a deep and caring friendship. Olin made her feel at ease, as if he were a long-lost friend from her own world. Her thoughts lingered on the chipper man as she and Soren ventured through the dense woods.

Aurora's mind drifted to Camryn. But instead of dwelling on the fact that her friend was probably beside herself with grief at having lost Aurora in the desolate wilderness, fearing the worst, Aurora wished Camryn were here with her on this strange journey in a mystical place. She knew her friend would see it as an adventure, a gift to explore. Aurora vowed to herself to keep some of Camryn's spirit through the ordeal, clinging to the hope it would give her courage and a good story for her friend when she made it back home.

Weary of the lingering silence, Aurora asked, "How did you and Olin become friends? It doesn't seem like you'd have much in common." Her eyes looked at Soren's expressionless face.

"Olin makes you his friend ... whether you like it or not," Soren said with a subtle annoyance.

Aurora chuckled, finding amusement in Soren's admission. "Yeah, I can believe that," she said. Camryn had the same gift.

Sensing Aurora's curiosity, Soren continued, feeling her gaze on him. "I moved to Riverholm as a young boy. Olin was the first child—the only child—who wanted anything to do with me." A momentary shadow crossed his face, his brow furrowing in a display of sad recollection.

Aurora thought back to her imposing question at Clara's, where she learned about the treatment he endured from other children, all because he lacked the pointed ears characteristic of the fae. She felt a pang of sympathy for Soren. Beneath the veneer of his stern demeanor lay someone who had faced challenges and experiences she had yet to uncover. His cool exterior was more like a shield forged from loneliness than the entitlement she initially perceived.

She considered the unseen depth of Soren. "Well, Olin seems like the best friend to make you feel welcomed and wanted."

Soren reflected on his friend. Olin's infectious cheer melted his guarded exterior, showing him the value of companionship. Each visit to Olin's farm lifted a weight from Soren's shoulders, replaced by the lightness of Olin's banter and the amusement dancing in his eyes. Olin's clever quips and deep conversations became fond memories in Soren's solitary journeys.

In moments of doubt or uncertainty, Soren found reassurance in Olin's unwavering support. Olin's indestructible optimism illuminated even the darkest times, offering Soren a lifeline to hope. Their friendship was one of contrasts that somehow made sense.

They rode in silence for several miles, and Aurora sensed a shift in Soren. With each conversation, his walls come down bit by bit.

She could relate to him. Aurora had always kept herself guarded, weary of others' motivations. She kept tight control of her emotions, never wanting to feel taken advantage of for letting people too close. Aurora cast a sideways glance at Soren, feeling as though an invisible thread had connected their lives across space and time, and her lips curved in wonder at the thought.

Above the thick canopy, Aurora noticed the clouds rolling in, darkening the sky. About to ask Soren about how far they were from Larkspire, a loud clap of thunder cracked overhead, startling both her and Beacon. The horse recoiled on its hind legs, and Aurora tightened her grip on the reins.

Casting a horrified glance at Soren, another thunderous boom sent Beacon into a full sprint.

Aurora's cry pierced the air. "Help!"

Soren's body responded, urging Ash forward with a determined kick to his flanks.

Aurora gaped at the swiftness of Beacon beneath her. As she glanced back, the landscape blurred.

"Soren! Soren, help," she cried out, her voice carried away by the wind.

From behind her, a deep, guttural growl bellowed, "Aurora!"

Aurora clung to Beacon as they darted between trees and brush. Branches whooshed past her head, and her cloak billowed behind her in a frenzy. Closing her eyes, she spoke to the horse, "Beacon, please, lovely girl, slow down. It's okay. It's just thunder. It can't hurt us. Please, we need to slow down."

Behind her, another roll of thunder echoed, but this one emanated from the ground. The rhythmic beats of Ash's hooves pounded the earth as Soren and his horse closed the distance. Aurora stole a glance backward, her heart flooding with hope and relief at the sight of Soren's gaze.

Soren's eyes remained locked on Aurora as he urged Ash to a greater speed, expertly maneuvering around to the side of Beacon. The two horses raced alongside each other, their thundering hooves echoing the urgency of the moment. Soren extended his arm toward Aurora. "Jump on!" he said.

Aurora's grip on Beacon tightened. "Are you crazy?!" Her voice trembled as she clung to the racing mare.

"I will catch you. You have to trust me. Now jump!" Soren's amber eyes bore into Aurora's. In that intense moment, she knew—without a doubt—she could trust this man with her life.

With a trembling hand, she reached out toward Soren, who clasped it firmly. The wind whistled and stung her face, but her focus remained on him. With a single nod, she knew it was time to leap. Aurora released her grip on the horse and used all her strength to propel herself off the racing mare.

In one swift motion, Soren pulled her onto Ash's back behind him. Aurora wrapped her arms around Soren's waist, feeling the solid strength of his form beneath her trembling hands. She pressed her face into his back as they sped onward.

Once he was certain that Aurora was secure, Soren lunged for the reins of the rogue horse, clutching them in his grip as he regained control of the mare. They burst through the edge of the forest and into an open meadow before coming to a complete stop.

"Whoa, whoa now," Soren spoke to Beacon, his voice a calming presence amid the lingering adrenaline rush. His attention shifted to Aurora, who clung to his back with a tenacious grip. "Are you alright?"

Aurora's eyes fluttered open, revealing a world that had resumed its normal rhythm. But she kept her firm grip around Soren, finding solace in the steadiness of his presence. "Yes, I'm okay," she whispered.

He glanced down, noticing how her hands wrapped around his waist. "That's good. It might be best for you to accompany me on Ash until we reach the inn," he said, a tone of protective concern lacing his words.

"Gladly," Aurora said, relieved.

Though Aurora couldn't see the gentle smile that appeared on Soren's face, a sudden clap of thunder overhead caused her eyes to slam shut, bracing for another swift motion. Meanwhile, Soren gripped the reins of Beacon, guiding the horse into a steady trot next to them.

It wasn't long before Aurora felt the solitary touch of a large raindrop atop her head. She cracked open her eyes, peering upward at the brooding sky. A smattering of raindrops kissed her face, foretelling the downpour that was to come. Then, as if on cue, the heavens unfurled, unleashing a torrent of heavy, icy rain. Aurora gasped.

Soren quickened their pace, the rain now an opaque veil obscuring his view. Rivulets of water cascaded through his hair, tracing a path down his back, and pooling in Aurora's lap.

"Hold on tight." Soren's voice cut through the howling wind.

Aurora drew herself even closer to him, her arms weaving tightly around his waist. The cold droplets splattered against her, extinguishing the burst of adrenaline that raced through her. With a silent nod, she affirmed her readiness, her heartbeat thundering in unison with the horse's powerful gallop.

Beneath them, Ash burst forth with renewed urgency. His muscles flexed, driving them across the expansive fields. The world around them transformed into a fluid canvas, painted by the relentless rain. It was as if they were moving through a world of liquid silver. Amidst the storm, Aurora's laughter rang out, blending with the wind's roar. She couldn't help but laugh at the absurdity of it all. Fate was hell-bent on throwing every obstacle in her way.

Soren's sturdy frame was a barricade against the raging elements. But the sound of her unbridled laughter sang in his ears like a long-forgotten song. Aurora, nestled close, found comfort in his strength.

As they advanced, the outline of Larkspire materialized through the rain's veil. The village shone through the dark like a beacon in the storm. Soren confidently steered Ash while Beacon matched the horse's vigorous pace.

Upon reaching the fringes of the village, the duo's pace subsided, the resounding beat of hooves on the earth now replaced by a gentler rhythm against the cobblestone streets. With a sigh of relief, Soren eased the horses to a stop. Aurora dismounted, her laughter a radiant chime amidst the sounds of the village.

Soren turned to face her. His golden eyes mirrored the storm's intensity and his fondness for her. "Quite the adventure," he mused.

Aurora's eyes sparkled in response, reflecting not just the storm, but the shared thrill of their escapade. "Yes, indeed," she said, her words laced with a playful, shared understanding.

As the rain persisted, Soren and Aurora found themselves in the bustling heart of Larkspire. They stepped into the warmth of a quaint tavern, and a shiver ran through Aurora as the cool dampness of her skin contrasted with the heat radiating from a roaring fireplace.

Soren turned toward her, his fingers sweeping a rain-drenched lock of hair from her face. His gaze locked onto her eyes. He leaned in, his lips hovering near her ear. "Find solace by the fire. I'll arrange rooms for us," he said, his breath hot against her rain-cooled cheek, sending a cascade of shivers down her spine.

As he retreated, Aurora's smile lingered. She drifted toward a plush chair by the fire. Settling in, she observed the tavern—a hive of activity, alive with spirited chatter and the merry clink of glasses. She realized this was the most crowded gathering she had seen since her arrival in Silverveil.

Her gaze swept across the room, and she noticed the unique characteristics of the fae that filled the space. Each individual was a fascinating blend of the familiar and the fantastical. Some sported delicate, translucent wings that shimmered in the firelight, while all of them boasted the distinct ears that tapered to elegant points. The variety was mesmerizing—from those adorned in vibrant, patterned garments to others whose simple, earth-toned attire blended with the natural world.

Their movements were fluid and graceful, an embodiment of the fae's ethereal nature. Their expressions ranged from deep contemplation to bursts of laughter, painting a vivid display of life in this enchanted realm.

Despite the buzz of the crowd, their rain-soaked, exuberant entrance had drawn only fleeting glances. Amidst the tavern's liveliness, Aurora found a comforting anonymity—a moment to reflect on the day's journey.

As Aurora basked in the fire's warmth, her thoughts drifted to her recent exchange with Soren. For the first time, she glimpsed a different side of him—a vibrant, human-like side that lay beneath his reserved sentinel exterior. The rain had washed away his indifferent shell, revealing a more lighthearted spirit. Aurora was eager to discover more of this playful side of Soren. At the very least, it was a welcomed distraction from the reality of her situation.

Soren appeared at her side a few minutes later, bearing a key and two fluffy towels. Eager to dry her rain-soaked body, Aurora followed Soren through the crowded tavern to a narrow stairwell near the back. He led her to the top of the landing, where he explained the inn was unusually crowded because of the inclement weather, leaving only one room available. Soren assured her, with a touch of chivalry, that he would take the floor while she enjoyed the comfort of the bed.

A flush of warmth tinged Aurora's cheeks at the thought of sharing such close quarters with Soren. She dismissed the notion, following him into a modestly furnished room. Soren placed his saddlebag on a wooden chair near the door and shed his heavy, drenched cloak, draping it over the back of the chair before toweling his hair. Aurora grabbed the other towel and watched him, noting the deliberate, gentle firmness with which he wrung the fabric through his hair—a simple, intimate act that offered a rare glimpse into his unguarded self.

After drying his hair, Soren moved with purpose to the fireplace, picking up a couple of logs from the stack beside it. With practiced ease, he kindled a roaring fire, filling the room with a comforting warmth.

Aurora, meanwhile, shed her cloak, admiring how it had remained remarkably pristine despite the day's adventures. She draped it over a chair near the window and sat down to remove her boots. Much of her attire was drenched, including her socks. She placed them near the fire, stretching and wiggling her toes.

Settled by the fire to dry her hair, Aurora's gaze lingered on Soren, who stood near the door. A soft knock diverted her attention.

"I've arranged for some dry clothes," Soren said.

Opening the door, he received a bundle of clothing from an inn staff member—a short, burly figure. Soren carried the bundle to the bed, sorting through it. He selected a long-sleeved shirt and dark pants for himself.

What remained in his hands was a single, thin smock, its parchment hue understated but revealing in its simplicity. Aurora's cheeks flushed at the garment's sheer fabric. She snatched it from his hands, as an amused smile curled on Soren's lips, and retreated to her chair by the fire.

Soren, meanwhile, began loosening his drenched shirt. Across the room, Aurora watched from her seat, a mix of nervousness and intrigue in her eyes. As he undid each button, his attention was on the flames, but he was acutely aware of Aurora's gaze upon him.

Soren worked his way down the shirt, each button he released unveiling more of his sculpted torso. The play of light from the fire accentuated the taut skin stretched over his well-defined muscles. Aurora contemplated the texture of his skin, wondering if it was as smooth as it appeared. The firelight cast a warm glow, highlighting the fine smattering of hairs that gathered in the center of his chest.

With the last button undone, Soren peeled off the shirt. He moved to lay it over a chair, and Aurora caught her breath. Her skin heated at the sight of his sculpted abs tapering into his waistband. As he turned, his biceps and broad shoulders flexed, revealing the latent power in his physique. The sculpted muscles of his back held Aurora in a trance.

When Soren faced Aurora again, he found her eyes fixed on him. They shared a prolonged look before he cleared his throat, his hands moving toward the fastening of his pants.

Aware of her gawking, Aurora flushed and turned away. Her heart raced from the thrill of the moment. Soren, with a knowing smirk, slid off his sodden pants, which landed on the floor with a wet plunk. An unspoken tension filled the room.

Aurora's cheeks flamed with a rush of unexpected heat, aware of her proximity to Soren's naked form behind her. This stirring of desire caught her off guard, and it sparked a thirst she hadn't realized was parched.

Memories of past intimacies, long forgotten, teased at the edges of her mind. It had been a while since she had slept with someone, and a primal urge tempted her to turn around, to feast her eyes on the extent of Soren's impressive physique, to surrender to the impulse to explore and yield to her burgeoning needs. But with disciplined restraint, she pressed her lips together and sat on her hands, quelling the rising tide of her desires.

Soren dried off and redressed in fresh clothes. He turned to Aurora with a playful note in his voice. "All yours," he said.

Moderately disappointed to find him fully clothed, Aurora picked up the fabric that barely qualified as a garment, and with a swirl of her finger, instructed him to turn around. He complied, his gaze lingering on hers. As he faced away, Aurora began shedding her wet clothes.

She tugged at the hem of her soaked shirt, the fabric emitting a squelching sound as it gave way. The sensation of peeling off her clingy bodice was a relief, like pulling off a restrictive bandage. Her pants suctioned to her legs. Every movement was a struggle, the wet fabric twisting and turning in her grasp. With a sigh of relief, she freed herself from the clinging material.

Soren, his back to her, stood with arms crossed, his lips pursed as he conjured up the image of Aurora behind him, her damp skin exposed.

Disrobed, Aurora moved closer to the fireplace. The warmth lapping at her skin was both rejuvenating and enticing. She kept a watchful eye on Soren, the heat from the flames mirroring the warmth that radiated from within her, igniting a mix of excitement and apprehension in the charged atmosphere of the room.

As Soren stood with his back turned, his mind wandered, indulging in vivid, sensuous fantasies about the naked woman behind him. He imagined exploring her body, the intimate caresses and kisses, each thought more delicious than the last. In his mind's eye, he savored every imagined detail, from the gentle touch of her skin to the imagined responses of her body to his attention. The fantasy was so intense, so stirring, that he was engrossed in it.

Aurora's voice suddenly interrupted his reverie. "You can turn around now."

Soren, aware of the physical manifestation of his thoughts, adjusted his posture to manage the growing tension in his pants, and turned to face her.

The firelight's play tempered his slight disappointment at seeing her clothed in a simple frock on the fabric, revealing subtle hints of the form beneath. But his gaze drifted, noting the gentle rise of her chest where her nipples pressed against the material, mirroring the flush of her cheeks. The shadowing of the fabric outlined the curves of her waist.

Soren had to restrain his eyes from wandering further, aware that his admiration was becoming increasingly difficult to conceal.

Aurora, aware of her revealing state, crossed her arms. She moved to the end of the bed, retrieving a blanket. Aurora wrapped it around her shoulders. The simple act of draping the blanket around her shifted the room's atmosphere, introducing a layer of modesty to the tension that had filled the space moments before.

Aurora's stomach broke the silence with a resounding grumble, taking both her and Soren by surprise. Her involuntary reaction drew a light chuckle from Soren, breaking the spell of the moment. They had been so engrossed in the storm's aftermath and the ensuing emotions they had neglected their basic need for food. Aurora's body, however, was not so easily ignored, and she placed her hand over her stomach as if to quiet its loud protest.

Soren, ever the gentleman, smiled. "I will head downstairs to the tavern. A hearty meal is what you need."

"That would be wonderful, thank you," Aurora said, her cheeks tinged with a soft blush. His thoughtfulness touched her, and her stomach fluttered at the prospect of sharing a private meal in the seclusion of their room, while she wore such delicate attire. *Objectifying men and food were all that consumed her here, apparently—outside of imminent death.*

The door closed behind Soren as he ventured downstairs, his final glance lingering on Aurora sitting by the fire.

Fifteen minutes later, a firm knock at the door signaled Soren's return. Aurora opened it, finding Soren balancing an assortment of plates and pints. He stepped inside, his focus intent on not spilling their meal, a sight that made Aurora smile. His attempt at playing the part of a waiter was both endearing and amusing.

Once Soren arranged the food on the floor near the hearth, he gestured for Aurora to sit before taking his place beside her. The meal was inviting—warm bread, a steaming bowl of soup, and smoked brisket. Aurora dived into the feast with an enthusiasm that delighted Soren. He watched, charmed by her unbridled enjoyment of the hearty fare.

Their meal progressed in comfortable silence, each absorbed in satisfying their hunger. As Aurora's appetite waned, she turned her attention to the ale Soren had brought. Although not a beer enthusiast, she found herself surprised by its light, citrusy notes. The drink was refreshing and complemented the meal.

Before she realized it, the pint glass was empty, resting at her feet, leaving her with a pleasant, light-headed buzz. The intimate setting, the satisfying meal, and the soothing ale were the perfect end to an adventurous day.

Aurora turned to Soren and asked with a playful grin, "So, what's the plan for tomorrow?"

Soren took a moment to finish chewing and wiped his mouth. "Our next destination is Eldersmoor, just beyond Raven's Ridge. The passage through the mountains is challenging, especially with the high winds we're likely to encounter at this time of year. And, hopefully, we won't cross any … unforeseen obstacles." His voice carried a hint of apprehension, but Aurora couldn't help but laugh in response.

"You're always so serious," she said with amusement. "Don't you ever just relax and enjoy yourself?" *Although she was sure people could say the same about her.*

Soren regarded her with a contemplative gaze. "Serious matters require serious thought," he said. "However, I am indeed enjoying this moment with you." His sincerity was clear in his softened expression.

Aurora, sensing the depth of his words, felt a twinge of guilt for her light-hearted jab. Her eyes flashed to the floor, afraid to meet his burning gaze. "Yes, this is nice. I just meant that everything seems to teeter on the brink of disaster. It would be nice to have one night free from the shadow of looming danger," she said softly. She looked up to see his amber eyes flickering in the firelight.

Soren responded with a gentle nod. "My priority is to ensure you're prepared for whatever lies ahead. You're under my protection, and I take that responsibility deeply to heart. I can't fathom what I would do if anything were to happen to you," he confessed. His voice was barely louder than the crackling fire. His gaze lingered on the flames, then shifted to Aurora.

The pain that flickered across his face struck a chord in Aurora, filling her with regret for her earlier light-heartedness. She leaned in, extending her hand to rest atop his.

"I'm stronger than you might think, but I have complete trust in you. I'll follow your lead," she assured him.

Aurora's smile was soft and radiant, mirroring the emotions that simmered just beneath the surface. In response, warmth spread through Soren, like sunlight piercing through clouds after a storm. His fingers itched with the urge to trace her features, to validate the emotions he felt in this moment. He glimpsed a future together, a vision of intertwined destinies forming an unbreakable alliance.

Aurora's impulse to lean forward, to close the distance between her and Soren, startled her. She abruptly launched to her feet, and the light-headedness from the ale tipped the room at a nauseating angle. She grasped the fireplace mantle for support, steadying herself against its solid frame.

Aurora caught her breath. "Well, it's been quite the evening. I think it's best to turn in for the night, to be well-rested for tomorrow." She swallowed the lie. She didn't want sleep—she wanted to give in to whatever this world had stirred in her.

Soren looked at Aurora with a mix of admiration and longing. How he wanted to pull her to him to guide her to the bed. He imagined a soft kiss, the warmth of their bodies under the covers. He envisioned the contours of her body molding perfectly against his as he formed a protective cocoon around her. In his imagination, he stroked her hair, the scent of lavender surrounding him, lulling both into a peaceful sleep. The fantasy reflected his deepening feelings, a silent yearning for a protective and intimate closeness.

Soren resisted the pull of his desire and stood, offering Aurora a respectful bow. Despite the emotions swirling within her, Aurora held strong. She wanted to invite him into her bed, to close the gap that propriety demanded they keep. But she held firm to the boundaries she had set, her actions evidence of her willpower.

Aurora moved to the bed, gathering an extra pillow and blanket. As she handed them to Soren, her fingers lingered for a moment longer than necessary. With a soft smile and a voice barely above a whisper, she said, "Goodnight, Soren."

Soren paused for a moment, his gaze lingering on Aurora with a softness that rarely touched his guarded expression. "Goodnight, Aurora," he said. His eyes held hers for a fleeting second before turning back to the hearth.

In the quiet hours of the night, Soren lay awake on the floor, the warmth of the fire a slight comfort against the turmoil of his thoughts. He listened to Aurora's soft, rhythmic breathing, a sound both soothing and agonizing. Soren grappled with the intensity of his feelings for her, emotions that were becoming difficult to dismiss or ignore. He had known physical attraction before, the simple fulfillment of primal desires, but what he felt for Aurora transcended that. His past encounters, though pleasant, had never stirred in him the depth of emotion that she evoked.

As the fire's glow waned, Soren's thoughts lingered on Aurora's face, illuminated by the dying embers. Her strength and spirit captivated him. She was an enigma, beautiful and complex, and he longed to delve deeper into the mystery of her being. His heart ached to understand her, to connect with her on a level beyond the physical. As sleep claimed him, he drifted into dreams of Aurora's laughter guiding him through the shadows of his own doubts.

CHAPTER 7

The sun, radiant and unforgiving, filtered in through the window and cast a harsh light that made Aurora wince. Soren was already awake, his figure silhouetted against the morning light. He sat in the chair near the fireplace, his back to her. The early light cast a golden hue across his hair, softening the usual sternness of his features.

As Aurora sat up, the sheets rustling with her movement, Soren turned toward her. His eyes, usually so piercing, carried a gentler light in the morning's calm.

"Good morning," he said, his voice a low rumble in tune with the quiet peace of the dawn.

Aurora, feeling the remnants of sleep still clinging to her, managed a small, groggy smile.

"Good morning," she replied. She brushed a stray lock of hair from her face as she took in the unusual softness in Soren's gaze.

She allowed her eyes to linger on his face, appreciating the rare vulnerability he showed the previous night. With a deep, steadying breath, she prepared to rise and face the day.

The soft chatter of early risers and the clinking of cutlery greeted Soren and Aurora as they stepped out of their room. As they made their way to the common room, the floorboards creaking under their steps, anticipation hung in the air.

Breakfast held an awkward silence, despite the glimpses of vulnerability the two shared the night before. To Aurora's dismay, Soren's guarded demeanor had returned. He decided he wouldn't let his mind wonder about what would happen if he acted on his growing feelings toward Aurora.

They left the shelter of the inn and stepped into the crisp morning air. Aurora wrapped her cloak tightly around herself, anticipating the drop in temperature as they approached Raven's Ridge. The mountain range loomed ahead, its onyx peaks standing as silent voyeurs over the obstacles they were bound to face.

Beacon and Ash navigated through serpentine paths, leading their riders across a vibrant valley. The landscape unfurled in waves of lush emerald and golden hues, forming a breathtaking vista. Wildflowers swayed in the soft breeze, the array of colors blending into a mesmerizing display. The air was rich with the sweet perfume of blooming flowers, intermingling with the deep, earthy scent of moist soil and the crisp aroma of pine.

Their journey continued into the valley's expansive fields, yielding to clusters of trees. The woods appeared as if they were gatherings of old friends, their branches interlocking. Above, the leafy canopies wove patterns of light and shadow onto the ground below, creating a tranquil sanctuary under their boughs. The forest was alive with the harmonious chirping of birds and the occasional rustle of small animals in the underbrush, each adding a layer to the valley's symphony of life.

Amidst this natural serenity, Aurora found the silence between herself and Soren not just tolerable, but comforting.

Soren broke the silence, much to Aurora's surprise. He tried to pull his mind from the dizzying fantasies they played as he smelled Aurora's enticing scent in the wind.

"When I was a boy, not yet strong enough to wield a sword, my father took me to this very valley," he said. "Back then, it was a vast canvas of golden wheat. We ascended a hill, and from the top, the land unfolded before us. I felt as if we were at the edge of the world."

Aurora listened, her heart captivated by the vivid picture Soren painted with his words. She watched the emotions play across his face as he delved deeper into the memory.

"My father rested his hand upon my shoulder, and in that instant, the burdens I didn't even know I carried lifted. He spoke of honor, of courage, and of the sacred duty to protect those we hold dear. There, gazing over the endless valleys and rolling hills, I felt a calling deep within me. I knew then that I would be a sentinel, to embody and uphold the values he imparted to me."

Aurora watched Soren, her heart swelling as he shared this memory with her.

"I discovered a purpose that day, a connection to something far greater than myself. And now, journeying with you through these lands, I am reminded of that young boy on the hill, the promise I made to my father and our people."

Tears welled in Aurora's eyes at the image of a young Soren, his face bathed in sunlight that infused his young soul with dreams and endless possibilities. She smiled, touched by the innocence of the image, but her mind couldn't help but wander to the journey that had sculpted the man before her. *What trials had the boy endured to become the resilient, guarded man he was? What happened to that child brimming with optimism and wonder?*

"That's a beautiful memory," Aurora said. "Thank you for sharing it with me. I wish I could have met that little boy." She smiled warmly at him.

Their conversation emboldened Aurora as if it had cracked open a door, and she ventured further. "Did you grow up around here, then?" she asked.

Soren nodded. "My family moved around a lot when I was young, but the home I'm most fond of is just outside of Eldersmoor. My parents were sentinels too, so my childhood was filled with travel and adventure. But returning home to Eldersmoor was always the highlight. That's where I saw my parents at their most relaxed. We'd gather around the dinner table, sharing laughs, and I'd spend hours listening to their stories by the fire." His words painted a picture of a loving household, a stark contrast to the disciplined life of a warrior.

The wistful expression that crossed Soren's face stirred a deep empathy within Aurora. She could sense the memories and emotions behind his gaze, prompting her to ask with a gentle hesitance, "And where are your parents now?"

The brief flicker of pain that dimmed Soren's features was answer enough. "They died—killed defending our lands. I was still quite young." His voice was steady, but his eyes, distant and reflective, betrayed the depth of his loss.

Aurora's heart ached. "I'm so sorry," she whispered. Her instinct to comfort him was almost overwhelming.

Soren bristled. "It's in the past." He allowed himself a moment to dwell on the memory, then, perhaps sensing the weight of the conversation, he redirected the focus. "What about you? Tell me about your home." His amber eyes looked at Aurora with intrigue.

Aurora's expression lightened, amusement coloring her response. She let out a sound that hovered between a scoff and a chuckle. "My home is rather unremarkable compared to this." Her eyes scanned the lush landscape. "Endless flat lands stretching as far as the eye can see. People busy themselves with their daily routines, living lives that tread a predictable path. You work, and eventually, you die. There's not much room for anything else." Her words painted a picture of a life vastly different from Soren's, one rooted in monotony rather than adventure. But they shared a common thread of longing for something more.

The frankness in Aurora's voice caught Soren off guard. He had pictured her returning to a life vibrant with anticipation and purpose. "Do you not like it there?" he asked.

Aurora sighed. She thought of her marketing job, managing projects that didn't add meaning to her life. "It's fine, I suppose. I could move, start over somewhere else. But in the end, what's the point?" She stared into the distance. "The novelty wears off, and you find yourself caught in the same routines, just in a different place. Life has taught me that nothing is permanent. The best you can do is excel in what you're good at and seek small joys to make the days bearable." It was as if she had resigned herself to accepting life's monotony.

Soren asked his next question with a depth of emotion that surprised even himself. "And what brings you joy?" he asked, his amber eyes glimmering beneath the sun.

Aurora turned to face him, taken aback by the intensity of his gaze. His focused eyes waited for her response. The question hung in the air between them, a bridge to deeper understanding, an invitation for Aurora to share more of her inner world.

Her face brightened as she spoke of her interests. "I've always loved reading and exploring various arts and crafts. Swimming is another passion of mine. I feel most vibrant and free when I'm in the water." Her spirits lifted at the thought of immersing herself in the tranquility of clear waters.

Soren, sensing a shift in the conversation, probed further. "And what about your family?" he asked.

Aurora's expression sobered as she delved into more personal territory. "Well, my family ... It's complicated. My parents divorced when I finished school. It had been a long time coming; our home wasn't always a happy one. I have a younger sister, but we're quite different and not very close. My dad moved to another state and remarried soon after the divorce. My mom lives nearby, so I see her occasionally. But honestly, I've been putting my focus on my own life and trying not to dwell on the past."

Soren eyed her. "And do you have a lover waiting for you at home?"

Aurora choked back a cough at his directness, and her cheeks flushed. "If you mean a boyfriend or a husband, no, I don't have a lover waiting for me." A pit of loneliness settled in her stomach at her words. There really wasn't anyone waiting back home for her, besides Camryn. Her lack of closeness with her family and her preference for getting lost in a book rather than socializing with peers meant she lived on an island of her own making.

Soren, recognizing the somber turn of their conversation, offered a gentle smile and steered the topic to a lighter note. "You like to swim?" he asked, a playful glint in his eye.

Aurora threw him a suspicious side-eye. "Yes..." His mischievous glance promised a welcomed departure from the heavier subjects.

"Then I have a surprise for you," Soren said, his voice laced with a hint of mystery. With a quick, conspiratorial smile, he nudged Ash into a brisk trot.

Aurora, her curiosity piqued, spurred Beacon to follow. The landscape rose more steeply, and as they ascended, Soren vanished over the crest of a ridge. Urging Beacon to quicken her pace, Aurora soon reached the hill's summit. There, she paused, her gaze descending from atop her horse to the scene below. Soren was descending toward a secluded pool, its waters a stunning shade of turquoise, nestled at the foot of the imposing mountains.

The pool glowed with a surreal luminescence, its beauty arresting. The ripples from Soren's approach danced across the surface. It was as if nature itself was playing a soft, visual melody.

Aurora watched, breathless. The contrast was striking—his commanding presence against the gentle allure of the turquoise waters. A blend of strength and tranquility, resilience and peace.

As Aurora's fingers clasped the reins more firmly, she remained a figure of quiet observation atop her horse, her heart resonating with the poignant beauty unfolding below her.

With a sense of urgency, she guided Beacon down the hill, closing the distance between her and Soren. He stood there, a sentinel beside his horse, his gaze fixed on Aurora as she approached. In her eyes, he could see the reflection of the sun and the shimmering water, her face illuminated with a joy he hadn't seen before.

As she brought her horse to a gentle stop at the water's edge, Aurora let out an awestruck gasp. "Soren ... it's beautiful." The sheer beauty of the spot took her breath away.

Soren's response was a radiant smile, his heart swelling with a happiness that had been foreign to him for far too long. "I thought you might like it," he said. "I spent many days here as a child, playing in these waters." His words painted a picture of a younger, carefree Soren.

Filled with excitement, Aurora dismounted her horse. She approached the water, where gentle ripples lapped against the smooth pebbles, and crouched to touch the surface. The water warmed her skin despite the coolness of the day, sending a pleasant shiver through her.

Turning back to Soren, her eyes sparkled with anticipation and delight. "Do we have time for a quick swim?" she asked, her voice brimming with eagerness.

Soren's response was a warm chuckle, charmed by her childlike enthusiasm. "Of course, as long as we leave before nightfall," he teased with an affectionate smile.

Without hesitation, Aurora shed her outer layers, leaving all semblance of her modesty in front of the sentinel on the shore of the water. She leaned against Beacon for support as she kicked off her boots and removed her socks. With a fluid motion, she draped her cloak over her horse's back and pulled off her heavy sweater. She slipped out of her pants, standing in just her undergarments.

Aurora gave Soren a playful grin as he watched her. "Can I get a little privacy?"

Soren raised his brows and slowly turned his back to the barely clothed woman, a mischievous smile on his lips. *Gods help him.* Aurora kept her eyes on him as she removed her bodice, letting it fall to the ground along with the delicate fabric of her underwear.

The gracious sentinel kept his gaze fixed on an invisible mark in the distance, while his ears remained attuned to his surroundings. When he heard the surface of the water break, he waited a few more moments for Aurora's body to be sheathed under the cover of the spring before he turned toward her.

The water, warm and inviting despite the autumn air, swallowed Aurora. She ventured deeper until the water lapped just below her shoulders. She turned back to face Soren, who remained at the water's edge.

"Are you coming?" she called out, her voice carrying over the water, resonating with a playful challenge.

Soren began to undress, his movements deliberate, aware of Aurora's attentive gaze. As he peeled off his shirt, Aurora couldn't help but admire his well-defined physique, each muscle defined and gleaming under the sun's rays. *Lord help her.*

It was then that she spied a tattoo—which she hadn't noticed the night before—on the left side of his chest, hovering over his heart. There, on his tanned skin was an inked black snake wrapped around a dagger, its yellow eyes gleaming. Her mind flashed back to the serpent in the forest that slithered up her leg as if beckoned by her.

Soren's eyes caught her gaze, and he looked down at the tattoo on his chest. His brow furrowed, and a curious look fell on his face. He thought often of the tattoo that he got to memorialize his parents—the sentinel strength of his father and the healing and protective power of his mother; the two wrapped around each other, irrevocably entwined.

The night when he dreamed he was a serpent searching through the forest, he felt his parents' spirits within him, as if they were guiding him to the woman he was destined to protect. His eyebrows rose at the divine connection he couldn't shake, and he looked at Aurora treading in the water.

He paused as his hands drifted to the buttons on his pants. As Aurora watched him from the water, a smile played on his lips, and he cleared his throat.

Aurora blushed as she gawked at the half-naked man, and she turned her back to him. Her golden curls trailed in the water behind her. As she heard the rustling of fabric fall to the ground, she bit her lip to keep herself from turning back. She stayed steadfast as she heard his powerful legs force the water around his body as he entered the spring.

Each step of Soren's entrance into the water sent ripples across the surface, the water rising and lapping against his skin. He approached Aurora with a measured pace until he was just a breath away from her, and she turned toward him.

Aurora looked up at him, her eyes sparkling with delight. She scooped up a handful of water and playfully splashed it against Soren's chest. Her laughter rang out as he recoiled in surprise.

Soren responded with a feigned glare, his eyes deepening with mock severity. He dipped his head and let out a playful growl, prompting Aurora to let out a gleeful scream. Her eyes flickered with excitement before she submerged herself, disappearing beneath the surface.

Soren's demeanor shifted, a sly smile playing on his lips as he watched the spot where Aurora had vanished. He dove into the water after her, his movements fluid and powerful. It was a playful pursuit, charged with an undercurrent of excitement and attraction. Perhaps here, under a cloudless sky and within the solace of the watchful mountains, he could let his guard down. Just a little.

As Aurora resurfaced, the sunlight caught water droplets on her skin, casting her in a radiant glow. Soren, his strokes strong and determined, closed the gap between them. Their laughter mingled with the gentle sounds of the water, creating a harmonious chorus that echoed around them.

In this moment, amidst the playful splashes and shared laughter, they found themselves immersed in a realm of sheer exhilaration. It was a space where the usual barriers faded away, leaving only the vibrant pulse of their shared moment, a dance of light, water, and unspoken affection under the vast, open sky.

In the water, Aurora showed off her strong swimming skills, but Soren caught up to her with ease. His large hands found her shoulders, halting her playful escape. As she ceased her thrashing and stilled, their eyes locked. The playful glint in Soren's eyes retreated, replaced by a more intense, serious gaze as he peered into Aurora's eyes, deep and unfathomable. He stepped closer, his body only inches from hers, his hands still resting on her bare shoulders.

The warmth of the water complimented the heat emanating from Soren's touch, sending waves of fire cascading through Aurora's body. She reached out, her hands and gaze resting on the tattoo on his muscled chest. Something sparked beneath her hand as she imagined Soren as the slithering snake who found her in the forest, letting her know she was safe.

Her glimmering blue eyes sent shivers down Soren's spine. The sensation of water droplets under her fingers intensified the connection between them, drawing Soren further into the depth of her gaze. For a moment, they stood locked in each other's gaze, the world around them melting into the water.

Caught in the spell of the moment, Aurora rose onto her tiptoes, her eyes never leaving Soren's. Fighting back every urge her rational brain was telling her to stop, she brought her lips to meet his, igniting emotion that coursed through her. The kiss was intense, filled with a mutual longing. Soren's response was equally passionate, pulling her closer, their bodies aligning into a perfect union. A whirlwind of desire, passion, and excitement enveloped Aurora in a sense of comfort and security. *Maybe there was something in the water.* She surrendered to the embrace.

A thunderous roar from above suddenly interrupted the gentle lapping of water against their bodies. Aurora broke the kiss, her attention drawn upward. An enormous shadow swept over them, revealing a dragon soaring across the sky, its scales shimmering like obsidian in the sunlight.

Disoriented by the intensity of her emotions, Aurora looked at Soren, searching for reassurance. Concern etched his face. Without hesitation, he grasped her hand and guided her swiftly to the shore, ignoring the fact that they emerged naked and dripping wet. Urgency propelled them as they dressed and neither dropped their gaze from the sky above. The beating wings of the dragon overhead were a reminder of the unpredictability and dangers of the world they inhabited.

They dressed quickly, and Soren swung Aurora up onto Beacon. Her heart hammered in her chest, breath catching in her throat as Soren mounted Ash with practiced speed, setting off at a gallop toward the mountains. Aurora urged Beacon to keep pace, the horse's powerful strides jarring her as they raced forward.

The dragon was relentless in pursuit, its mighty wings slicing through the air, creating a thunderous roar that shook Aurora to her core. Soren's heart pounded, adrenaline surging through him as he navigated the rough terrain, the rush of air against his face almost drowning out the monstrous roar behind them.

Beside him, Aurora's heart raced in tandem with his. They charged through the dense forest, dodging low-hanging branches and leaping over gnarled roots. The path was a hazardous maze, each twist and turn presenting a new challenge, but the urgency of their escape sharpened their reflexes, driving them onward.

Sweat dripped down their foreheads, the physical exertion of their escape compounded by the terror of their pursuer. Aurora risked a fleeting glance back and her breath hitched at the sight of the dragon bearing down on them. Its massive body glided through the air, scales glistening like dark jewels in the sunlight above. The dragon was a magnificent yet terrifying sight, a creature of raw power and majesty. And it was closing in on them.

As the danger intensified, Soren's grip on the reins tightened. He navigated Ash with expert precision, darting between the dense forest trees and vaulting over obstacles with a deftness born of desperation. Aurora, shadowing him, matched his every move.

The dragon's roars continued to thunder through the woods, a terrifying sound that sent tremors through the ground and dislodged leaves in a flurry. Its fiery breath nipped dangerously close, singeing the air at the horses' heels. In Soren's chest, his heart beat a rapid drum of fierce conviction, each pulse a silent vow to keep Aurora safe.

In a moment that teetered on the edge of despair, Soren spotted a sliver of salvation—a narrow break in the dense foliage. With a burst of speed fueled by raw adrenaline, he steered his horse through the slim opening, Aurora following close behind. The pathway constricted even further; the trees pressing in on them like the walls of a narrowing corridor, but Soren's determination never wavered.

As they navigated the complex maze of the forest, their breathing became labored and ragged, and their vision tunneled to the path ahead. Behind them, the dragon's terrifying bellows receded, its presence diminishing as they maneuvered away from its clutches.

Breaking free from the dense forest, Soren and Aurora urged their horses onto a stretch of open terrain, guiding them toward a towering rocky outcrop The relief was palpable as they dismounted, pressing their backs against the cool, jagged surface of the rock.

The dragon's distant roars still echoed through the trees, a haunting and relentless sound that underscored the gravity of their escape.

Sheltered by the outcrop, they found themselves in a stone sanctuary. Their breathing steadied, and the pounding of their hearts subsided. But the memory of the chase, the fiery breath at their heels, and the shadow of the dragon overhead remained caged in Aurora's mind.

Chapter 8

Nestled within the sanctuary of the rocky outcrop, the surrounding forest paused—its very pulse slowing. Aurora focused on her breathing, creating a natural rhythm that soothed her frayed nerves. The adrenaline that had propelled them through the forest still lingered in her bloodstream.

A sense of relief settled around them. Aurora met Soren's eyes, and the rest of the world faded away.

Amidst the stillness, Aurora's hand reached out, her fingers trembling as they brushed against Soren's. The contact filled both with a wave of comfort. Their fingers entwined, as if compelled by a force greater than themselves.

Soren, his heart aching with the desire to rekindle the intimacy they'd shared at the spring, knew that the moment and setting were not right. Aurora deserved more than a hurried jaunt against the cold, damp rocks.

His face still marked with concern, Soren led Aurora out of the shelter. They reluctantly unclasped their hands as they stepped out from the rocky outcrop.

Without a word, Aurora launched at Soren, shoving his shoulder. She shook her hand when her palm hit his hardened muscle.

"You didn't tell me there were dragons here!" she yelled with a scowl.

Soren whirled in surprise. "I didn't expect we'd cross one. At least I was hoping we wouldn't." He gaped back at her.

"What else lives here that wants to kill me?" she asked, glaring at him.

Soren's jaw twitched. "I can tell you all about the creatures here as soon as we are safe. We should get moving." Aurora fought the urge to recoil at the sternness in his voice. She simply turned away from him and mounted her horse.

Aurora, rendered speechless, longed for the tranquil shores of the lake. There, amidst the serene waters and under the open sky, she had tasted a sense of freedom that now seemed like a distant dream. She yearned for that brief, idyllic escape where she had basked in the warmth of a different side of Soren—a side that was relaxed and playful, different from the relentless intensity of their current predicament.

They resumed their journey in silence. The forest around them breathed a sigh of relief, its dense foliage giving way to clearer vistas. With each step forward, the memory of their shared ordeal infused Soren with a renewed sense of purpose.

As they journeyed on, the terrain softened into a more forgiving landscape. It was as though nature itself was extending an olive branch, a kind hand guiding them toward a new chapter. The imposing mountains that had once loomed over them now receded into the backdrop, giving way to undulating hills and meadows that stretched out toward the edges of a village.

Upon reaching the crest of a hill, a scene of striking beauty unfolded before them. Eldersmoor, nestled in a valley cradled by mountains, revealed itself in all its splendor. Sunlight danced upon the tiled rooftops, turning them to molten gold, while plumes of smoke ascended from chimneys, sketching delicate patterns against the sky. The buzz of the town blended with the rustling of nature, creating a peaceful atmosphere.

As Aurora and Soren entered the village, they became the focus of many curious gazes. The townsfolk halted their daily activities, their intrigue clear in the way they watched the newcomers. The cobbled streets were filled with hushed conversations and subtle smiles. There was an energy in the air, a buzz generated by the rare appearance of strangers in their secluded haven.

Despite the intensity of the interest they garnered, the atmosphere in Eldersmoor was light. Here, amidst the quaint streets and the warm glances, the travelers found a brief reprieve from their journey.

Wandering through the heart of Eldersmoor, the town square thrived with activity, bustling with townsfolk and lined with a variety of stalls and shops. Each storefront displayed all the town had to offer, from the brightly colored fabrics fluttering in the breeze to the handcrafted goods that spoke of skilled artisanship.

As they moved through the town, the weight of many curious glances fell on Aurora. Her sense of being an outsider was palpable.

"Do I really stand out that much?" she asked, wary of the beings that watched her.

Soren's tone had lightened. "It's not just you," he said. "Visitors are rare in these parts. And you ... You are certainly not easy to overlook." His statement caused a warm flush to rise in Aurora's cheeks. *Was it because she was human?*

For a moment, Aurora found herself lost in the depths of Soren's gaze, the hum of the town around them fading into a distant murmur. It was as if they were alone amid the crowd, their connection forming a quiet island in the sea of Eldersmoor's unsuspecting residents. In his eyes, she saw a reflection of her own curiosity and wonder.

As evening approached, the sunset painted the sky in a breathtaking palette of gold and crimson. The surrounding air cooled, and a shiver ran through Aurora. A tranquil calm settled over the town, punctuated only by the sounds of villagers winding down their day.

Soren brought his horse to a gentle stop outside a quaint inn nestled near the village center. Its windows were lit with a warm light that spilled onto the cobblestone street, creating a magical display reminiscent of fireflies on a summer evening. Forcing herself to suppress the mental images of the dragon chasing them, Aurora found herself captivated by the inviting contrast of light and darkness, the inn's beckoning warmth promising a soothing escape from the cool kiss of the evening.

Her heart fluttered as she watched Soren dismount with a fluid grace. Eager for the shelter the inn promised, Aurora dismounted her horse, leaving it in the care of the local stable hand, before following Soren inside.

A tangible warmth enveloped her as they crossed the threshold, driving away the evening chill that had clung to her skin. A roaring fire in the stone hearth casting an enchanting play of light across the inn. Sturdy wooden beams lined the ceiling. The atmosphere was thick with the essence of many years and many travelers, all converging to create a space that felt both timeless and comforting.

As Aurora's eyes traveled across the inn's interior, she absorbed the mix of its patrons. Some were tucked into corners, lost in deep conversation, while others sat at tables laden with hearty fare, reveling in the evening.

Her gaze settled on Soren, who found them a vacant table. His eyes had softened. Aurora let out a quiet sigh, releasing the lingering stress of their adventurous day. She relaxed into the moment, the inn's atmosphere washing over her.

The promise of a comforting fire and a nourishing meal filled Aurora with a deep sense of satisfaction. Across from Soren, the fire's flickering light danced in his amber eyes, hypnotizing her.

A barmaid approached their table, her presence almost unnoticed until she placed two tall pints of chilled ale before them. The drink, frothy and cool, sloshed over the rims of the glasses as they made contact with the wooden surface, leaving small, glistening trails down the sides.

Aurora's gaze settled on the woman—undeniably fae and breathtakingly beautiful. Her stature was slim, with sun-kissed skin that shimmered in the firelight's glow. Her hair, a cascade of sleek, ebony locks, flowed over her shoulders, reaching down to her lower back. She carried a tray in her long, slender arms, while a tight black leather corset accentuated her enviable curves.

Aurora's eyes shifted away from the striking fae to gauge Soren's reaction, expecting him to be as captivated by her as she was. To her surprise, she found his attention remained on her, oblivious to the enchanting fae who stood beside them.

With a soft "Thank you" to the barmaid, Aurora watched as the woman moved away with a graceful, unconcerned air, barely acknowledging the human sitting at the table. Aurora's gaze lingered for a moment on the retreating figure, her mind a whirl of thoughts about the striking beauty of the fae and the undivided attention Soren had given her.

Soren's words were light, his tone tinged with both relief and renewed optimism. "It's remarkable, isn't it? How the warmth of a fire and the promise of a satisfying meal can turn everything around," he said, a soft smile playing on his lips.

Aurora stared into his amber eyes and wanted to follow his lead and fall into lighthearted conversation. But her cautionary brain reeled her back in.

"So, what else do I need to worry about besides a fire-breathing dragon?" she asked. She couldn't believe the words she was saying.

Soren appraised her sky-blue eyes, darkened with worry. He sighed and dipped his head to look at the weathered table. "For the most part, Silverveil is safe. But there are dark creatures who lurk in the lands north of the Silverveil Mountains. Occasionally, they leave their boundaries and venture south." His eyes flashed to her waiting face, etched with concern. "They often prowl when a tear in the veil has appeared." Aurora's eyes widened. "That's what I do—my duty as a sentinel is to fight off any creatures with malicious intentions," he continued. "I apologize for not making you aware of the dangers sooner. That is why we must reach Whispering Glen as soon as possible and return you home."

Aurora quieted, feeling the weight of Soren's words. She saw the pain and disappointment on his face and her heart sank. It was clear this wasn't easy for him, and she wasn't making it any easier. She grabbed her frosty mug of ale and lifted it to her lips.

"Well, there's nothing like a brush with death to make you appreciate the simpler things in life," she said, taking a long pull from her glass.

Soren's lips curled into a slight smile at Aurora's attempt at lightening the conversation. "Ah yes, the art of survival." His voice warmed Aurora's bones.

Aurora lifted her heavy mug of ale, her blue eyes flickering. "To survival, and the art of maintaining high spirits in the face of adversity." She smiled softly at Soren.

He marveled at Aurora's resilience. At her ability to ask the tough questions, weigh the information, and then proceed. He lifted his own frosty glass to hers. "Cheers to that," he said. Their mugs clinked together in agreement.

As they sipped their ale, a comfortable silence enveloped them, the crackling fire casting a soothing warmth.

Breaking the silence, Soren said, "You know, this journey keeps unfolding in the most unexpected ways. I can't help but wonder what other surprises lie ahead for us." His golden eyes danced with intrigue.

Aurora lurched forward, placing a warm hand across Soren's gaping mouth. "Shh! You're just asking for trouble!" Surprised at her actions, she retreated to her chair, her eyes watching Soren.

Her fingertips sparked Soren's lips in a delicious jolt. A smile curled on his face. "It appears trouble has a way of finding me." His voice was low, and his amber eyes burned into Aurora's.

Aurora couldn't stop the rush of heat that filled her cheeks at the enticing sound of Soren's voice. "Well, I apologize for the disappointment," she said, her eyes flashing to his under thick lashes as she sipped her ale, her tongue lapping at a lingering drop from her lips.

Soren noticed and his eyes hung on her wet mouth, entranced. He leaned back in his chair, desperate to flee Aurora's intoxicating scent and flirtatious actions.

Aurora smiled into her glass. Maybe she'd lean into this unexpected adventure more than she typically would. More than she should.

***

To Aurora's subdued dismay, Soren had arranged for separate rooms. Part of her had hoped the evening's conversation might extend into another night in a shared space. But Soren insisted on the need for rest, with an early start awaiting them in the morning.

Weary from the day's events, Aurora ascended the narrow stairs of the inn. The hallway was dim, the lanterns casting a soft, flickering light that played upon the walls. She reached her room, her hand turning the key in the lock with a faint click. The door swung open to reveal a modestly furnished space. Turning to Soren, who stood just outside her door, she found a comforting reassurance in his presence, a silent sentinel in the darkened hallway.

Aurora's voice was cautious. "Would you mind checking the room? Just to be sure everything's alright," she asked, her smile gentle but weary.

Soren responded with an understanding nod, eager to extend their time together. "Of course. After everything that's happened today, we can't be too careful," he said, stepping past her into the room.

He moved with practiced ease, his eyes sweeping over the space. Years of being a sentinel had honed his ability to assess his surroundings for any potential threats. Satisfied the room was secure, he turned back to Aurora, his expression one of calm assurance.

"All clear," he said, his gaze meeting hers in a silent promise of safety.

"Thank you," Aurora said, her gratitude laced with something more inviting.

Soren leaned casually against the doorframe, watching her. "Anything to ensure your peace of mind. Besides, it's a good excuse to linger a little longer in your company." He smiled at her.

Aurora's knees weakened at the sight of his sly smile, and warmth flooded her cheeks. His presence, once a source of mystery, had become a comforting constant, and his willingness to put her at ease only deepened her appreciation for him.

Her smile widened, eyes alight with amusement. "Well, I'm quite happy to have you as my knight in shining armor. It suits you," she said, her tone light and teasing.

Soren's chuckle filled the quiet hallway. "Let's not get too carried away with the titles," he said with a playful glint in his eye.

"Oh, it's far too late for that," Aurora said. "You've more than earned it, Sir Soren."

His laughter, rich and genuine, echoed down the corridor, filling the space with a sense of warmth and comfort. They lingered in the moment, their gazes locked.

"This journey ... it's full of surprises, isn't it?" he said.

Aurora nodded, her eyes still fixed on him. "It certainly is."

His amber eyes sparkled at her words, a smile tugging at the corners of his mouth. "I'm glad to add a bit of excitement to your life," he said.

Aurora's heart fluttered at the earnestness in his voice. She leaned into the playful banter. "Just try not to let it all go to your head."

Soren feigned a look of shock, his hand over his heart. "Me? Let something go to my head? Never," he said, the twinkle in his eye belying his mock indignation. Their laughter mingled in the air, a delightful harmony that brightened the dim hallway.

Beneath the laughter, there was a charged undercurrent, a truth that neither of them voiced—the undeniable, magnetic pull between them that intensified with each shared moment.

Aware of the advancing hour, Aurora glanced toward her room with a reluctant smile. "Well, it's getting late. I should get some sleep. Tomorrow is another day full of your surprises," she said, her voice soft. She bit her lip, holding back an invitation.

Soren's gaze held Aurora's with an intensity that rivaled his calm exterior. Inside, he was a storm of emotion, each wave crashing against his determination to part ways for the night. He imagined a different scenario, one where he could stay, where closing the door would shut out the world, leaving them in a timeless space of their own. He longed to hold her, to express the depth of his feelings, kindling a night alive with passion.

But reality held its ground, and with a deep, steadying breath, Soren grasped Aurora's hand. He lifted it to his lips and placed a kiss on the back of her hand. The warmth of his breath against her skin sent a shiver through her, a silent yearning for more. As he released her hand, Aurora's eyes lingered on his face, her heart echoing with unspoken wishes and the quiet hope of what may come.

Soren's eyes held Aurora's with a depth that bridged the space between them, communicating all the words that remained unspoken. His lips formed a gentle farewell, a whisper laden with the complexities of their situation.

"Goodnight, Aurora," he murmured, his voice a soft echo of their shared emotions.

"Goodnight, Soren," Aurora replied.

With a grace that hid the turmoil within, Aurora turned and retreated into her room, closing the door behind her with a soft click. Inside, she was overwhelmed by its quiet solitude. She leaned against the door and sighed, her thoughts swirling like leaves in a whirlwind.

In the quiet of her room, Aurora confronted a dizzying mix of emotions. This journey had taken her far from the realm of her familiar life, challenging the very rules that had once guided her—*don't let anyone get too close*. The unexpected intensity of her feelings for Soren was a surprise she hadn't prepared for. For so long, she had guarded her heart, wary of the vulnerability that came with romantic connections.

But, as she stood there, she couldn't help but wonder about the possibilities that lay in surrendering to these feelings, even if just for a single night. The thought of embracing the unknown with Soren, of finding solace and freedom in his arms, tempted her with its promise of liberation from her usual restraints.

In this fleeting, moonlit moment, the line between caution and desire blurred. Could she allow herself to be carried away by this sudden rush of passion? The thought of giving in to the magnetic pull between them held an intoxicating appeal. Perhaps she could push away her doubts and fears and take a chance on whatever connection was forming with Soren. Break free from the constraints of her usual self-imposed boundaries.

With her heart pounding, Aurora made a choice that defied her usual caution. Driven by a burst of boldness, she reopened her door and crossed the hallway to Soren's room. She stood in front of his door and took two steadying breaths to quell the flutter in her chest before knocking. The door swung open, illuminating Soren, shirtless and looking just as surprised and breathless as she was.

Her eyes traced the contours of his well-defined chest, the curves of the snake tattooed over his heart, then lifted to meet his intense gaze. In a charged moment, Aurora stepped forward, closing the gap between them. Her hands found his face, and she pulled him into a kiss, her heart racing in tandem with his responsive passion.

Soren backed into his room, Aurora's presence an insistent flame against him. He pushed the door shut behind her, his hands finding their way to her back, pressing her closer. The urgency of their movements spoke of a deep hunger, a longing that had been simmering beneath the surface.

His hands moved lower, contouring the shape of her, his grasp firm. In a single caress, he grasped the flesh of her thighs beneath her rounded backside and lifted her. Aurora's legs wrapped around his waist, anchoring herself to him. With their lips still locked in a passionate dance, Soren navigated toward the bed, each step fueled by a mixture of desire and a deep, undeniable connection. This was more than just physical; it was the culmination of a quiet bond that both had felt.

When his shins hit the wood frame of the bed, he bent forward, bracing Aurora's back as he lowered her onto the bed. She pulled her lips away from his, still framing his chiseled face with her hands. She looked into his amber eyes, which burned back at her.

Still holding her gaze, Soren lowered his knees to the bed. Aurora scooted back, making room for his mighty form. She lifted the hem of her sweater over her head before tossing it to the floor. Her corset-like undergarment held her breasts, raised and heaving with her quickened breaths.

Soren's eyes lingered on her chest before he moved closer to her. His fingers reached out to the delicate string that held the garment closed, just below where her breasts pressed together. He pulled, and the string fell loose, allowing Aurora to breathe deeper. He further tugged until the fabric loosened. Soren eyed her hardened, rosy nipples poking through, begging to be released. With both hands, he pulled the rest of the bodice away, and it fell open against the bed's downy covers.

Soren took a moment to appreciate her naked chest. Aurora's breasts were full and hung with a gentle slope. Her skin was fair and softer than he imagined, and it glistened under the flicker of flame that lit the room.

He moved to her, his lips pressing against hers, forcing her on her back as he hovered over her. Aurora's hands trailed along his muscular arms to his firm shoulders and down his ridged back. Her smooth touches sent chills down his spine, further encouraging him. Soren moved his lips from Aurora's and traveled down to her neck, the scent of lavender intoxicating him.

His lips trailed to her collarbone, and she gasped with delight. His tongue escaped his lips, tracing a small circle down his path. Aurora moaned with anticipation. Pressing on, Soren moved down her chest until his mouth found the hardness of her nipple. His lips on one, he moved his hand to the other full breast, wrapping his gentle fingers around it. He rubbed his fingers back and forth over her nipple, and it hardened further in response. His tongue traced small circles around the other, and his lips enveloped it, sucking lightly. His movements sent shockwaves throughout Aurora's body and further moans escaped her lips.

Spurred by her sounds, Soren continued his journey, kissing down Aurora's stomach. He looked up at her before tugging her leggings over her hips and sliding the material down her legs. He tossed them to the floor and sat back on his heels as he took in the sight of a fully nude Aurora. She lay raised on her elbows, watching him. Her knees raised, sliding her feet against the covers of the bed and obstructing Soren's view of the pulsating warmth between her legs.

After taking in the ample beauty of her body, Soren rose forward off his heels. He placed one hand on her knee, nudging it to the side. His other hand rested on her hip bone before sliding down her thigh, igniting her skin before reaching her other knee and spreading her legs open.

He watched her as he slid both hands up from her knees to her inner thighs, his thumbs gracing the skin at the apex. Aurora's breath hitched. Soren moved forward, his mouth returning to her chest, his lips tugging against her nipple. One hand cupped her breast while the other lingered against her inner thigh. He moved closer to the growing heat between her legs until his fingers felt her arousal. His thumb teased, and he traced gentle circles against her most sensitive spot. Aurora moaned and her breath quickened.

Soren moved with purpose. He retreated from Aurora's chest and his lips resumed their journey downward toward the wetness his fingers enjoyed. As his mouth moved closer to the warmth between her legs, he watched her. She returned his stormy gaze, anticipating the destination of his mouth.

He slid his hands under Aurora's thighs, gripping her hips and pulling her toward him. Her legs spread further open and rested against his firm arms. His lips kissed the soft skin outside the apex of her thighs before he unleashed his tongue on her warm skin, tasting her. She moaned at the sensation of his tongue against her.

Soren's mouth pressed further into her wetness, his tongue moving in small circles. She writhed beneath him, and he tightened his hold on her hips. As his lips sucked gently, Aurora squirmed beneath him and her moans grew louder.

Soren slowed his movements and released one arm from his hold on her and moved to unbutton his pants. With one last flick of his tongue, he pulled away from Aurora's wetness while she panted beneath him. He pushed back to the edge of the bed and stood, lowering his pants to the floor.

Aurora raised herself to look at him, his eyes darkened with desire. Soren stood before her, naked and radiating sensual energy. She gasped at his hardened length. He moved to the bed, stalking toward her heaving body with his powerful arms. He hovered over her before lowering his lips to her mouth once again. Passion and desire fueled Aurora's lips.

Soren moved his hips to align with hers, lowering himself while Aurora spread her legs wide and lifted her hips, ready to receive all of him. He pulled his lips away, his nose brushing her cheek. His amber eyes burned into hers as he pressed into her. Aurora's mouth opened in pleasure, and a soft moan escaped her lips.

He studied her face, full of euphoric bliss, before moving rhythmically. Every thrust of his hips filled her more deeply. Her breath quickened with the rock of their bodies, and her moans grew louder. Soren increased his pace and deepened his thrust when she was close to release. Aurora felt him harden inside her and thought she would explode from pleasure. Her hands gripped his rigid back, desperate to keep herself in the hypnotic rhythm that brought her closer and closer to climax.

Soren moved his lips to Aurora's breast while continuing the movement of his hips. Her nails dug into the skin of his back, and her breath hitched. He stayed focused on her hardened nipple as her head tilted back, and she released the most primal moan, her body shaking beneath him. She pulled tighter against his back as waves of pleasure crashed against her.

Satisfied by her body's response, Soren let himself fill with pleasure, a wave of heat building inside him before exploding through his body. He heaved several more thrusts as he pulsated inside her, emptying himself. A deep, guttural groan escaped him as he finished, and the two lay breathlessly together.

Aurora caught her breath and brushed away the strands of hair that clung to Soren's glistening face. His amber eyes moved to hers, and they kissed, sharing a delicate moment of pure intimacy.

Soren shifted off her, but pulled her close to his chest, his hand holding hers against his body. The exhaustion and exhilaration surprised her. Aurora nestled closer to his chest and heard the melodic thumping of his heart. She ran her fingertips over the black snake that curled on his chest, feeling the inked skin of the tattoo. Her brow furrowed as her hand traced the ink.

"You're my protector," she whispered.

Soren tilted his head to look at her. "I am," he said with confidence.

Her blue eyes gazed up at him. "In the forest, before I fell through the portal, there was a snake that slithered up my leg while I was daydreaming. When I realized what was happening, I wasn't afraid. It's like I knew it wouldn't hurt me. Like it was just letting me know it was there and that I wouldn't be alone."

Soren's brow furrowed. "I dreamed of you," he said. "That I was a snake in the forest, compelled to find someone—you. Only I couldn't see your face. I didn't know it was you."

Aurora's heart beat faster. "How?" she whispered.

Soren's face softened. "I think it was my parents ... guiding me to you. You needed me. That's why I went to the river that day. I just knew you'd be there."

What did it mean? Were they destined to find each other? Why? Aurora's head swirled with questions, but she felt safe in his arms. Her eyelids drifted shut at the warmth of Soren's body, and the entanglement of their fingers comforted her. He pressed a soft kiss to her forehead as she drifted to sleep.

In the quiet of the room, Soren lay awake, his mind replaying the passion of the night. The soft sound of Aurora's gentle breathing against his chest was a sweet serenade, a soothing rhythm that brought a smile to his face. He appreciated the vulnerability she displayed in her sleep, her gentle breaths a lullaby to his thoughts.

Soren wished to capture this moment, to hold on to the serenity and closeness they had found in each other. He turned his head to gaze upon her peaceful face and planted a soft kiss on her forehead, inhaling the lingering scent. His eyelids grew heavy, his breath synchronizing with hers in a harmonious rhythm, as sleep claimed him too.

Outside the safety of their room, the night in Eldersmoor held more than just peace and slumber. High above the village, in a secluded cavern with a commanding view, a figure lurked in the shadows. No longer in the guise of a fearsome dragon, the figure's form shimmered and shifted, revealing its true identity—a shadow weaver, her features marked by a dark, enigmatic beauty. Her violet eyes, alight with a malevolent curiosity, surveyed the village below.

The shadow weaver, skilled in the powers of illusion and deception, watched, a malicious smile playing on her lips. She harbored a secret agenda, driven by a relentless search for a rift in the veil that imprisoned her. Her gaze sharpened, filled with calculated plans that would intertwine her path with that of the sleeping lovers. Soren and Aurora remained unaware that their fate had become intricately linked with this malevolent figure, who harbored sinister intentions that would unfold in unimaginable ways.

CHAPTER 9

The first light of dawn filtered through the window, casting a gentle warmth across Aurora's face. As she stirred, her senses slowly reawakening, she became acutely aware of the comforting presence of Soren beside her. She allowed herself a moment to bask in the remnants of the night before.

Aurora's heart expanded with a complex blend of emotions. There was something deeper that she hadn't expected. The night they had shared lingered in her mind, a vivid collection of moments that she replayed with a sense of wonder and introspection. Soren had so easily cracked her protective walls. *She'd let him do it.* Maybe her unguarded actions were a coping mechanism for her uncertain situation. Or maybe she was letting herself feel emotions that she hadn't allowed herself to feel in years, and act on them.

But Aurora couldn't help but feel their union had been more than physical—it was an intertwining of souls, a search for understanding and comfort in each other's arms amidst the unpredictability of their journey. Her fingers grazed the texture of the blanket, her thoughts meandering through the intimate memories of their passionate encounter. The bond that had formed between them was undeniable, leaving Aurora excited, but uncertain about what lay ahead.

Soren, sensing her awakening, stirred beside her. His touch, roughened by the life of a sentinel, traced a path along her arm, igniting a cascade of sensations. Their eyes met, and in that gaze, a silent conversation unfolded. The room pulsed with the depth of their shared emotions, a blend of desire, fragility, curiosity, and a faint whisper of apprehension about the future.

Soren's morning voice, rough with sleep, broke the stillness of the room. "Good morning," he said, tracing his fingers along her arm.

Aurora smiled. "Good morning," she said, her voice barely above a hush, but laden with the complex emotions that had blossomed within her. Their gazes remained interlocked, creating an intimate world that eclipsed everything else around them. In that silent exchange, they acknowledged the depth of their connection—they were on the precipice of exploring something intense and uncharted.

The morning light spilled into the room, bathing them in its golden glow, casting a serene ambiance over their entwined figures. Soren shifted closer, their bodies mirroring each other, heads propped on bent arms. He traced his finger down the length of Aurora's other arm, eliciting a trail of goosebumps in response to his touch. His smile deepened at her reaction.

Soren broke the silence. "We should eat." His voice was smooth and inviting, like the comfort of the morning.

Aurora rolled her eyes at his incessant sentinel practicality, but asked, "Where are we headed today?" Her question hung in the air. Each destination was a step further into the unknown but made less daunting by his company. He intrigued her. Soren was unlike any man she'd met back home. His chivalry was endearing and slightly annoying. She didn't want to be thought of as weak—a damsel in distress. But she knew there was more to him than his protective side. And she was ready to pull back more layers.

Soren's gaze grew distant, his eyes reflecting the gravity of their mission as he contemplated their next steps. "Whispering Glen is our next stop, a day or two's ride from here. We don't have the exact location of the tear in the veil, but there's a place we can stay while I search for it," he said, his voice tinged with a sense of duty.

Aurora felt a pang of sadness at his words, her heart sinking with the realization that their time together was drawing closer to its end. It was a strange contrast to her initial desperation to return to her own world. Now, the prospect of leaving this world, and Soren, filled her with a sense of loss and longing. It was as if a piece of her had become irrevocably tied to this realm. And leaving it meant she would have part of her ripped away. She'd only ever wanted to feel whole, and now she was being pulled in two different directions.

Masking her emotions, she mustered a smile. "Well then, let's have breakfast," she said, forcing a note of cheerfulness into her voice.

Soren returned her smile with a gentle one of his own, sensing the shift in her mood. He rolled out of bed, stretching his naked body. Aurora couldn't help but admire his form, the memory of her hands tracing the contours of his back, sending a thrill through her. She remained silent, watching him as he dressed, his gaze contemplative as he looked out the window. Unspoken emotions and the poignant awareness of the inevitable crossroads approaching in their journey filled the quiet moment.

Soren peered out the window, his eyes scanning the horizon. "Looks like storm clouds are gathering. We might need to hold off on leaving until they clear," he said, his tone carrying a mix of caution and a hidden pleasure at the thought of spending more unhurried time with Aurora.

After he dressed, Soren collected Aurora's scattered clothes from the floor and laid them neatly at the foot of the bed. He lingered for a moment, tempted by the desire to stay and watch her dress in the morning light that bathed the room. But he chose the more respectful option, deciding to afford her some privacy.

"I'll go down and secure a table for breakfast. Take your time getting ready," he said, casting a final glance at Aurora, who sat in bed, sheets pulled loosely to her chest, offering him a side view of the curve of her bare breast. There was a hint of disappointment in her eyes, reflecting their mutual regret at the end of their secluded time together.

With a warm smile, Soren quietly exited the room, softly closing the door behind him, and leaving Aurora in the serene ambiance of the morning.

She sat for a moment, reflecting on the unexpected turn their journey had taken. Rising from bed and slipping into her clothes, she couldn't help but recall the previous night—the way Soren had eagerly untied the same laces she now fastened. Memories of his touch played through her mind. His lips left a lingering warmth on her skin. She took deep, steadying breaths to calm the flurry of emotions and vivid images of their night together.

Aurora navigated her internal conflict, grappling with the unexpected depth of her feelings for Soren. She had assumed that giving in to her desires might somehow resolve the emotions she harbored for him, filling a primal need. But she found that their night together had only intensified her feelings. She shook her head as if to clear away the swirling thoughts. She smoothed her sweater and stepped out of the room, leaving the echoes of their shared night behind as the door clicked shut.

In the inn's common room, Aurora spotted Soren seated at a small table in the corner. As she approached, he stood, a gesture of respect that didn't go unnoticed. Even now, after the intimacy they had shared, Soren was captivated by her presence, his gaze lingering on her with an air of admiration. "You look beautiful," he said.

Heat tinted her cheeks at his straightforward compliment. "Thank you," she said softly.

They settled into their seats, and a comfortable atmosphere settled around them. Soren leaned forward, his voice low and smooth. "I've been chatting with some locals this morning. There's talk of impending storms and heavy rains. It seems staying in Eldersmoor until the weather improves would be wise." He couldn't conceal his delight at the prospect of being delayed by the weather. It was an unexpected but not unwelcome development.

Aurora's face brightened at the news. The possibility of an extended stay in Eldersmoor made her heart flutter, particularly at the prospect of spending more time with Soren. "Are you certain the locals weren't just trying to keep an impressive sentinel like you in town?" she teased.

Soren's smile broadened, a soft chuckle escaping him as he played along with her jest. "Well, I can't say for sure. I suppose my sentinel charm might be hard to resist," he said, the laughter in his eyes reflecting the light-hearted nature of their conversation.

Aurora laughed, a pleasant sound that tugged at Soren's heart. Their interaction was effortless, marked by an ease that suggested a familiarity far beyond the brief time they had known each other.

As Aurora reached for her tea, her fingers brushed against Soren's on the table, sending a jolt of awareness through her. It was a small but significant reminder of the attraction that continued to grow between them, a silent acknowledgment of the unspoken emotions that were gradually rising to the surface. She stifled her desire to reach for him, to guide him to the privacy of her room and tear off his clothes with passionate intensity.

Aurora restrained herself, and an unexpected question bubbled to her lips. "Do you have someone waiting for you? Someone to go home to?" She chewed her fingernail, anxious about what he might say. But if history told her anything, men weren't forthcoming about other partners they may have—at least in her world.

Soren's gaze flashed to her, a serious expression on his face. "No, of course not. I would not have shared a bed with you if that were the case."

Heat flooded Aurora's cheeks at her assumption. "I just thought I'd ask. What happened last night was unexpected, and I didn't know if you had someone who cared about you like that."

Soren's amber eyes burned into Aurora's. "I don't know what it's like where you're from, but it is a great dishonor for a man to betray his woman like that. I could never do such a thing."

Flutters filled Aurora's stomach hearing Soren talk about a man's loyalty to his lover.

His gaze narrowed, and he clenched his fists. "Has someone done that to you? Betrayed your trust in such a way?"

The deep timbre of his voice swirled heat through her body. She blushed again and dropped her gaze to the table, trying to sound as indifferent as possible. "Once, yes. We'd been dating for a few months when I found out he was also seeing other people. So, I like to ask now—better to know what I'm getting myself into than be surprised." Aurora looked back up at Soren, who was watching her intently. "But it's obviously different, me just being here until I can get home. I just wouldn't want to be the reason for someone else's pain," she said.

Soren was quiet, but his face softened. "I'm deeply sorry someone betrayed you like that. He must have been a fool for having eyes for anyone other than you."

Aurora blushed again at the compliment and the burning intensity in Soren's eyes. A shy smile curled on her lips. "Thank you," she said. "And he was a fool." Soren chuckled and flashed Aurora a brilliant smile.

The morning passed in a blur of conversation and laughter. The easy flow of their dialogue did not escape her attention. With each word, the invisible thread that linked them grew stronger, reinforcing a surprisingly natural intimacy.

Despite the looming uncertainties and the shadow of the pursuing dragon, Aurora found comfort in Soren's company. The storm that threatened to unleash its fury on Eldersmoor felt distant, overshadowed by the warmth and connection that flourished between them. As they talked, Aurora couldn't shake the feeling that perhaps fate had guided her to this realm for a purpose yet to be unveiled, a thought that lingered in her mind like an unsolved mystery.

Following their morning meal, Aurora and Soren readied themselves to venture outside. Donning their cloaks, they stepped into the lively streets of Eldersmoor. Soren extended his arm, to which Aurora accepted with a smile. She slipped her arm under his and they walked in sync, their steps harmonizing as they walked the uneven streets.

The market square, vibrant and bustling, beckoned them with its array of sights and smells. The air was rich with the aroma of baked goods and savory stews. They wandered among the stalls, each one a treasure trove of foods and handcrafted items.

The time spent wandering around the town was rejuvenating. Aurora couldn't help but feel uplifted by the noticeable change in Soren's mood. He was lighter, his mood pairing with the vibrant atmosphere of the market.

At one stall, Soren paused to admire wooden figures, masterfully carved and rich in detail. His fingers traced the craftsmanship. Soren's eyes lingered on one particular figure—a woman, standing tall with a serene look on her face. In her hands, she held a dagger, and a celestial sun hung above her head. When Aurora called to him, it was difficult for him to look away from the curious figurine.

In the heart of the market, the air was alive with music. A group of musicians played spirited tunes on their stringed instruments, casting a spell of joyfulness over the gathering crowd. The music drew the people of Eldersmoor, young and old, and they clapped their hands and swayed their bodies to the infectious rhythm. Aurora, tangled in the festive atmosphere, laughed freely, feeling a sense of liberation and pure bliss. She glanced at Soren, his attention captivated by the musicians, his face alight with a wide grin.

He turned to Aurora, a playful spark in his eye, and extended his hand toward her. "May I have this dance?" he asked.

Aurora, surprised by his sudden invitation, couldn't help but laugh. "Dance? Here, in front of everyone?" she asked, her eyes sparkling at the image of Soren dancing in the crowd.

"Yes," Soren said, his smirk widening. "Dancing and celebrating life—I take that very seriously."

"Well then," Aurora said, her voice laced with playful sarcasm, "how could I possibly deny you such a pleasure?" She placed her hand in his, and they stepped forward, joining the rhythmic sway of Eldersmoor's lively gathering.

Aurora and Soren blended into the crowd that spun and swayed with infectious energy. The musicians, sensing the growing excitement, shifted into a livelier tune, the notes leaping into the air. A thrilling mix of anticipation and nervousness swirled within Aurora, but the welcoming smiles of the townspeople eased her into the festive spirit. The square had transformed into a communal space of shared happiness, where the barriers between strangers dissolved in the rhythm of dance and music.

Soren's gaze was steady, a silent promise of his support. His presence was both reassuring and invigorating, giving Aurora the confidence to join the dance. With a slight nod and a smile, he silently assured her of his guidance through the lively jig.

As the music swelled, Soren's hand found its place at the small of Aurora's back, his touch igniting a spark within her. She placed her hand in his, their fingers intertwining. They inhaled in unison and began to move, their bodies responding intuitively to the vibrant melody that surrounded them.

Soren led with a natural grace, his movements perfectly in tune with Aurora's. Together, they danced, each step and turn a seamless expression of their synchronized rhythm. Their gaze remained connected, creating an oasis of calm amidst the vibrant whirl of the dance. Around them, the world became a kaleidoscope of swirling colors and harmonious sounds, but in each other's gaze, they found a point of steady focus. Soren's smile was a constant, reassuring presence that encouraged Aurora to abandon her inhibitions and fully immerse herself in the rhythm and jubilation of the dance.

With each turn and step, they moved as one, their laughter mingling with the music, embodying the shared emotions of the moment. The drum's rhythmic beat mirrored the pulse of Aurora's heart, a guiding cadence for their synchronized movements. A wave of pure exhilaration swept away any initial apprehension, connecting her not just to Soren, but to the entire gathering around them.

The town square thrummed with collective energy, a vibrant, communal pulse that unified everyone in a celebration of the present. The music rose to a crescendo, and with it, Soren's and Aurora's dance quickened, their movements a whirlwind of euphoria. Their laughter flitted through the air, adding its own unique note to the symphony of the square.

The lively dance came to a close, and with it, Soren's and Aurora's spirited movements slowed to a gentle sway. As the music dwindled into silence, they stood close, hands still clasped, breaths mingling in the cool air. Their eyes met and for that moment, Aurora had completely forgotten how far she was from home.

A soft, familiar voice calling out to Soren interrupted their intimate moment. He turned, his expression shifting from curiosity to recognition as his eyes settled on a petite elderly fae woman with sparkling green eyes.

"Soren? Soren, is that you?" The woman's voice carried a mixture of surprise and delight.

As Soren's gaze met hers, his confusion giving way to recognition. "Elara?" he asked.

"You remember me, sweet boy?" Elara's joy was palpable as she hugged Soren, her small arms barely reaching around his broad shoulders. The warmth of their reunion was clear, a connection rooted in memories of years gone by.

Aurora watched the exchange with a gentle smile. It was a glimpse into Soren's past, a piece of his life that she had yet to know.

After a moment, Elara released Soren and turned her inquisitive eyes to Aurora. "And who is this lovely young woman, Soren?" she asked, her gaze alight with curiosity.

Soren introduced Aurora with pride. "Elara, this is Aurora. She's been traveling with me." His eyes drifted to Aurora's curious face.

Aurora's eyes lingered on Soren, wondering how he might introduce her. She extended her hand to the woman and smiled. "It's a pleasure to meet you, Elara," she said.

Elara's gaze held a sparkle of mischief as she appraised Soren and Aurora. "A companion, then?" she asked, her voice rich with humor and an unspoken insight.

Soren blushed. "Yes, something like that."

Elara's response was a gentle chuckle. "There's a unique charm in adventures shared with good company," she said, her eyes twinkling with understanding.

Aurora's cheeks flushed at Elara's words. The older woman's playful and welcoming nature helped bridge the gap between them, making Aurora feel more comfortable in this unexpected encounter.

Elara motioned toward a quaint, ivy-covered cottage that lay nestled in the trees nearby. "Let's continue this conversation indoors. I'm eager to hear about your journeys and what brings you to Eldersmoor," she said with an inviting smile.

Soren and Aurora shared a glance before they followed Elara. As they walked, the late afternoon sun bathed the scene in a golden light, adding a serene glow to the quaint village. As they stepped into Elara's home, an ambiance rich with memories and comfort greeted them. The cottage was a repository of stories, each corner whispering tales of the past.

Gathered around a small table in the heart of Elara's cottage, the flickering candlelight cast a warm, intimate glow over them. Elara settled in her chair. Her eyes, reflecting the candlelight, held depths of emotion. At some point, the conversation had turned to Soren's parents.

Elara's words carried the weight of fond remembrance, her voice tinged with a blend of sadness and reverence. "Ah, Soren, your parents were remarkable people. Their presence was valued by all. They extended their hands and hearts, never wavering in their commitment to our people."

Captivated, Soren leaned in, his eyes reflecting a deep longing to reconnect with the fragments of his past. "Can you tell me more about them? My memories are fragmented pieces."

As Elara spoke, her gaze drifted to a place far away, her mind traversing the corridors of time. "Your father, Cathal, was a pillar of honor and dedication. His vow to protect and preserve the balance of our world was unmatched. A master of the sword, yes, but his greatest strength was his ability to unite, to kindle a sense of solidarity among us, especially in our darkest hours."

A smile graced Soren's face, his heart warmed by the image of his father, a man of principle and courage. "I remember him saying that, emphasizing the virtue of standing for what's right," he murmured, the words echoing the teachings of his youth.

Elara's expression softened, a light flickering in her eyes as she spoke of Soren's mother. "And Orla, your mother, she possessed a captivating grace. Her connection to nature was a dance of spirit and life. She could nurture the most forlorn garden into a haven of blooms, and her hands held the power to heal. She was a guardian of life, her essence intertwined with the very soul of our land."

Soren's voice carried a depth of emotion as he reminisced, a blend of admiration and a wistful yearning for the past. "I have vivid memories of her tales about the forest, its mysteries, and hidden treasures."

Elara, her emerald eyes misty with memories, nodded slowly. Her gaze transcended the walls of the cottage, reaching back through the years. "Indeed, Orla had a profound connection with the land. She saw life and stories in every aspect of nature, in every rustle of leaves, in every stone on the path. Together, Cathal and Orla were the embodiment of harmony. His strength was the perfect counterbalance to her gentleness. Her magical touch found its match in his determination. They were not just partners but two halves of a whole, their qualities merging to create a remarkable connection that was felt by everyone around them."

While sitting at the table with Elara, Aurora immersed herself in the richness of the stories that unfolded, feeling the weight and emotional depth of the conversation. She watched Soren, seeing the blend of love and loss reflected on his face as he listened to Elara speak of his parents.

Elara's smile carried both joy and sadness. "Your parents' love was profound, Soren. And their love for you was beyond measure. You brought so much joy into their lives."

Soren's response was quiet, his voice carrying a subtle undercurrent of grief. "But they're no longer here," he whispered.

Elara extended her hand across the table, resting it on Soren's. "Their physical presence may be gone, but they live on through you. In your eyes, I see their spirit, and in your actions, their kindness. You are their legacy, Soren, a living testament to their love and strength." She beamed at him.

Aurora's heart swelled at this exchange. The bond he shared with his parents deeply moved her, a connection made of memories she could only imagine. She felt privileged to be part of this intimate moment, offering her silent support.

Elara then turned her gaze to Aurora, her eyes warm and insightful. "And you, Aurora, you've become a part of this story. Your path crossing with Soren's is no small matter. There's a purpose to your presence here, I believe."

Soren shared a reassuring look with Aurora, encouraging her to share her story. Aurora turned to Elara, her voice soft. "I was near Riverholm when Soren found me. I was in trouble, and he saved me."

"That's quite fortunate. But what were you doing out there alone by the river?"

Aurora hesitated, glancing at Soren, who nodded with encouragement. Taking a deep breath, she revealed the extraordinary circumstances that had led her to this moment. "I had an accident. I was out looking for a friend of mine and fell down a ravine in the night. And then I woke up by the river, disoriented." Aurora paused, wondering how much more she should reveal about her violent tumble from another world.

Aurora's recounting of her arrival in their realm painted a vivid picture of her ordeal. "So, I've been traveling with Soren since then, trying to find a way back to where I belong." Her eyes shifted to the woman.

Elara's response was thoughtful, a nod of understanding forming as she processed Aurora's story. "A traveler, then," she murmured, more to herself than to them. Her gaze shifted to Soren, a look of realization dawning. "Well, that does shed light on a few things," she said. Soren stilled.

Turning her attention back to Aurora, Elara's expression warmed. "You were indeed incredibly lucky to cross paths with Soren. He's renowned as one of the finest sentinels of Silverveil." She smiled, a reflection of the high regard she held for Soren.

Soren offered a humble grin. "Thank you, Elara, for the memories. As for our journey, we're headed to Whispering Glen. There have been some reports of a new tear in the veil, and it seems like our best chance to get Aurora back to her world." His voice tapered off, the thought of Aurora's departure casting a shadow over his words.

"We had planned to continue our journey this morning," Soren added, glancing at Aurora with a grateful smile for the unexpected delay. "But it looks like the weather has granted us another day here."

Elara watched the subtle exchange of glances between them, the unspoken connection between Soren and Aurora evident in the air. "It's a pleasure to meet you, Aurora. I'm sure Soren has appreciated the company on his travels." Her tone held a knowing quality, a gentle teasing that hinted at the deeper bond she sensed between them.

As Aurora sat at Elara's table, her cheeks warmed with a blush, the memories of the night spent in Soren's arms flooding back. She had always been a solitary soul, often preferring the company of a good book to idle conversations. But in the whirlwind of events that had brought her to this realm, Soren had become more than just a protector or guide—he was someone deeply significant to her. And that realization frightened Aurora. It was a novel feeling. The only bond she held at any depth was with Camryn, and even that was one of friendship, not an intimate connection.

Soren's presence illuminated the past days, though filled with fear and uncertainty. What started as a source of comfort had blossomed into a profound connection. His presence, initially a reassuring calm in the chaos, had grown into an essential part of her daily life. Aurora had to admit to herself that this man from another world had effortlessly found his way into her heart, leaving her with a fear of the emptiness his absence would bring. *What would happen to her when she returned home?*

Soren, noticing the change in Aurora's expression, decided it was time to leave. "Elara, it's been a pleasure revisiting these memories with you. Thank you for welcoming us into your home," he said. "We should head back to the inn now, though, to avoid the storm."

Elara stood up to bid them farewell, her smile filled with warmth. "Seeing you has brought back so many wonderful memories, Soren. You've made this old woman incredibly happy today."

As Aurora watched them, tears welled in her eyes, moved by the scene before her. This unexpected trip was fraught with danger but had also been a journey of discovery and lasting connections. It was a poignant reminder of the impact of each moment and relationship had on her life.

Elara reached out to clasp Aurora's hands. Her emerald eyes, vibrant and full of emotion, shimmered as she spoke. "Aurora, like the first light of dawn, it's been a true joy to meet you. You're an extraordinary young woman, and I hope our paths cross again. But for now, I wish you safe travels home." Elara's eyes flickered briefly to Soren. "Remember us, and the time you spent here."

Aurora's smile wavered as she fought back tears. "I don't think I can forget any of this," she said, her gaze sweeping across the room before settling on Soren. "This experience, this place, you, Soren ... it's all been like a dream." She noticed the intensity in Soren's eyes, reflecting a myriad of emotions. She swallowed hard.

***

The setting sun, casting its vibrant hues across the mountains, greeted Aurora as she stepped outside Elara's cottage. While engrossed in the woman's stories, she had forgotten about the outside world and the passage of time.

But as Soren and Aurora left the comfort of Elara's home, the reality of their situation settled back upon them. Challenges and uncertainties loomed ahead, but their bond had strengthened. The connection they had forged provided a glimmer of hope. It was a reminder that, regardless of what lay ahead, they had each other's support, a source of light amid any looming darkness.

As they made their way back to the inn, Soren and Aurora moved in a comfortable silence, their steps synchronized, their arms occasionally brushing against each other in a soft, unintentional dance. The natural chorus of chirping birds and the gentle rustle of leaves in the breeze provided a serene backdrop to their walk. Amidst the tranquility, Aurora grappled with a sense of sadness, the thought of leaving this world and Soren weighing heavily on her heart.

Soren, perceptive of Aurora's mood, reached for her hand. His fingers intertwined with hers, offering a silent reassurance. Aurora looked up at him, meeting his comforting smile with a mix of gratitude and sadness.

A gusting wind soon disrupted the atmosphere, signaling the impending storm. Dark clouds rolled in overhead, casting a foreboding shadow over the landscape. Soren, with a wary glance at the sky, quickened their pace toward the inn. Around them, the townspeople hastened their steps, closing shop shutters and scurrying toward the safety of their homes.

As soon as they stepped into the inn, there was a palpable sense of unease. The main room buzzed with the anxious chatter of the residents, their voices a blend of concern and speculation. The whispered mention of a shadow weaver caught Soren's attention, heightening his vigilance.

Without wasting a moment, Soren guided Aurora upstairs to her room, his urgency clear. As he ushered her inside, his mind was already racing with the need to protect her from whatever danger the whispers of the shadow weaver might reveal.

Aurora pressed for answers, her voice tinged with anxiety. "What's wrong?"

Soren's expression was grave, his brows furrowed in concern. "I don't know yet," he said. "But I need to gather some information. Please, stay in your room. Keep the door locked and stay clear of the windows." His tone was firm as he drew the heavy curtains closed, ushering the room into a dim light.

Aurora watched, her anxiety escalating into fear, as Soren moved swiftly around the room, securing each lock and checking every entry point. His actions spoke of imminent danger, heightening her sense of alarm. Frustration and fear mingled in Aurora's voice. "You can't just leave me here without explaining what's going on." She stared at him, her blue eyes searching for answers.

Soren paused, turning to face her. "Do you remember the dragon that chased us?"

The memory of the dragon was vivid in Aurora's mind, a terrifying encounter she could not easily forget. "Yes ..." she replied, her voice barely above a whisper.

Soren's gaze was steady, his voice low. "That was not just a dragon. It was a shadow weaver—a powerful sorceress who can take any form. I heard some townsfolk whisper of a shadow weaver. I need to find out what they know and why she might be here."

Aurora's heart sank as she processed this information. *So, the dragon chase wasn't a simple encounter, but potentially the work of a powerful sorceress.* The idea was almost too fantastic to believe, yet in this world, it appeared anything was possible. It was a stark reminder of how little she knew of this realm.

"I won't be long," he said. "Just stay in here, and remember, only open the door if you're sure it's me," Soren reassured her as he moved toward the door.

Aurora's voice held a tinge of fear as she contemplated the deceptive abilities of the shadow weaver. "But if this shadow weaver can mimic anyone, how will we ever be sure of who we're dealing with? Could she impersonate you?"

Soren's confirmation was sobering. "Yes, she could." He paused, deep in thought, and then an idea struck him. "Do you remember what Elara said about my childhood visits? I used to bring her flowers. Can you recall which one was my favorite?" He looked intently at Aurora, hoping she would remember the details of Elara's stories.

Aurora's mind raced back to Elara's tales, recalling a story about a flower, a favorite of Soren's, linked to the wind gods. "Windflower," she whispered.

Soren's face brightened with a gentle smile, relieved and impressed by her memory. "That's right. Windflower. When I come back, I'll knock four times and say 'Windflower.' That way, you'll know it's truly me." He clasped her hands in his as his amber eyes settled on hers.

Understanding the gravity of the situation, Aurora nodded, her throat tight with emotion. Anxiety coursed through her at the thought of being alone, but she trusted Soren's plan.

Soren's expression was serious as he turned to leave. "Lock the door after I leave." With those words, he stepped out of the room, leaving Aurora to face the silence and her own fears, fortified only by the promise of the secret code they had shared.

Panic coursed through Aurora as she rushed to the door, her hands fumbling with the lock in her rush to secure it. After locking the door, she retreated to the sanctuary of the bed, her eyes fixed on the door. The room was dimly lit by candlelight, the flickering flames casting an array of shadows that danced hauntingly across the walls. Wrapping herself in the protective comfort of the bedcovers, Aurora lay there, her gaze watching for any sign of movement outside.

Her breaths came in short, ragged gasps, and she tried to quiet them, straining her ears for the sound of Soren's approaching footsteps. The silence that enveloped the room was oppressive, broken only by the sound of her uneven breathing.

Aurora was so far from the carefully crafted pieces of her life. She had no control over what was happening to her and no idea how to stop it. She was slipping into oblivion.

A sudden knock on the door caused her to jolt, her heart pounding fiercely against her ribcage. She stifled the urge to scream, remaining silent despite the rising fear. The door received three more knocks, followed by a deep, familiar voice uttering a single word, "Windflower." The sound of the secret code spoken by Soren did little to ease her anxiety. With trembling hands, she cautiously approached the door and unclasped the locks.

As the door creaked open just enough to reveal the figure outside, Aurora's eager eyes met Soren's. In his gaze, she sought reassurance, her heart still racing. He gazed back at her, repeating the word, "Windflower," in a whisper.

Flooded with relief, Aurora flung the door open. Soren swept into the room, immediately noticing her trembling form. "It's me, Aurora. It's really me," he said. He wrapped his arms around her, pulling her close, his chest a comforting shield against her fears.

Despite his reassurance, the terror of being separated from Soren, even momentarily, continued to grip her. Soren sensed her distress and pulled back, cradling her face in his hands. His amber eyes locked onto hers. "It's me," he whispered again and pressed his lips to hers. A kiss filled with the promise of safety and the depth of their bond.

Although still frightened by the thought of a sorceress hunting them, Aurora melted into Soren. Under his lips and within his arms, she was safe. Fear left her mind and her body took over. They quickly discarded their clothes before moving to the bed.

Soren, feeling as if he returned home after a long journey, already knew the curves of Aurora's body. He knew where to touch her. He knew the softness of her skin and the firmness of her muscles just beneath. Her breasts were in his hands, full and responsive. The roundness of her backside in his grasp. Her hypnotic scent of lavender. But there was always something new to discover, and he took his time exploring her body.

Safe in the moment, the two took their time. Aurora found pleasure beneath Soren, rocking in sync with his movements. He softly kissed her face, romantic passion guiding his every move.

Feeling as though she were losing control of everything in her life, Aurora shifted, forcing Soren onto his back. She mounted him, sliding over his full length. Moving her hips in a rhythmic motion, she enjoyed sweet friction between her legs, feeling stretched and filled.

Aurora moved slowly at first, looking down at Soren lying beneath her, watching her so intently. His honey eyes burned, and his face darkened with desire. His hands slid up and down from the curves of her waist over to the fullness of her hips and around to her backside. Aroused by watching Soren's hands on her body, Aurora quickened her pace, feeling the heat within her growing.

Soren watched Aurora rock back and forth on top of him, taking pleasure in her control. Her stormy eyes erupted and her face contorted with gratification. As she moved faster, Soren moved his hands to cup her breasts, tugging her nipples gently between his fingers, making her spur even faster.

Aurora's moans became louder as Soren's hands ignited her body. She could feel her climax growing deep within her, and as she watched Soren recognize her closeness, one of his hands moved to the sensitive area just above where they joined. One hand kept the pressure on her breasts and nipple while the thumb of his other hand rubbed soft circles between her thighs.

Aurora's pace matched her growing climax. Her face was a picture of pure vulnerable pleasure, and her eyes burned with passion and desire. Soren's hands kept on their targets as Aurora's head flung backward and a guttural moan escaped her lips, her orgasm rocking through her body.

Knowing Aurora had found her release, Soren allowed himself to climax, warmth throbbing inside of her. As he finished, Aurora's movements stopped, and she curled into Soren's chest, panting. He brushed her wild curls away from her face, letting her catch her breath.

Aurora lay on Soren's chest, easing with the rise and fall of his breathing. Soren stroked her hair and rubbed his warm hand up and down her back while she listened to the beating of his heart.

"What's happening to me?" she breathed.

"What do you mean?" Soren asked, concerned.

Aurora shifted to look at him. "I am in a foreign world, ripped away from my friend and what I knew, being chased by a powerful creature, and yet I can't get enough of you. I've known you barely longer than a week, but I feel such a pull to you, like metal to a magnet." She looked at him with wonder in her eyes. "I'm not usually like this. I don't fall hard and fast for people, or really ever. But there's something about you and this place that just feels ... right."

Soren gazed down at her, a deep emotion swelling in his chest. "I feel the same. And I can't explain it. But I will embrace it while you're here." He smiled softly at her.

Aurora's chest ached to look at him and hear him share his feelings with her. She wasn't alone. He was here. She closed her eyes and before she knew it, all thoughts of whatever churned within her ceased, and she slept soundly.

Chapter 10

The lace curtains did little to contain the morning light filtering through the window. With the quaint room bathed in a delicate, luminous glow, Aurora slowly awakened from the guarded cocoon of her dreams. Wrapped snugly in the plush quilts, her sleep had been undisturbed, a rare luxury as of late. The inn, with its tranquil charm, had provided a brief escape where Aurora's fears and dangers were kept momentarily at bay.

Aurora stretched, feeling the quaint creak of the wooden bed beneath her. Her eyes, a clear shade of blue, fluttered open, lingering in the serene moment as the room basked in the golden morning light. The gentle chirping of birds just beyond the windowpane added to the room's peaceful ambiance.

As the haze of sleep cleared, a subtle sense of unease crept over her. The space beside her on the bed, now empty, sent a jolt of alarm through her. Her heart rate quickened as her gaze swept across the room, a flurry of thoughts racing through her mind.

Memories of the shadow weaver moved to the forefront of her thoughts. Soren, her steadfast protector, had vowed to keep her safe, but now his absence felt like a breach of that promise. The empty space next to her was a stark reminder of their precarious situation, a symbol of vulnerability in a world where danger lurked just beyond the veil of safety they had momentarily woven around themselves.

Awakening to find herself alone, Aurora's heart pounded with a mixture of fear and confusion. The memory of Soren's last words to her, laced with concern and a deep-seated conviction, echoed in her mind. His touch, once a source of warmth and security, was now replaced by a cold emptiness, leaving her feeling exposed and unsettled.

The room echoed her fears in its stillness. Torn between the urge to wait for his return and the impulse to seek answers, Aurora's emotions roiled like turbulent waves. The haven of the previous night had transformed into a space filled with uncertainty and apprehension. She scolded herself for letting her guard down, for placing her security in another's hands.

As she sat there, trying to steady her racing heart, the door creaked open. Soren stood in the doorway, his tall figure outlined against the morning light. His tousled hair and weary eyes reflected a hint of fatigue.

"Hello," he greeted her, a soft smile gracing his lips. His familiar voice, a soothing presence in her life, enveloped her, easing some of her anxiety. "Sorry for slipping out. I had to check on something," he said, his tone carrying an undercurrent of something unsaid, a hint of the weight he carried on his shoulders. Aurora, concern still lingering within her, searched his face for clues, trying to piece together the puzzle of his unannounced departure and hasty return.

Aurora saw the subtle, but unmistakable signs of strain etched across Soren's face. His eyes darted with a hidden anxiety, and his movements carried a careful deliberation that was uncharacteristic of his usual demeanor. Despite the undercurrent of tension, her heart swelled with relief at his return. She let out a small, involuntary sigh, her feet carrying her across the room to where he stood.

"Where did you go?" Her eyes searched his.

Soren stilled. "I scouted the woods nearby, to make sure it was all clear." There was something guarded in his eyes.

Aurora noticed his hesitation but let the relief over his return wash over her. "I was beginning to worry," she breathed, reaching out to intertwine her fingers with his. Their hands connected, a familiar and comforting sensation.

Soren responded with a softness that contrasted his troubled expression. He leaned in, planting a gentle kiss on her forehead. "I'm here now, and everything's okay. You're safe," he whispered, his voice a comfort.

For a moment, Aurora found solace in his presence—a temporary refuge from the world outside. A lingering apprehension laced her sense of calm, silently acknowledging the dangers that still lurked in the shadows.

Aurora's initial sense of relief slowly gave way to a resurgence of doubts and unease. The thought of venturing back into the open, potentially exposing themselves to unseen dangers, gnawed at her. *But how could she not place her trust in Soren, who had thus far been her steadfast protector?* Torn between her apprehensions and her faith in Soren, she wrestled with the decision, knowing that each step forward brought its own risks and uncertainties.

At breakfast, everything felt slightly off balance. Soren interacted with Aurora in an unusually formal manner. He spoke with a strained effort to appear at ease, but it came across as if he were playing a part. His laughter, once so effortlessly joyful, now seemed rehearsed, a poor imitation of the spontaneous amusement she had come to love. His memory faltered as he attempted to recall shared moments, and his looks toward her carried an unfamiliarity, a glint that was out of place in his eyes.

Aurora tried to dismiss her growing unease as paranoia, attributing it to her heightened anxiety. But, as they concluded their meal and Soren outlined the plans for the day, her doubts refused to be silenced. Seeking reassurance, she leaned in and kissed him, longing for the familiar warmth of his affection. However, the kiss was hollow, missing the usual spark that had always been a hallmark of their connection. It was like fitting a mismatched piece into a puzzle, and the sense of wrongness was palpable.

Aurora's unease was not without reason—her apprehensions were indeed well-founded.

Unbeknownst to Aurora, the shadow weaver was engaged in a delicate act of imitation. Having observed Aurora and Soren from a distance since their encounter in the clearing, she had pored over their behaviors, their speech patterns, and their interactions. Disguised in her human form, she had blended in seamlessly with the townspeople, watching and learning, preparing to step into a role she believed she could convincingly play. But despite her efforts, the subtle nuances of Soren's true character eluded her, and the facade began to crumble under Aurora's intuitive scrutiny.

***

Luring Soren into the forest under the veil of twilight had been a simple task for the shadow weaver. The ruse she employed was as cunning as it was cruel. Setting Elara's cottage ablaze proved to be an effective decoy, knowing well the bond Soren shared with the elderly fae woman. The fire acted like a beacon in the night, drawing him with a sense of urgency and fear. But when he arrived, it was too late; the cottage was engulfed, and the woman slipped into a smoky slumber from which she would not awaken.

The shadow weaver watched from the shadows as Soren approached, his face contorted with horror and fury at the sight of the burning cottage. She savored the moment of his despair before confronting him, casting a powerful binding spell that made him helpless, his limbs bound by an unseen force as he lay seething on the forest floor. The shadow weaver had prepared for Soren's retaliation, fueled by anger and grief. With a swift flick of her wrist, she neutralized his strength, rendering his efforts futile. "What have you *done*? She didn't know anything." Soren's voice was thick with anguish and outrage.

The shadow weaver feigned regret. "Oh, I know. But I needed something … impactful to draw you away from the mortal." Her voice dripped with insincerity, revealing the true nature of her ploy.

Realization dawned in Soren's golden eyes; the burning cottage had been a mere distraction, a tragic and manipulative tactic. Before he could voice another word, the shadow weaver silenced him with a simple gesture, her power effortlessly muffling his protests.

With a casual snap of her fingers, she transported Soren to a new location—a dark, dank root cellar. As he lay there, struggling against the magical restraints that sealed his mouth shut, he scanned the dim room. Faint beams of light filtered through the cracks of a wooden door, casting an eerie illumination over the cellar. Trapped and powerless, frustration and concern for Aurora left unknowingly unprotected from the hands of a dangerous imposter consumed Soren.

In the darkened cellar, Soren's gaze slowly focused on the shadow weaver's figure lurking ominously in the corner. Her deep purple gown cascaded heavily to the ground, a stark contrast to the dusty, earthy surroundings of the cellar. Despite the dirt and grime of the underground space, her velvet gown remained pristine. Her dark, lustrous curls fell in a tumbling cascade, brushing against the small of her back.

As she turned to face him, her violet eyes cut through the darkness, fixing Soren with a piercing, unnerving stare. A smirk played on her lips, a hint of vanity, as she noticed Soren's instinctual attention to her appearance. "It's a captivating figure, isn't it?" she said with self-admiration. "It's my natural form, but I much prefer the freedom and intimidation the dragon affords me. But this form, while less forbidding, has its … advantages."

The shadow weaver moved toward Soren. Huddled in the middle of the room, he watched her approach with a mix of wariness and defiance. Despite his compromised position, he kept his eyes fixed on her, trying to gauge her intentions.

She glided across the room, reaching him in mere moments as she floated above the ground. As she descended to his level, their gazes remained locked, creating a tense, charged atmosphere. "I know I'm not quite your type—I'm not blonde nor human," the shadow weaver taunted, her voice dripping with malice. "But you must admit, there's a certain allure to this form, isn't there?" She laced her words with a manipulative charm, a dark seduction meant to disorient and confuse. Soren remained focused, aware of the dangerous game she was playing.

The shadow weaver's insidious reference to Aurora caused Soren's heart to race with concern. It transported his mind back to the inn, where he had spent intimate moments with her that now seemed like a distant memory. He thought of the deepening of their bond, the way each touch had not only stirred his desire but also solidified his feelings for her. But he needed to stay focused on the task at hand—he had to return to Aurora, to ensure her safety.

The shadow weaver, sensing his internal struggle, moved with a predatory grace. She leaned forward, her hands supporting her as she slowly crawled over Soren's immobilized form. Her approach was deliberate, each movement calculated. As she drew nearer to his face, Soren recoiled, his body stiffening as he found himself beneath her menacing presence.

Her violet eyes bore into him with a curious intensity, studying his reactions. Despite his precarious situation, Soren refused to show any signs of fear or vulnerability, understanding that displaying such emotions would only fuel the shadow weaver's malevolent satisfaction. His unflinching gaze met hers.

Soren's breath caught in his throat as the woman leaned in and pressed her lips against his without warning. The touch was soft but jarring. Searing cold, like the bite of winter frost, nipped at his lip. It was a sensation so startlingly frigid it was as if a shard of ice had grazed him. A shiver coursed through his body, a chilling reaction to the icy air emanating from her. The coldness of her enveloped him, a stark contrast with the natural warmth of his skin. It was as if her very presence drew the heat from his body, leaving a trail of goosebumps in its wake.

Her laughter, cold and mocking, filled the air, chilling him further. "Ah yes, I have many gifts," she said, her tone laced with malice. "But a beating heart is not one of them." The lack of warmth in her voice matched the icy temperature of her touch. Soren, still reeling from the passionless kiss, braced himself for what she might do next, his mind racing to find a way out of her chilling grasp.

"I wish I had more time with you, but your precious human will be frantic soon if you don't return," the shadow weaver crooned. "But maybe I can give you a little glimpse into the pleasure I could give you." She smiled wickedly.

Soren, bound on the floor by her magic, eyed her with rage. But then his ice prickled on his skin. It licked up his arms and wrapped around his head, seeping into his brain. He stilled, frozen by the image pouring into his mind.

The shadow weaver cast her and Soren's images into his mind like a reflection of reality, and he could not look away.

Soren saw himself, bound on the ground with the shadow weaver looming next to him. In a moment of eerie stillness, the projected shadow weaver's eyes fluttered closed. When they opened again, her image had transformed. The eyes that met Soren's were hauntingly familiar, mirroring the blue of a temperate ocean, filled with an unsettling mix of anticipation and some-

thing darker. Cascading around a face kissed by the sun were soft, golden curls, framing features that Soren knew all too well—features that molded perfectly under the touch of his hands.

A giggle, light and playful, sounded from those all too familiar lips. It wasn't Aurora's voice; it was a cruel imitation, a twisted echo. A smokescreen designed to disorient and manipulate served as a stark reminder of the shadow weaver's penchant for deception.

The shadow weaver, reveling in her trickery, ran her hands over Soren's chest. Her touch was like an icy breeze, leaving a trail of icy prickles on his skin. She lowered herself, positioning her body to straddle his waist.

Soren writhed on the ground, desperate to free his mind from the horror the sorceress was imparting on him. He felt a surge of anger and repulsion at this dark magic. The shadow weaver's ability to twist and contort the image of his beloved into something so cold and calculating was a torment all its own. And the actions taking place in his mind were too real.

The shadow weaver gazed down at Soren on the ground with a look of perverse desire, her eyes alight with a twisted glee. "How I look forward to seeing the shock and hurt in your woman's eyes when she discovers your infidelity."

"It's not real," Soren said through gritted teeth. "It's just an illusion."

"Well, she doesn't need to know that. I will push it into her feeble mind, and she will believe you betrayed her," the shadow weaver said with malice.

Anger and disgust coursed through Soren as he recognized the shadow weaver's vile plot. He knew he couldn't stop this grotesque charade. But then an unexpected weight descended upon his head, clouding his thoughts. A scent, deceptively sweet and familiar—lavender warmed by the sun—enveloped him, causing his tense muscles to relax. It was the same scent that always lingered on Aurora, a scent that had become a drug in their time together.

His vision blurred, and the figure in his mind morphed into a haze of confusion. Struggling against the disorienting sensation, Soren spoke. A mix of hope and disbelief tinged his voice, a frail thread clinging to reality. "Aurora," he uttered, the name more a question than a statement, as he grappled with the illusion the shadow weaver had woven around him. The bewilderment in his voice was palpable, a clear sign of the shadow weaver's cunning ability to manipulate his senses and emotions.

"Shh, now. Yes, Soren. I am your Aurora, and I need you. Now." The melodic voice danced in his head, and memories of Aurora's embrace twisted with the projection in his mind. Before he could stop himself, his hands were free from their invisible bindings, and he was clawing for the woman who was rocking her hips on top of him. He felt himself grow hard from the friction and his hands cupped round breasts, cold but soft and full beneath her velvet bodice.

Soren's hands glided quickly behind the slim back of the glamoured shadow weaver, pulling at the delicate strings of her garment. Her head tipped toward the sky at Soren's passionate movements to free her breasts, excited to feel his strong, warm hands graze across her hard nipples.

Soren's hands clawed the sleeves of her gown until they slid off her delicate wrists. A sharp moan escaped the shadow weaver's lips as Soren's anticipated grip on her breasts tugged deep in her stomach. Soren launched himself toward her, moving his lips to the breasts that heaved in his hands.

Watching him writhe on the ground, the shadow weaver laughed in victory. It was sweeter than she imagined. She almost pitied him. He was powerless against her magic and deceptive illusion.

Immersing herself back into the vision, she tore open Soren's shirt and pushed him until his chiseled back hit the packed dirt with a delicious thud. He looked up at her with slight surprise before his eyes darkened with desire. The shadow weaver couldn't imagine Aurora being so forceful with him.

She exuded such submissive energy. The seductive aggressiveness the shadow weaver was wielding would unravel Soren. She imagined catapulting him into her darkest fantasies, torturing him with pain and pleasure he couldn't imagine until she allowed him the most explosive release of his life. Oh, the things she could show him.

But she controlled herself, slinking back into the illusion he longed for. She felt how hard he was beneath her. Her icy tongue traced a trail from his navel to his sculpted chest, his tanned skin glistening beneath a soft smattering of dark hair. Her tongue circled each of his nipples, ice shocking to life every cell of his body. She glanced up at him as her mouth moved slowly, and he looked down with pained desire. She knew he was ready, but she couldn't resist the slow burn.

She continued to watch him through her thick lashes as her tongue worked its way back down toward his waistline. A sharp intake of breath drew from Soren's lips as she reached the top of his pants. She watched him for a moment before a knowing grin spread across her glamoured face.

With slow hands, she undid the few buttons that held back his glorious length, and a moan of relief escaped from Soren, as he was no longer restrained. With his eyes closed, cool, soft lips closed around the tip of him. Emotions and memories swirled in his mind as the delicate mouth moved up and down. The icy flick of her tongue was almost enough to unravel him right then. But he wanted to please her. He wanted to plunge himself into her warmth until she shook with pleasure.

With that thought, he pulled his Aurora to his lips and kissed her passionately before flipping her over onto her back. The swift rustle of movement excited the shadow weaver, and she spread her legs in response, raising the skirt of her gown. Her head tilted back as Soren filled her, and she moaned at the deep warmth of him.

Soren was eager to pleasure her, to bring her to climax. There was a surprising chill as he thrust himself into her. It wasn't the familiar warmth he had grown to know and desire. But he thrust harder, deeper. The shadow weaver's glamoured body moved in response and her moans grew louder, so he moved with intention.

As her back arched and her body stiffened with climax, Soren held onto his own release until he had watched every feeling of passion explode from her body. As he let himself fill himself inside her, he looked down at his lover's face, a sudden headache pounding into awareness. His eyes blurred and when he could focus once again on the face of the woman beneath him, it was not Aurora's.

Soren recoiled in horror and disbelief as the true nature of the shadow weaver's deception became painfully clear. The shadow weaver's grin widened at Soren's reaction, her amusement evident.

She taunted, saying, "The next time we meet, I won't keep our actions in our minds. It's been ages since I've indulged in such pleasures, and the mind games are only a tease. But I believe we both found some enjoyment in it." Her cold, violet eyes shone with a sense of triumph over her successful ruse as she eyed Soren's pants.

Soren's voice trembled. "What do you want? Why are you doing this?" he demanded, struggling to maintain his composure. His stomach churned from the disturbing display the shadow weaver had forced into his mind.

The shadow weaver leaned back. "Your precious human inadvertently trespassed into our realm, didn't she? And she's so desperate to return to her world. Well, I find myself yearning for a change of scenery, too. This world has grown dull, its mysteries all too familiar. But her world, ah, that's a realm ripe for the taking. A world in chaos, teeming with weak, easily swayed minds. Imagine the power, the control I could wield there. I plan to accompany her back, to find a new kingdom where I can reign. Your Aurora's world seems the perfect new dominion for someone of my ... talents." Her words dripped with malice and ambition, painting a terrifying picture of what she intended for Aurora's world.

Soren's face flushed a deep red, his anger boiling over at the shadow weaver's insinuations. "Aurora doesn't know the portal's location, and I certainly won't help you," he declared with defiance and fury.

With venomous confidence, the shadow weaver said, "I wouldn't be so certain, Soren. Your bond with Aurora, while touching, is an obvious vulnerability. I'm surprised that you, of all people, would be so naïve. You should know the dangers of such attachments, especially after what befell your parents." Her eyes gleamed with cruelty.

Soren's heart clenched at the mention of his parents, their tragic end flashing before his eyes—the attack and chaos that had shattered his world. He forced the memories away, aware that the shadow weaver was manipulating his emotions, aiming to weaken him.

"Yes, you remember, don't you?" she taunted, her voice cold and calculating. "Would you want Aurora to suffer a similar fate?"

The mere thought of Aurora in harm's way ignited a fire within Soren. With a burst of righteous anger, he roared, "You will not lay a finger on her!" His voice echoed in the confined space. He had to protect Aurora at all costs.

The shadow weaver's posture shifted into one of feigned surrender, her hands raised as if in retreat, but the malicious glint in her eyes remained. She stood before Soren. "It's quite simple," she said. "Tell me where the rift is, and I promise, I will leave you and your beloved in peace."

Soren, however, remained determined. "No. That's not what Aurora wants. Her desires are what matter to me." There was a clarity in his tone, a reflection of his inner certainty.

In that moment, amidst the shadow weaver's temptations, Soren realized the depth of his feelings for Aurora. Yes, part of him yearned for her to stay—to share a life filled with love and laughter in his realm. He envisioned a future where they traveled the valleys, danced in village squares, and stood side by side facing whatever challenges came their way. A life where happiness was constant, within his reach.

But Soren understood this realm was not Aurora's home. She yearned for the familiarity of her world, for the life she had known. His love for her extended beyond his own desires; he was selfless, willing to sacrifice his happiness for hers. It was this realization that solidified his purpose. He loved her too much to keep her in a world where she did not belong and did not want to be. With a heavy heart, Soren knew that despite everything within him that wished otherwise, he had to help Aurora return to her world—to the place where she truly belonged. And he had to protect not only his world but Aurora's from the shadow weaver's malicious plan.

As Soren grappled with the painful realization that he couldn't keep Aurora in this world, the shadow weaver observed him with a mix of annoyance and envy. It irked her to witness such profound love, a sentiment she was incapable of understanding or receiving.

"Very well," she declared. With a breath, the shadow weaver faded into darkness, her form shimmering as it disappeared into the void. Soren's gaze remained fixed on the spot and his eyes widened when what replaced the space was not the cruel woman's figure, but that of his own.

In front of him stood a perfect reflection of himself, dressed and poised as he was. He stared in disbelief at the figure before him, the realism of the replica so uncanny it felt surreal.

When the replica spoke, it was in Soren's timbre, now twisted with a sinister undertone. "Have it your way. But don't worry, I'll take wonderful care of your precious Aurora." The words, laced with malice, sent a chill down Soren's spine.

Before he could react, the shadow weaver disappeared with a flick of her fingers, releasing Soren from her spell. He collapsed to the floor, momentarily overwhelmed. His mind raced with urgency. He did not know where he was or how far he was from Aurora, but he knew he had to act fast. The imposter was with Aurora, and time was of the essence. With renewed determination, Soren prepared to make his way back to her. Whatever it took.

***

The shadow weaver, reflecting on her deceitful encounter with Soren, found maintaining her guise as the sentinel increasingly challenging as the day wore on. Her struggle lay in replicating the emotional connection and deep-seated familiarity that Aurora and Soren shared.

Throughout the day, the shadow weaver navigated a complex paradox. Her mission was clear—to sustain the illusion of being Soren, gain Aurora's trust, and extract information about the portal. She tried to mirror Soren's characteristic warmth, his laughter, and his words, but enacting a convincing performance of affection proved harder than expected.

The delicate balance between trust and deceit was slowly unraveling. Each kiss and look they exchanged carried contradictions. The day's events unfolded like a dance on a razor's edge, a continuous oscillation between artificial and something unexpectedly real.

Their journey had taken them through the rugged terrain high above Whispering Glen. As the evening light waned, casting long shadows over the landscape, Aurora observed with a hint of surprise as Soren guided his horse toward a shadowy cave entrance. Her intuition nagged at her; their pace had been uncharacteristically slow throughout the day.

"We'll stay here for the night and then continue at dawn," Soren said.

Aurora, suspicion chewing on her mind, questioned their decision to stop so close to their destination. "Isn't that Whispering Glen down there? Aren't we nearing the portal?"

She caught a fleeting but telling reaction from Soren—a subtle curl of his lips at her mention of their proximity to the portal. "Yes, but we can't do much in the dark. It's best to wait until morning," he replied.

Dismounting her horse, Aurora remained cautious. Something troubled her, and her instincts were on high alert. She needed to devise a plan, but for now, she had to bide her time. She watched as Soren disappeared into the cave's dark entrance. Hesitating for a moment, Aurora followed, her eyes struggling to adjust to the pitch blackness that enveloped her the moment she crossed the threshold, the figure of Soren vanishing into the depths of the cave.

As Aurora stepped into the cave, a chill swept through her, the stark contrast from the outside air making her shiver. She blinked rapidly, trying to adjust her eyes to the enveloping darkness that swallowed the faint light from the cave's entrance. Instinctively, her hand reached out, fingers brushing against the rough, cool surface of the cave wall, seeking a guide in the oppressive blackness.

She had barely taken a few cautious steps into the cavernous space when a heavy blow struck the back of her head. It came without warning, a forceful thud that echoed in her ears and sent a sharp pain radiating through her skull. Her legs buckled under her, and she collapsed forward, her body succumbing to the darkness that pulled her down into its depths. The last thing Aurora was aware of before succumbing to unconsciousness was the cold, hard ground rushing up to meet her.

Chapter II

Aurora blinked against the hazy daylight filtering into the enclosed space and focused her gaze. Soren's figure stood in the mouth of the cave, with his back turned to her and his broad shoulders silhouetted against the brightening sky. His contemplative gaze was on the valley spread out below them. A wave of relief washed over her as she rose to her feet, moving with purpose toward him.

What happened? Confusion clouded her mind as she grappled with fragmented memories of the preceding events. As she walked toward Soren, her heart raced.

She yearned to close the distance between them, to feel the familiar comfort of his presence, to be wrapped in the reassurance of his embrace. She longed to hear him say that everything was under control, that her return home was imminent.

But deep within her, there was a conflicting desire, a reluctance to leave this realm that had become unexpectedly dear to her. In the span of a few weeks, this otherworldly place had felt like a lifetime's journey. The concept of 'home' had transformed—it was no longer just a place but a feeling, one she found in the shared moments of laughter and intimacy with Soren. He had become her sanctuary, her sense of belonging.

A smile broke across Aurora's face as warmth flooded her veins, fueled by the memories of their closeness. Visions of them entwined in sheets, their bodies bare and bathed in the soft glow of the lamplight, filled her mind.

In these moments, amidst the chaos and uncertainty, Soren had become more than a protector; he had become a part of her, a piece of what she now considered home.

Standing just behind him on the ledge, emotions stirred within Aurora as she watched his dark hair dance in the cool mountain breeze. Compelled by a deep-seated need to reconnect, she reached out to touch his shoulder, intending to draw him to her, to seal their reunion with a kiss.

But the moment her hand touched his shoulder, an unnerving chill shot through her, a sensation so jarring it was as though she had touched a slab of ice. She recoiled, her eyes widening in shock as the man turned toward her. The face that met her gaze was not the familiar, comforting visage of Soren.

Instead, she stared at a being that appeared to have stepped out of the chronicles of time itself. Its face bore the burden of eons, each line and crease telling a tale of ancient existence. The skin had an eerie, spectral glow, a luminescence that spoke of a realm far removed from the human world.

Soren's dark locks transformed into a flowing mane of raven-black hair, framing a face that was a study in haunting contrasts. Dark eyes, void of warmth or humanity, gazed out from beneath heavy, shadowed brows. A thin, cruel smile twisted the creature's lips, revealing a row of sharp, jagged teeth—a predator's tools designed for rending.

As Aurora stepped back in horror, the creature lunged toward her with a bone-chilling scream, a sound so terrifying it embodied the essence of nightmares. Aurora's heart pounded in her chest, fear and adrenaline spurring her to act, to escape the clutches of this monstrous apparition.

Jolted awake, Aurora's heart raced furiously in her chest, her breaths coming in sharp gasps. Her hands extended in defense against an unseen assailant, the remnants of her nightmare still vivid in her mind. She hurriedly scanned her surroundings. She lay on a bed of cold, damp rock, the chill of the ground seeping into her bones. The absence of natural light and the musty, earthy smell of the air confirmed she was deep within the rock.

In the dimly lit chamber, the only source of warmth and illumination was a small fire, its flames casting an orange glow that danced eerily against the rocky walls. A haunting echo of laughter reverberated through the cavern with a chilling resonance that broke the silence.

Beyond the fire's flickering light, Aurora spied a shadowy figure. As her eyes adjusted, the silhouette of a woman emerged from the darkness, her form outlined by a ghostly silver-blue luminescence. The woman moved with an unnerving grace, each step deliberate, as she approached Aurora.

"See something ... shocking?" Aurora's gaze widened in shock as the woman stepped into the full light of the fire. The creature before her was of unnatural beauty—her skin was like creamy porcelain, smooth and flawless, stretched across a delicately structured face. The faintest hint of pink tinged her small and perfectly proportioned lips.

But it was the eyes that truly captivated and unnerved Aurora. Violet and piercing, they stood in stark contrast to the cascade of raven-black waves that framed the woman's face. They bore into Aurora with a soul-penetrating intensity. This being, with her otherworldly elegance and unsettling gaze, was like nothing Aurora had ever encountered.

The shadow weaver's voice flowed with the same grace and darkness as the deep purple gown that clung to her form. Aurora, feeling a growing threat, moved backward, her limbs scraping against the rough, cold rock beneath her. The sudden impact against a jutting stone sent a sharp pain through her back, and her head struck the wall behind her, a wave of pain radiating through her skull. She reached back, her fingers probing her hair, and they came away stained with the warm, sticky evidence of blood.

The shadow weaver saw Aurora's discomfort. "Force was necessary, I'm afraid," she said. "I sensed your growing suspicion. Rendering you unconscious was a more merciful option than allowing you to resist."

"Who are you?" Aurora's voice trembled, betraying her effort to sound courageous despite her shaky breaths. "What do you want from me?"

The shadow weaver flashed an exaggerated eye roll. "Humans and their incessant questions," she muttered. "Since we're indulging in introductions, I am Isolde. And you, my dear, have something I want. You hold my key to freedom." Her eyes bore into Aurora, a cold, calculating glint within them.

"Freedom? Freedom from what?" Aurora asked, her voice a mix of curiosity and fear, as she struggled to comprehend the situation and the intentions of this enigmatic, formidable being named Isolde.

Isolde tossed her head back, her laughter ringing out, melodious but haunting, echoing off the cavern walls. "Your feeble human mind couldn't even begin to comprehend the freedom I seek," she taunted with cruel amusement. "You needn't trouble yourself with my motives. What matters is that I'm aware you know the portal's location to your world, and I will do whatever it takes to extract that information from you. Humans, though fragile, can endure torture for weeks under the right ... methods of persuasion." Her smile broadened, revealing a set of opulent white, unnervingly sharp teeth.

Aurora, despite her fear, demanded to know more. "How did you find me?" she asked.

Isolde's gaze upon Aurora was predatory. "The moment you passed through the veil, it sent ripples through the fabric of our world. Anyone with a hint of power felt it. And then I simply followed your disgusting human scent." Her eyes lingered over Aurora, examining her from head to toe, causing Aurora to squirm under her unsettling scrutiny. Isolde's grin widened into a gleeful expression that belied the malice beneath.

"Why do you think your sentinel was so desperate to escort you away? He knew beings like me would flock to you, each of us eager for the secret to crossing realms. You're a siren's song to us, my dear."

Aurora's heart sank at this revelation. "Are there ... are others like you after me?" she asked, her voice barely concealing the fear that gripped her. The thought of being pursued by more creatures like Isolde, each with their own sinister intentions, was a terrifying prospect.

Isolde's laughter was brief, but it carried a chilling edge before her voice hardened. "There is no one like me. Other shadow weavers, yes, but none possess my level of ... lethality." Her violet eyes sharpened as they focused on Aurora, as cold and unyielding as the words she spoke. "This realm teems with bloodthirsty beings yearning for a portal to escape through, willing to spill blood for such an opportunity."

Aurora, driven by a mix of fear and curiosity, questioned the rationale behind such a desire. "But why? Why would you want to leave for a world without magic like mine?"

Isolde's face lit up with a dark glee at the question. "Exactly because of that. Your world is a blank canvas, ripe for someone like me to dominate. A realm where I can rule without bounds, satiating my deepest cravings." The intensity in her eyes was unsettling, revealing the depth of her ambitions. But then her face turned solemn. "There's nothing left for me here."

Aurora's voice was barely a whisper, a faint breath of sound as she contemplated the fate of her world. "But what about the people there? Humans like me ..."

Isolde scoffed, her disdain for humanity clear in her tone. "Fools, every one of them. They're already ensnared in their petty squabbles, their violence fueled by selfish, senseless desires. They chase after power without understanding its true nature. Why not serve someone who truly wields power? I'll indulge their greedy appetites, their materialistic yearnings, while they grovel at my feet. My plans for them are grand." Her words dripped with a menacing excitement, painting a picture of a dark future under her reign.

Aurora's question hung in the air, heavy with unspoken fears. "And those who'd refuse?" she asked, mustering the courage to meet Isolde's gaze.

Isolde's response was a sinister smile, one that transformed her delicate features into a mask of devilish intent. "My creatures have to eat," she said, her voice laced with malice. Her words made it clear and horrifying: anyone who resisted would face a fate worse than servitude.

The gruesome image of creatures devouring human flesh and bone sent a wave of nausea crashing over Aurora. She fought to suppress the rising bile, but the revulsion was overwhelming.

Isolde shifted her tone to mock concern. "Oh, you must be famished after today's journey. How silly of me to forget that humans must eat too." With a casual flick of her fingers, a bowl filled with a steaming greenish-brown liquid materialized in front of Aurora. The pungent smell that wafted from it was repulsive, turning Aurora's stomach.

The sight and smell of the concoction were too much for Aurora, who had not eaten in hours. Her body reacted involuntarily, and she retched, the contents of her empty stomach splattering onto the cold, rocky floor.

Isolde's laughter echoed through the cavern. "Aww, not the fine cuisine you are used to? Silly me," she taunted, her voice dripping with feigned pity.

Aurora, overwhelmed with disgust and despair, could only look up at her captor through eyes blurred with tears, her mind racing to find a way out of this nightmare.

Isolde's words dripped with malice, adding to the already suffocating tension in the air. "This may be even easier than I thought. Just lead me to the portal, and as a reward, I'll leave you a feast beyond your wildest dreams."

Desperate to steer the conversation away from Isolde's sinister plans, Aurora seized on another thought. "Where's Soren?" she asked. "What did you do to him?"

A spark of mischief glinted in Isolde's eyes, a harbinger of the cruel words to follow. "Oh, what *didn't* I do to him?" she said with a sinister chuckle. "Meeting the famed Sentinel of Silverveil was ... enlightening. To taste him, to touch him ..." She paused, savoring the memory of the illusion she had cast in his mind. "I understand why you're so enamored with such a creature. A protector. A lover. And quite the lover, indeed." The look of perverse satisfaction on Isolde's face, as she uttered those last words, sent a chilling wave of revulsion through Aurora.

In a blind fury, Aurora launched herself at Isolde, her eyes ablaze with rage. Her fingers reached desperately for Isolde's throat. But just as she was inches away from her target, an unseen force yanked her violently back. She crashed against the cold, hard wall of the cavern with a painful thud, collapsing to the ground, gasping for air.

Isolde watched Aurora's failed attack with a smug smile. "Oh dear, did I forget to mention? You're on a short leash here." She clicked her tongue in mock disappointment.

Struggling to regain her composure, Aurora spat defiantly at Isolde's feet. Her act of rebellion, however small, was evidence of her unbroken spirit.

Isolde crouched down, her slender, icy finger lifting Aurora's chin, forcing her to meet her gaze. "Come now. What would Soren think of such unladylike behavior?" she taunted—her voice a chilling whisper that echoed around the cavern.

Aurora's attempt to avert her gaze and retaliate with words was futile; she found herself physically incapable of looking away or speaking, completely at the mercy of the creature that ensnared her.

Isolde continued with a taunting nonchalance. "Luring away your sentinel was simple. Unfortunately, that dear old woman, Elara, had to suffer for your inadvertent trespass. Fate can be so cruel, can't it?" The malicious glee in her tone was unmistakable.

The mention of Elara's fate hit Aurora like a physical blow. Her heart ached as she remembered the warmth of Elara's smile, the kindness in her eyes. The thought of such a gentle soul meeting a grim end because of her brought tears to Aurora's eyes.

"Manipulating him was child's play," Isolde boasted, while she forced the illusion of the tangled image of her and Soren into Aurora's mind. "I merely had to take the form of his deepest desire—you. And once I had what I wanted, I left him. He's resourceful; he'll find his way out. I couldn't extinguish such ... vigor. Such ... primal talent." Her lips twisted into a smirk, reveling in the torment her words inflicted.

A surge of fury and heartache overwhelmed Aurora as she watched the scene play out in her head. The thought of Isolde violating Soren's mind and body, using her image to deceive him, was unbearable. It was a violation, a betrayal, though she knew Soren had no control over it. The knowledge that the shadow weaver had crossed such a sacred boundary with such ease was a cruel twist to her already frayed emotions.

Reading Aurora's tormented face, Isolde's voice dripped with mock sympathy. "You can't entirely blame him. It was the magic of glamour, shaping me into the person he most desired." Her giggle was like a knife twisting in Aurora's heart, a cruel reminder of the depth of her manipulation and deceit.

Isolde's words were like venom, each one designed to inflict maximum pain. "I mean, I have never had a lover dismiss me in this form," she said, gesturing at her alluring figure. "But he gave himself so willingly, thinking it was you. Oh, the pleasure he gave me, believing he was with you. His determination to satisfy was … amusing, but *deeply* appreciated. But I grew tired of his earnest attempts. You are far more intriguing."

Isolde's face drew dangerously close to Aurora's, her icy lips almost grazing Aurora's skin. Aurora strained to close her eyes, to shut out the torturous scene before her, but Isolde's cruel magic kept them open. A tear escaped Aurora's eyelids, sliding down her cheek, only to be captured by Isolde's chilling tongue, which traced the salty path with perverse delight.

"Mmmmm." Isolde savored the taste. "The flavor of human tears … so rich with emotion." Her icy fingers then traced a path across Aurora's shoulder, gliding down to the center of her chest, eliciting a reactive shiver. Isolde's eyes gleamed with a predatory desire as she saw the physical response of Aurora's body.

As Isolde continued her torment, a fiery rage ignited within Aurora. The thought of Soren, deceived and used in such a manner, fueled her anger. It burned within her, growing more intense with each touch of Isolde's icy hand.

Aurora struggled against her invisible restraints, her gaze locked on Isolde, who was now attempting to press her icy lips to hers. The heat inside Aurora rose, a roaring sound filling her ears, the fury becoming almost unbearable.

Just as she thought her rage would consume her, her mouth flew open, releasing a deep, guttural roar. A brilliant flash of light erupted, forcing Isolde to recoil in surprise.

A curious smile flickered on Isolde's lips as she recovered, an intrigued glint in her eyes. "My, my. There may be a fire in you yet … How interesting." Isolde placed a slender finger on her lips, pondering. Aurora's unexpected display of power hinted at an untapped strength, a resilience that even Isolde hadn't anticipated.

Aurora stood in defiance, her body tensed, each breath coming in sharp, ragged gasps. Her face, once rigid under Isolde's magical control, regained its mobility, allowing her to blink back the angry tears that welled in her eyes. "You. Will. Not. *Touch* me."

Isolde, unflustered, responded with an exaggerated gesture of surrender. "Perhaps you'll reconsider after a meal," she said, her gaze shifting to the neglected bowl of unappetizing slop on the cavern floor, now cooled and even less appealing.

Aurora's eyes darted to the bowl a few steps away. With a sudden burst of defiant energy, she strode to it. Grabbing the dish and facing Isolde, she flung the contents toward the shadow weaver. The bowl shattered spectacularly against an unseen barrier just inches from Isolde's face, the greenish concoction oozing down an invisible wall.

With a casual wave of her hand, Isolde dispelled the protective shield, leaving the remnants of the bowl and its contents in a sordid heap on the ground. "Tsk, tsk. Such wastefulness. You might regret that decision later. Strength comes from sustenance."

Her tone was patronizing, her gaze pitying. "But perhaps you need time to reflect on your choices. We'll revisit this conversation at dawn." With that, Isolde gave Aurora a final, disdainful look before she shimmered out of sight, taking with her the comforting light and warmth of the fire, plunging Aurora into cold, unsettling darkness.

In the overwhelming darkness of the cavern, Aurora's senses sharpened, focusing on the sound of her labored breathing and the subtle drip of moisture echoing off the stone walls. In just a thin undergarment, Aurora felt vulnerable. The shadow weaver must have changed her while she was unconscious. She pushed aside the unnerving thought of Isolde's invasive touch.

Aurora navigated the cavern's floor on her hands and knees. The cold, rugged ground was unforgiving, causing discomfort and pain with each movement. Her hands, searching blindly, met a cold, sticky substance. The familiar, nauseating stench confirmed it was the remnants of her earlier sickness, and she fought back a wave of nausea.

Turning away from the mess, Aurora continued her exploration until a sharp, jagged edge sliced into her palm. She recoiled, settling back on her heels and clutching her hand. The warm trickle of blood was unmistakable, even in the pitch black. Realizing she had reached the broken pieces of the bowl, she braced herself against the sharp sting of the wound.

Desperate to stem the bleeding, Aurora tugged at the hem of her undergarment, imagining the stark contrast of her blood against the white fabric. The physical pain, coupled with the emotional torment of the day's events, overwhelmed her. Her throat constricted, and despite her best efforts to maintain composure, a heart-wrenching cry escaped her lips. The sound reverberated off the cavern walls, amplifying her anguish. Tears streamed down her face as her sobs grew louder, each one a visceral manifestation of her fear and despair.

In her mind's eye, she pictured Soren—confused, anguished, and desperately searching for her. The thought of him in such distress only deepened her sorrow, intensifying the sobs that shook her entire body in the cold, unforgiving darkness of the cavern.

In her heart, Aurora yearned to turn back time, to return to the serene and loving moments she had shared with Soren just the night before. Their encounter had been a sanctuary, a fleeting glimpse of a world where everything was perfectly aligned. The memory of their closeness, the way her heart swelled with wonder in his presence, was what she clung to in the bleakness of her current predicament.

Summoning the strength of those memories, Aurora calmed her sobs, recognizing the futility of tears in her desperate situation. Cradling her injured hand against her chest, she navigated the cavern's floor with cautious movements. She inched forward, her feet tentatively sweeping aside the scattered shards of porcelain.

Her toes brushed against something unexpectedly soft and substantial—her cloak. A rush of gratitude washed over her as she grasped the familiar garment, thinking of the woman who had given it to her. The memory of Clara's warmth and generosity brought fresh tears to Aurora's eyes, a poignant reminder of the kindness she had encountered in this strange land.

Despite the oppressive chill of the cavern, the cloak retained a mysterious warmth. Aurora couldn't fathom why Isolde had overlooked the item, but in that moment, she was grateful for the oversight. She wrapped the cloak tightly around her shivering form, pressing her wounded hand close to her body for warmth.

Exhaustion soon overtook her, and Aurora succumbed to the need for rest. Her eyelids grew heavy, and her breathing deepened into the steady rhythm of sleep. In her dream, she escaped to where Soren's radiant face awaited her, his arms outstretched, ready to fold her into him, a comforting contrast to the cold, unyielding darkness of her reality.

Chapter 12

Soren emerged from the root cellar's confinement with a force that shattered the serenity of the forest. His sudden entry into the daylight was abrupt, the sharp contrast of light and shadow momentarily disorienting him. Above, the forest canopy teemed with life, birdsong filling the air, but he focused solely on his urgent mission.

Whirling around to survey the cellar he had exited, he found it had disappeared, as if it had never been there. A boulder replaced the mound that had concealed the cellar, seamlessly blending into the forest's rugged landscape. A sense of familiarity washed over him; he recognized this part of the forest, not far from where Elara's cottage once stood, but deeper in the woods.

Soren dropped to one knee, placing his hand on the forest floor, seeking a connection with the earth beneath him. He closed his eyes and tilted his head forward, attuning himself to the natural world around him. He absorbed the sounds of life in the underbrush, the rustling of leaves, and the distant calls of animals. A gentle breeze caressed his neck, guiding his senses, and helping him find his bearing.

Soren rose and launched into a swift sprint, heading northward. The slivers of sunlight filtering through the trees indicated the lateness of the afternoon. Time was of the essence.

He knew the shadow weaver would move toward Whispering Glen, drawing Aurora inexorably to her perilous fate. The mere thought of that vile creature touching Aurora, harming her, fueled his urgency. His legs pounded against the forest floor, each stride faster and more determined than the last, propelling him through the wilderness with a singular goal—to reach Aurora before it was too late.

As Soren emerged from the shelter of the trees, the outlines of the town appeared before him, a stark reminder of how much had changed since the seemingly idyllic day he and Aurora had spent there. His heart raced with a mix of hope and dread, propelling him forward with palpable haste.

He sped through the village, his mind replaying the warm memories of their time with Elara, now tainted by the harsh reality of the present. The villagers turned to watch as he passed, his expression grim.

Reaching the inn, Soren burst through the door with such force that the common room fell into a sudden hush. The innkeeper looked up, startled, as Soren approached the counter with quick, heavy steps. "Have you seen the woman I was with? Golden hair, blue eyes?" he asked, filled with fatigue and urgency.

The innkeeper, taken aback by the intensity of Soren's gaze, shook his head. "Not since you left with her this morning," he responded quickly, sensing the gravity of the situation.

Soren's heart sank. Cursing under his breath, he slammed his fists onto the counter in frustration, the sound echoing through the quiet inn. Without wasting another moment, he charged upstairs, his movements driven by a desperate hope of finding Aurora.

He threw open the door to Aurora's room, startling a young maid who was tidying up. The room was devoid of any sign of Aurora. A wave of despair washed over him, but he didn't allow it to linger. Every second counted. Soren turned on his heel and dashed out, his mind racing to devise a plan to find Aurora before the shadow weaver could harm her. The direness of his mission left no room for hesitation.

Soren fled the inn, leaving behind a trail of confusion and concern among the innkeeper and patrons. He made his way to a nearby horse, realizing the shadow weaver had taken Ash. He quickly untied the reins, and with a fluid grace, vaulted onto the horse's back. In an instant, they were off, galloping through the heart of the village. Villagers stepped back in surprise as Soren and the horse weaved through the streets, heading northward and out of town.

The village soon faded into the distance as Soren pushed the horse into a faster gallop. An icy wind lashed against his face, but Soren focused on tracking the shadow weaver. The distinctive, smoky scent he had picked up in Aurora's room filled his nostrils, guiding him. A gut feeling assured him that the trail would lead to Aurora, and his heart clung to the hope that she remained safe.

As the horse thundered across the countryside, thoughts of confronting the shadow weaver consumed Soren's mind. His desire to exact vengeance on the creature that had threatened Aurora's safety matched his determination to rescue her.

***

Aurora awoke to the sound of howling wind, an eerie presence in the sealed confines of her dark prison. The pain from her wounded hand was a constant reminder of her plight, the dry blood creating a tight sensation across her skin. She cautiously held her hand in a protective curl, fearful that any movement might worsen the injury.

In the oppressive darkness, she couldn't see her hand before her face, leaving her to rely solely on her other senses to navigate the cavern's confines. Despite the bleakness of her situation, the hope of Soren's return and her eventual escape fueled her.

Aurora's disheveled state mirrored her inner turmoil. Cold sweat clung to her, matting her hair against her skin. Despite the warmth offered by her cloak, a shiver of terror ran through her body, leaving her feeling vulnerable.

The silence of the cavern was broken only by her shallow breaths and the distant, haunting sound of the wind. She wondered about Isolde's whereabouts, the uncertainty of the shadow weaver's return gnawing at her already frayed nerves. Hunger twisted her insides, a physical reminder of her situation. The revolting smell of the unpalatable food Isolde had offered mingled with the scent of her sickness, creating a nauseating atmosphere that hung in the air.

Trapped in her thoughts, Aurora considered her options. *Could a shard of the broken porcelain bowl serve as a weapon against Isolde?* She pondered the feasibility of such an act of defiance. The likelihood was that Isolde's magic was the true barrier to her escape or Soren's potential rescue, and her violent undoing. The idea of using the shard was a faint glimmer of hope in the overwhelming darkness of her captivity.

Her mind inevitably drifted to Soren, picturing him frantic and determined to find her. She clung to the belief that he was out there, searching for her.

But reality crept in, reminding her of the grim truth. She possessed the vital information that Isolde craved—the location of the portal to her world. Aurora knew Isolde sought more than escape; she hungered for a new realm to dominate, a place to satiate her lust for power. The thought of such a tyrant unleashed upon her world was unbearable.

But Aurora was uncertain of the portal's exact location. She knew only that it lay somewhere in Whispering Glen, a piece of knowledge shared between Soren and Thorn. The ambiguity of its whereabouts was both a curse and a blessing. She could not lead Isolde to the portal, but neither could she use it to escape her current predicament.

As she sat there in the darkness, Aurora curled under the weight of her situation. She was the key to Isolde's ambitions, a pawn in a game she barely understood. But she was also the only one who could prevent Isolde from achieving her sinister goals.

Aurora sat huddled in the dank cavern, grappling with the gnawing fear of the unknown tortures that might await her. The thought of the shadow weaver's disappointment at her lack of knowledge of the portal's location sent icy shivers down her spine.

Terror clutched at her heart, but she could not, would not, betray her world by leading Isolde anywhere near the portal. The thought of her friend Camryn, already tormented by her disappearance, possibly facing a fate worse than death or enslavement under Isolde's reign, steeled her determination.

As Aurora contemplated her limited options for defense, her mind wandered back to when her emotions had erupted in a surprising display of power. Recalling Isolde's taunting words about Soren, burning rage ignited within Aurora. It had manifested itself as a burst of light, a spontaneous reaction that had caught Isolde off guard.

Aurora focused on this budding power, trying to understand its origin. As she fell deeper into the memory, a strange sensation prickled at her fingertips. Glancing down, she saw what appeared to be tiny sparks of electricity dancing across her skin. Her heartbeat accelerated, a mix of fear and awe coursing through her.

She brought her hands close to her chest as if to protect this newfound ability from unseen eyes. *Could this be an untapped power she had, or was it a temporary gift bestowed upon her in this realm of magic?* Regardless of its source, Aurora sensed that this mysterious energy might be her only chance at survival and resistance against the shadow weaver.

With cautious optimism, she focused on harnessing this energy, wondering if it could be the key to her escape. The stakes were high, and time was of the essence. Every spark that danced across her skin brought a glimmer of hope, a possibility that she could fight back against the overwhelming odds. In the darkness of the cavern, Aurora's courage flared. She vowed to protect her world and defy the darkness that threatened to engulf her.

Aurora's breath caught in her throat as she saw a dragon prowling through the entrance of the cave. Just as she was about to scream, the looming form transformed into the intimidating figure of Isolde. The icy blue glow emanating from her cast an eerie light on the cavern walls, deepening the sense of anxiety that gripped Aurora's heart. The juxtaposition of Isolde's beauty against the immense power she wielded was unnerving.

The cruel smile that twisted Isolde's lips sent shivers down Aurora's spine. Her words dripped with malice and hinted at a disturbing delight at the prospect of tormenting both her and Soren further. Aurora's mind raced. The thought of Isolde using her as a pawn to lure Soren into another trap was excruciating.

Aurora's gaze hardened as she met Isolde's chilling stare. Despite the fear clawing at her insides, she refused to let it show. She couldn't give Isolde the satisfaction of seeing her crumble. Aurora knew she had to remain strong, not just for her own sake, but for Soren as well.

The standoff between them was palpable, a silent battle of wills in the dimly lit cavern. Aurora's determination to protect Soren and her world was unflinching, even in the face of such daunting power. She clung to the hope that the mysterious energy within her could be her salvation, her secret weapon against the darkness that threatened to consume her.

As Isolde's menacing presence loomed over her, Aurora braced herself for whatever came next, ready to fight with every ounce of strength she had. "Oh good, you're not dead. That would make finding the portal much more difficult. Although it would give me another crack at your sentinel." A devious smile spread to Isolde's lips.

"Fuck you," escaped from Aurora's lips before she could stop it.

"Ouch. But you can do that anytime you wish. I could warm your body better than that pathetic cloak." Licking her lips and holding Aurora's gaze, Isolde changed topics. "You really must eat something. It will be morning soon and I have an especially important date with my destiny. Just tell me where the portal is and with the snap of my fingers, I could return you to that sweet little inn with Soren, a table of hot, delicious food waiting for you. And you will never see me again. What do you say?" Her violet eyes bore into Aurora.

Aurora shivered at the idea of lying in front of a warm fire, nestled between the warmth and safety of Soren's arms. Her stomach growled at the promise of a meal. "I will not allow you to go into my world just to burn it to the ground," Aurora said through gritted teeth.

"Oh darling, your kind will burn it to the ground themselves soon enough. I can give them hope for a new life. I can fulfill their deepest desires. Give them a real higher power to worship than their pathetic invisible gods. Leave it to humans to cast their gods in their image. So arrogant."

"Never," Aurora spat.

"Ugh. Your pathetic attempt at courage is nauseating." Isolde's face turned bitter. "I guess you just need some more encouragement." With an outstretched hand, Isolde's fingers curled into a tight fist and twisted. Aurora's stomach clenched in pain as if someone had stabbed her.

She writhed on the cold floor, her agony reaching unbearable heights. The pain was all-consuming, a relentless assault on her very being. She struggled to catch her breath, and her knees curled to her chest as she lay in the fetal position on her sweat-soaked cloak.

Isolde towered over her, a figure of unyielding cruelty, her hand still clenched in a sadistic grip. Her icy eyes glinted with malice, reveling in Aurora's suffering. The air around them crackled with malevolent energy, a tangible manifestation of Isolde's power and fury.

Amidst the excruciating pain, Aurora's thoughts turned to Soren. His face appeared in her mind's eye, urging her to endure, to hold on. She clung to the memory of his touch, his voice. The bond they shared that transcended realms and circumstances became her anchor in the storm of pain.

Isolde's expression twisted into a snarl of frustration. She had underestimated the depth of the human's strength—the resilience born of genuine love and sacrifice. In that moment, as Aurora lay there, battered but unbowed, she embodied the defiance of the human spirit, a stark contrast to the darkness that sought to consume her.

Aurora's determination shone as a solitary light against the overwhelming shadow of Isolde's malevolence. She lay there trembling, the weight of Isolde's threats crushing her spirit. Her breaths were shallow, each one a struggle, as she fought against the darkness encroaching on the edges of her vision. In the dim light of the cavern, Isolde's figure loomed over her like a specter of doom, her words echoing in Aurora's mind like a death toll.

Sensing the verge of Aurora's unconsciousness, Isolde released her hand, ending the pain that tore through Aurora's stomach. She caught her breath in quick, jagged inhales.

"Now then. The portal location, my dear." Isolde's voice was crisp and impatient.

The room spun, and Aurora shut her eyes to keep herself from heaving. The words she didn't want to say escaped from her lips. "You'll have to kill me. I will never tell you."

"How little you must care for your sentinel. The man who has kept you safe here. The man you've fucked. The one you won't say you love." Her violet eyes flickered to Aurora. "Oh yes, I know you love him, or whatever pathetic meaning love has in your world. But you must care more for the moronic human creatures of your world to so carelessly risk his life to save them. Because after I eviscerate you and leave your disemboweled corpse for him to find, I'm going to torture him until he relents. Days, weeks, years. Whatever it takes, I am getting through that portal one way or another. So, your very death in this cave will be in vain. There's no saving that pathetic world of yours. No saving the life of the man who would freely give his own to save yours. You must choose."

Terror, guilt, and shame spread over Aurora's face as Isolde's words pierced her soul. *How could she do that to Soren? How could she betray him?* But she felt betrayed. Betrayed by her own heart for allowing herself to get close to someone. To allow herself to so freely fall into uncharted territory.

But the thought of Soren suffering because of her decision was unbearable. He had risked everything for her.

Isolde watched Aurora intently. "Maybe I will keep you around. A front seat as I torture your beloved. Watch him fuck me over and over as I scramble his mind and leave him only a shell of who you know. Ah yes, that could be more fun."

Bile rose again in Aurora's throat, but rage sparked within her. She swallowed hard and fixed her gaze on the icy shadow weaver. "You won't touch him *ever* again."

Isolde's cruel laughter echoed throughout the cavern. "Oh good, are you coming to your human senses again? I mean, is it really that bad for you here? For someone like me, it's a prison, but for a human like you? Paradise. But oh, how I'd love to watch you two in a passionate dally. His powerful hips against your soft curves." Isolde licked her lips.

"I can still feel him inside me, still feel his hands and mouth on my breasts," she teased. "Oh, he wanted to take his time, but I was too much for him. I made him explode and fill me with such delicious warmth." Isolde's eyes danced as she told Aurora of her and Soren's imaginary rendezvous.

Aurora, her breaths ragged and heavy, remained defiant, power coursing through her veins. The revelation of her latent abilities, though shocking, ignited a spark of hope within her. Her fiery eyes bore into Isolde, challenging the shadow weaver's arrogance.

Isolde, surprised by this unexpected display of strength, scrutinized Aurora with intrigue. The air in the cavern crackled with tension, an electric current that danced between the two women.

"You may have some tricks up your sleeve, but they are mere child's play compared to my centuries of mastery," Isolde sneered, her voice dripping with contempt. But, beneath her words, there was a hint of uncertainty, a crack in her facade of invincibility.

Aurora clenched her fists, feeling the energy pulsating within her. She knew she was no match for Isolde's vast powers, but she also knew she couldn't give in to fear. She had to fight—for Soren, for herself, and for the world she called home.

"Whatever power I have, I will use it to stop you," Aurora declared, her voice steady despite the swirling chaos around her. "I will not let you take what isn't yours."

Isolde's eyes narrowed, a sinister smile playing on her lips. "Bold words, but let's see how long your courage lasts."

The standoff between them was a battle not just of magical might, but of wills—a clash between darkness and light, tyranny and freedom, despair and hope. Aurora, standing in the face of overwhelming odds, was ready to fight for everything she held dear.

Fire roared to life under Aurora's skin, and her ears sizzled with electricity. Golden red danced in her vision, and, in one swift and powerful motion, she thrust an arm toward Isolde as if to strike her across the jaw.

But instead of the crack of fist meeting bone, a blast of light ricocheted off Isolde's invisible crystal shield and sent sparks throughout the cavern, briefly illuminating the space. Aurora's hands buzzed and sparks flickered from her fingertips. Strands of hair floated over her shoulders, charged with electricity. She panted with anger and exhaustion.

"My, my, what a wonder we have here," Isolde said curiously. "There must be some magic that lingers in your world, or something has awakened in you since arriving in Silverveil. Very interesting indeed." Isolde cocked her head at Aurora and strode closer, unafraid of another flash of lightning being unleashed.

"Perhaps this is where you belong. Have you considered that, dear Aurora? Have you considered it could be Fate that led you through the veil that day, knowing the power you have? Certainly, it has no place in your mortal world. Our realm has stirred something in you, something that could be powerful if you give it the proper attention. And what better guide to have than your loyal sentinel? Would you really trade that power to save a world that has done nothing for you? You'd rather return to your measly insignificant life? Something tells me it no longer appeals to you."

Isolde's voice was bitter. The words danced in Aurora's ears. *What had happened to her? What was she becoming?* She didn't have those answers, and she was honestly too tired and hungry to question Isolde.

"Please," Aurora exhaled softly. "Leave me alone." The notion that Isolde might perceive her as unraveling was unsettling to Aurora, but her ability to think clearly was faltering. Hunger gnawed at her stomach, and her eyes ached for rest, heavy with the need for sleep. The gash in her hand stung.

Isolde's head tilted as she pondered. "Maybe you're right. Maybe I've been too harsh with you. After all, I didn't know you had such a fire inside you." Isolde said. "At the very least, filling your belly and regaining your wits will give you strength for a better fight later." Isolde lowered her head and flashed Aurora a wicked smile.

Aurora looked at her with hesitation, uncertain if Isolde was calculating a trick. But with a familiar snap of her fingers, a roaring fire crackled in the center of the room, its white smoke billowing up through a circular hole in the roof of the cavern. The floor was clean, all evidence of Aurora's vomit and broken bowl of sludge erased from the space.

Aurora sat next to a spread of thick pelts. Woolen blankets and a silk pillow sat invitingly on the fur. Next to the fire were plates of roast chicken, steaming vegetables, a crystal pitcher of water, bottles of wine, and thick, molten chocolate cake.

The aroma was tempting, a stark contrast to the earlier offering. Aurora eyed it warily, knowing that accepting food from Isolde could be a danger-ous concession.

Isolde observed Aurora with an air of amusement and curiosity. "Eat, dear Aurora. You'll need all the strength you can muster. Our game is far from over, and I am eager to see how it unfolds with your newfound abilities." With a final sinister grin, Isolde vanished into the darkness, leaving Aurora in the silence of the cave. A feast spread out before her.

Aurora's stomach rumbled, her hunger betraying her.

She couldn't help but marvel at the magic that surrounded her, even in her dire situation. She turned her attention to the feast before her. The aroma of roasted chicken mingled with the earthy scent of steamed vegetables, inviting her to satisfy her gnawing hunger. She hesitated for a moment, wary of any trickery, but the rumbling in her stomach overpowered her caution. At least, if there was poison, it wasn't a terrible way for her to go.

With a deep breath, she reached for a piece of chicken, its warmth comforting her chilled fingers. She took a small bite, savoring the tender, flavorful meat. It was delicious, far beyond anything she had expected in this grim cavern. She tried the vegetables, finding them perfectly seasoned and cooked. Each mouthful brought a small measure of comfort, easing the tension in her body.

The wine and chocolate cake beckoned to her, promising further indulgence. She poured herself a glass of wine, its rich aroma blending with the warmth of the fire. The first sip was like velvet against her tongue, a luxurious contrast to the harsh reality of her captivity. She allowed herself a humble piece of the chocolate cake, its sweetness a brief escape from her worries.

As she ate, Aurora wrapped herself in the pelts and blankets, their softness a stark contrast to the cold, hard floor of the cavern. The silk pillow cradled her head as she leaned back, allowing the warmth of the fire to seep into her bones. For a moment, she allowed herself to relax, to forget the danger she was in. But even as she relished the comfort, her mind raced with plans and possibilities.

She knew she couldn't trust Isolde, but for now, she needed to gather her strength and wits. She needed to be ready for whatever came next. With each bite of food, each sip of wine, she grew a little more fortified, a little more prepared to face the challenges ahead.

Her thoughts were a whirlwind of confusion and fear. Despite her physical weakness, a stubborn flame of defiance still burned within her. She was not ready to succumb to Isolde's manipulation, nor was she willing to abandon her quest to return home. But the shadow weaver's words had planted a seed of doubt. *What was her true destiny? Was there a greater purpose for her in this mystical realm, one that her old life could never offer?*

As the fire crackled and the shadows danced on the cavern walls, Aurora's thoughts turned to Soren. She wondered where he was and if he was safe—if he was searching for her. Aurora held onto the hope of being reunited with him, of overcoming this nightmare together. She had to survive, to outsmart Isolde, and find her way back to Soren. Aurora would not give up. Not now, not ever.

As Aurora lay there, enveloped in the warmth of the blankets, her mind drifted between the realm of wakefulness and the edge of sleep. The wine's comforting buzz hummed through her veins, a gentle lullaby that eased the jagged edges of her stormy thoughts. The fire's crackling rhythm became a distant melody, blending with the ebb and flow of her heartbeat.

In this liminal space, the harsh reality of her captivity blurred into the background, replaced by her vivid memories with Soren. She recalled the softness in his voice when he spoke her name, the way his laughter resonated like a song in her soul. His presence was a soothing reminder of something sturdy amidst the chaos.

Her thoughts lingered on him. She remembered the heat of his skin against hers, and the sweetness of his touch. The memories were so tangible that, for a moment, she could almost feel his arms around her, his breath against her skin.

Aurora allowed herself to sink deeper into the comfort of her memories, letting them wrap around her like a protective cocoon. In her mind, she saw Soren's face, his eyes sparkling with that same starry light that had captivated her from the start. She imagined him searching for her, fighting for her.

As sleep finally claimed her, Aurora drifted into a dream where Soren was with her. In this dream, they were safe and free from the dangers that lurked in the shadows of this world. They were in a place where time and fear had no hold, where only their love existed, as boundless and enduring as the stars themselves.

***

As Soren ascended the mountain, the wind intensified around him, swirling in a dance against the stark landscape. The distinct aroma of the shadow weaver filled the air, growing more potent with each step, assuring him he was following the correct path. Amidst this, a deep longing stirred within him—a yearning for the familiar and captivating scent of Aurora, a blend of fresh lavender and vibrant citrus that had become so enticing to him.

The night had enveloped the world hours ago, and Soren knew that the first light of dawn was not far off. He had journeyed relentlessly through the darkness, urging his horse onward with a sense of urgency. As they traversed the shadowy terrain, creatures of the night peered out from their hidden enclaves in the underbrush, their eyes glinting ominously in the moonlight.

There was an unmistakable energy about Soren, a palpable intensity that served as a silent warning to any who might dare cross his path. The smoky scent of the shadow weaver grew stronger, and his eyes, sharp and inquisitive, scrutinized the darkness. Then he noticed it—the faintest glimmer of light. A fire was burning within a cave nestled within the tree line above. Soren's mind raced with the implications. The shadow weaver, a creature of the night, had no use for fire. This could only mean one thing—there was a human inside that cave.

Chapter 13

Soren's heart quickened at the realization. The faint light in the cavern could only mean Aurora was there. His Aurora, the woman whose laughter had become his favorite song, whose presence was his solace. Without a moment's hesitation, he turned toward the cave, every sense heightened.

The night air was crisp, biting at his skin, but he paid no mind. His focus was singular—to reach Aurora, to ensure she was safe. He moved with stealth, the lessons of his youth as a sentinel guiding each silent step.

As he approached the cave, Soren was on high alert. He knew the dangers that the shadow weaver posed. This creature, a master of deception and malice, had woven a web of darkness around them. But Soren's conviction was unbreakable. He had faced fear and death before, but nothing frightened him more than the thought of losing Aurora.

Soren reached the mouth of the cave before the sun peeked over the horizon. He paused at the entrance, his breath forming clouds in the chilly air. He peered into the darkness, trying to discern any sign of movement. His eyes remained vigilant, scanning the shadows.

The scent of the shadow weaver lingered but told Soren that the creature wasn't nearby. Instead, there was a soft thrumming of vibration. The subtle movement reverberated through his ears.

As Soren approached the shadowy cave entrance, his boot unexpectedly collided with something solid, sending a sharp, echoing thud reverberating off the rocky walls. He thrust his arms forward, only for his hands to connect with an unseen barrier—an invisible wall that veiled the cave's mouth and what lies within.

Pressing his body against the cool, smooth surface, he peered through it, his gaze drawn to the soft, flickering light within. The gentle glow of fire revealed the confines of a small, secluded cell hidden in the cave's depths.

And then he saw her—Aurora. Wrapped in a cloak, her face was serene as she slept. Relief washed over him, followed by protectiveness. He pressed further, his heart aching to wake her, to hold her, to tell her everything would be alright.

He carefully surveyed the cave, looking for any sign of the shadow weaver. His hand reached for the hilt of his sword, ready to defend, to fight for the woman who had unknowingly captured his heart. He would stand against the darkness, against all odds, for her. For Aurora, he was her light in the shadow.

Soren's fists pounded against the unseen barrier with a sense of urgency and desperation. Each thud resounded with his increasing fear and determination. He called out Aurora's name, but she remained motionless.

Panic gripped Soren when Aurora didn't stir. His mind raced with possibilities, each more terrifying than the last. He needed to break through this barrier, to reach her, to ensure she was safe. The thought of her being in danger, potentially hurt, tore through his heart and clouded his vision.

Soren stepped back and launched himself at the barrier, his entire being focused on breaking through. The impact sent reverberations through the cave, but the invisible wall remained impenetrable.

With a breath, he unsheathed the sword from his back. The blade sang with magic as he swung his arm, but when the sword clashed with the barrier, the sound of metal meeting ice rang out. It failed to leave even the slightest mark on the barrier. The magic of his sword was no match for the unbreakable magic of Isolde's shield.

Frustrated but undeterred, Soren's mind raced for another solution. His eyes never left Aurora's still form, his heart aching. He needed to find a way—any way—to break through the barrier. His gaze turned skyward, imploring the universe for a solution.

His thoughts turned inward, focusing on the connection he shared with Aurora, the unspoken bond that had grown between them. Closing his eyes, he reached out with his mind, calling to her, wishing her to sense his presence, to find the strength to wake up, to break whatever spell held her captive.

Soren's voice softened, his words a heartfelt plea. "Aurora, please hear me. I'm here." His words floated into the cave, a silent prayer for the woman who had captivated him.

His gaze swept over Aurora with a mix of terror and scrutiny. Despite the dirt smudging her skin and the flecks of blood on her face, she appeared uninjured. A wave of relief washed over him. His amber eyes, alight with determination, focused on her as he called out, his voice reverberating against the cave walls, "*AURORA!*"

At the sound of Soren's deep, familiar voice, Aurora jolted awake, her heart leaping. She pivoted toward the sound, her eyes instantly welling with tears as they met his. Rising, her voice trembled with hope and disbelief. "Soren?" She couldn't believe he was there, that he had found her. Clutching her white cloak tightly around her battered and trembling form, she moved closer to him, yearning to breach the cruel barrier that separated them.

Her hands pressed against the cold, invisible wall as she peered up at Soren, her eyes brimming with urgency and fear. She glanced briefly over his shoulder, noting the first light of dawn creeping over the horizon, a stark reminder that Isolde's return was imminent.

Aurora shifted her focus back to Soren, and in doing so, she saw his features cloud over with concern. He fixed his attention on the deep cut in her palm. "You're hurt," he said, his tone threaded with unease.

"Yes, but ... I'm okay," she said with panic in her voice. "Isolde—the shadow weaver—she's going to return soon. We need to get out of here," Aurora said, her eyes begging Soren, silently conveying the urgency and seriousness of their predicament. Her voice trembled, the thought of Isolde's imminent return sending chills down her spine.

Soren's thoughts whirred at a frantic pace, wrestling with the immediacy of their perilous circumstance. Sensing her growing panic, he instructed, "Okay. Stand back," determination written on his face. Aurora stepped back, watching as Soren retreated a few paces before launching his large body against the crystal shield with all his might. The shield remained unyielding. Not even the faintest sound of fracturing filled the air.

Over and over, Soren rammed into the barrier with relentless force. Each impact timed with Aurora's mounting dread. She feared for Soren's well-being, seeing the strain of his efforts, and the potential for injury. But more than that, she feared what would happen if they couldn't find a way out before Isolde's return. The thought sent waves of panic coursing through her, each thud of Soren's body against the barrier amplifying her terror.

Aurora fixed her gaze on Soren, and her eyes reflected the deep well of emotions that his relentless efforts stirred within her. In this moment of peril, she recognized a truth she hadn't fully grasped before—the profound depth of her feelings for this man who had become her protector, her confidant, her unexpected love in this strange world.

She approached the invisible barrier, her movements slow, as if she were walking through a dense fog. A gentle smile, tinged with the sadness of acceptance, graced her lips as she extended her hands, placing them against the cool, smooth surface that separated her from the sentinel. "Soren, stop. Stop. It's okay," she whispered, her voice a soothing balm amidst the chaos of their situation.

Despite his exhaustion, Soren continued to hurl himself against the barrier, driven by a desperation born of love and duty. But at her words, he paused, his chest heaving with labored breaths. He turned to her and met her gaze. The look in her eyes struck him, a reminder of what they shared, however fleeting it might have been.

"Isolde will return soon," Aurora said, her voice filled with an underlying current of sadness. "I can't stand the thought of her harming you because of me. You have to go. Close the portal. Protect your world." Her voice softened, reading the unspoken thought behind his eyes. "And know that you haven't failed me. You've given me more than I ever knew I needed."

Her words hung in the air. In her plea for him to leave, she offered Soren the greatest gift she could—her love and the freedom to fulfill his duty, even if it meant sacrificing herself.

"I won't abandon you," Soren said. His hands, previously clenched in tight fists of frustration against the unyielding barrier, relaxed as he pressed his palms against Aurora's, separated only by cool glass. It was a futile but deeply symbolic gesture, their fingers yearning to intertwine through the invisible divide.

He sighed heavily, his breath fogging the shield, and bowed his forehead to rest against the barrier, mirroring Aurora's position. His eyes, usually a reservoir of strength, now shimmered with an unspoken sorrow.

Aurora gazed at him, drinking in the sight of his face—an image that was too perfect, too extraordinary to belong to any world but this one. A pang of bittersweet realization hit her; this man, this realm, had given her experiences and emotions she had never known in her world. She rose on her toes, her lips brushing the cold glass where Soren's forehead rested, her gesture a silent kiss goodbye, filled with all the love and longing she felt.

"I'm sorry," Soren whispered, a quiet confession laden with the weight of their impossible situation. His voice trembled with a blend of love and the excruciating pain of impending loss. Of inevitable failure—breaking his spirit as a sentinel, a guardian sworn to protect his realm at all costs. But the portal, their conduit between worlds, represented both their meeting and their parting—a passage that had to be sealed to safeguard his world and hers.

Soren's eyes opened to see terror on his lover's beautiful face. Her eyes, usually a serene shade of blue, now roiled like a tempestuous sea, darkened by fear. The first light of dawn cast a surreal glow on her features, accentuating her expression of stark terror.

He pivoted sharply, positioning himself protectively in front of the barrier that separated him from Aurora. His eyes narrowed, focusing on the looming threat that hovered ominously above.

Isolde, embodying the essence of a predator, floated against the backdrop of the rising sun. Her eyes, alight with a manic glint of excitement, locked onto Soren with a predatory focus.

Aurora, though retreating from the barrier, kept her eyes steadfast on the shadow weaver, her body tense and prepared for whatever may come next.

Isolde's voice echoed through the crisp morning air. "Hello again, lover," she purred, her tone a twisted blend of mockery and desire. "I thought I might have to hunt you down, but how fortunate that Fate has conspired to bring you to me just as the day unfolds!"

Her gaze shifted between Soren and Aurora, reveling in the palpable tension. Soren, a figure of muscle and conviction, stood his ground, every line of his body radiating defiance and protection. In that moment, the scene they formed was as dramatic as it was poignant—a warrior sentinel, a terrorized but determined woman, and a malevolent creature, all under the watchful eye of the rising sun.

Aurora's scream, a harrowing sound of pure terror, pierced the morning air. "No!" The desperation in her voice sent a ripple of tension through Soren, his muscles coiling like springs, ready to unleash his fury.

Isolde, reveling in the chaos she had conjured, turned her gaze back to Aurora, her smile a sinister curve. "So, have you reconsidered? Are you ready to forsake your insignificant world for eternal bliss here, in exchange for your lover's life?"

Panic gripped Aurora, her heart hammering against her ribcage. "Don't hurt him," she pleaded, her eyes darting between Isolde and Soren. "I'll do what you want. Just don't hurt him."

As she spoke, she saw Soren's reaction—time slowed, magnifying every detail of his defiant stance. Sword in hand and his arms stretched out toward the heavens, his face a mask of vengeance. Suddenly, the sky erupted, a brilliant flash of lightning tearing through it, followed by the rolling thunder that shook the earth.

Soren's eyes blazed with an otherworldly intensity, a vivid amber against the gathering storm clouds.

But Isolde was unfazed. With a graceful flick of her hand, a wave of dark purple energy surged forward, enveloping the scene in a shroud of impenetrable darkness. The sound of something shattering, followed by

Soren's roar—a guttural, primal sound full of pain and rage—filled the air, resonating with the storm's fury.

Aurora, trapped behind the barrier, could only watch in horror as the darkness swallowed Soren's figure, her heart sinking with dread at the realization of what might have happened to him.

With her heart hammering in her chest, she lunged toward the unseen barrier, her frantic gaze scouring the shadows for any sign of the unfolding nightmare. As the darkness dissipated, Isolde appeared, standing ominously on the ledge. At her feet, Soren was a figure of pain and defiance, kneeling and contorted in agony, his arms unnaturally pinned to his sides by an invisible, unyielding force. His breaths were heavy with pain and fury, echoing in the tense air.

Isolde's taunting voice broke the tense silence. "Behold the consequence of your defiance," she said, circling the incapacitated Soren like a predator. "A simple bone, yet so vital. There are many more to play with," she mused, her gaze cruel and calculating.

Aurora's horror became palpable as she realized the extent of Isolde's brutality—Isolde had shattered Soren's leg with chilling ease. "Enough!" she cried out with fear and fury.

But Isolde was already advancing, her chilling gaze fixed on Aurora as she approached the now flickering barrier. "I'm only just getting started, my dear," she said.

Behind her, Soren's voice, rough with pain, was defiant. "Stay away from her!" He struggled to rise, pain etching his features, his arms still trapped by the unseen bonds.

Isolde paid no heed to his words or his struggle. With a mere touch, she dissolved the invisible wall into a cascade of shimmering particles. Aurora's eyes darted back to Soren, who, despite his pain and immobility, was trying to position himself between Isolde and Aurora, his body a shield even in his weakened state.

Incapable of bridging the widening chasm separating him from the malevolent creature, Soren's valiant struggle waned, and he collapsed onto his knees with a pained groan. His arms strained against the invisible restraints, seeking the solace of the earth's strength beneath him, but to no avail. Isolde's magic held him in an unyielding grip.

Retreating toward the flickering fire, Aurora shuddered as Isolde advanced with menacing grace. "A touch of warmth for our journey, perhaps?" Isolde mused, noting Aurora's flimsy attire beneath the white cloak.

With a deft snap of her fingers, Aurora's clothing transformed. She found herself clad in fur-lined leather, her feet now encased in sturdy boots warmed by thick woolen socks. A charcoal sweater hugged her form, and a black leather coat, fleece-lined, enveloped her against the cave's chill. Her golden hair was now tightly braided and coiled into a bun.

Isolde's gaze then fell upon Aurora's injured hand. "Oh dear, your hand. How clumsy of you." Aurora looked down at her gash, dried into a deep russet. "Let me fix that for you," she remarked, her tone dripping with feigned concern. With another effortless motion, she healed the gash, the pain and blood disappearing under a wave of icy sensation.

Fury consumed Soren. With a primal roar, he lunged forward, his face striking the ground as he strained against his bonds. His eyes blazed with an untamed wrath, and his voice, a powerful reverberation, shook the very foundations of the cave. The earth trembled in response to his rage, loose stones cascading from the cavern's ceiling as Aurora stepped further back into the shadows, her heart pounding in sync with the seismic fury he unleashed.

Isolde's irritation was palpable as she glared at Soren, who she suspended in mid-air. The sentinel, a picture of defiant strength even in his constrained state, glowered back at her with unyielding determination. His left leg dangled lifelessly, a stark contrast to the rigid line of his right, while his broad shoulders strained against the invisible bonds.

As Isolde advanced, Soren's taut form radiated resistance. The dark cloud that enveloped him pulsated with his every labored breath, his shirt billowing open to reveal the contours of his strained muscles. His intense gaze never wavered from the shadow weaver, his expression a blend of fury and torment.

"You are a vexing impediment," Isolde snapped, her voice sharp and cold, slicing through the tension-filled air. Each step she took toward him was deliberate, a predator closing in on her prey. Soren's jaw tensed. Despite his precarious position, there was a raw, unspoken defiance in his posture, a sentinel ready to endure whatever torment she had in store, all for the sake of the woman and world he was sworn to protect.

With each hesitant stride, Aurora's heart pounded as she measured her steps toward the suspended form of Soren. She flinched as an unseen force tore Soren's shirt, leaving tattered remnants fluttering in the chilly breeze, exposing his sculpted chest to the harsh elements.

A horrified gasp escaped her lips as another spectral swipe left a cruel red gash across his skin, painting a stark contrast against his bronzed flesh. Each subsequent slash that marred his body was a blow to her soul, and she could barely stand to watch, but found herself unable to look away.

Soren's growl reverberated through the rocky outcrop, a deep, primal sound that echoed off the stone walls. Witnessing his agony, a wave of dizziness and nausea washed over Aurora, the sight of his suffering unsettling her to the core.

Isolde reveled in the display of her power. "I will disembowel you right here in front of your weak beloved with one more slice," Isolde said, reveling in the display of her power as her face twisted into a grotesque mask of pleasure at the sentinel's pain.

As Soren lifted his head, his eyes met Aurora's in a moment that transcended the physical agony he endured. The depth of emotion in his gaze was palpable, a silent declaration of his profound love for her. In his eyes, Aurora saw a reflection of her own heart's turmoil—a maelstrom of love, fear, and an unyielding desire to protect. Despite the brutality of the moment, their connection remained unbroken. She shared his pain.

As Aurora approached Soren, her heart was a storm of emotions—fear, love, power—all swirling together in a tempest that echoed in her every step. Her eyes never left Soren's. His eyes, though filled with pain and fatigue, shone with an undiminished warmth that reached deep into her soul.

Soren gazed at Aurora, and his eyes, usually so fierce and guarded, softened betraying his acceptance of their grim fate. He looked into her tear-streaked face and silently mouthed, *I love you*.

A profound ache bloomed in Aurora's chest as she discerned the silent confession on Soren's lips. A rush of warmth enveloped her, a stark contrast to the chilling anticipation of Isolde's final, devastating blow. Her eyes remained locked on Soren's anguished expression as she slowly advanced toward Isolde, who was grimly intent on completing her dreadful deed.

Within her, the warmth evolved into a deep, searing energy coursing through her veins, making her tremble with a powerful vibration. A flicker of white light danced at the edge of her vision. She glimpsed sheer astonishment on Soren's face just as an earth-shattering roar erupted from deep within her.

Her world turned into a cascade of blinding white light, obliterating everything else in her sight. Beams of a pure, unstoppable force were radiating from every inch of her skin, her hair standing on end as relentless waves of light burst forth.

When the onslaught subsided, leaving her breathless and her mouth snapping shut, Aurora's vision cleared. Soren was no longer suspended in mid-air, but now lay on the ground near the ledge. Isolde was gone, vanished without a trace, except for a charred fragment of her purple velvet gown that descended from the air, landing solemnly at Aurora's feet.

The heat that had surged through her, igniting a light so fierce and blinding, still tingled at her fingertips as she stood in front of Soren. Her mind was still reeling from the incredible force she had unleashed, a force she didn't understand.

The charred fragment of Isolde's gown lay discarded at her feet. Picking it up, she jolted, as if the singed fabric was reminding her of the fiery strength that lay within her. Letting it slip through her fingers, she turned her full attention to Soren, her heart aching at the sight of his injuries.

As she cradled his face in her hands, their eyes locked. In his gaze, she saw a mixture of awe and respect, a silent acknowledgment of the power she had wielded to save them both. His lips parted as if he wanted to speak, but no words escaped.

In that moment, they were more than a human from another world and a sentinel from a realm of magic. They were two souls, bound by something greater, united by a love that had defied impossible odds.

The dawn's light bathed them in a golden glow, casting a serene ambiance over the scene of their quiet reunion. In the stillness that followed the storm of their ordeal, they found solace in each other's presence, a harbor amid havoc.

Aurora's eyes shimmered with unshed tears as she gazed at Soren's battered form, her heart clenching at the sight of his wounds. Each drop of blood that traced down his taut, muscular chest was a stark reminder of the peril they had faced. Her voice was a whisper of regret, tinged with guilt for not recognizing the shadow weaver's deception sooner.

Soren, despite his injuries, enveloped her hands in his, their fingers intertwining in a silent promise of solidarity. His eyes, deep pools of amber, met hers with an intensity reflecting the turmoil and love that intertwined within him. He drew her close, their lips meeting in a kiss.

The kiss was a fusion of warmth and desperation, a silent proclamation that this moment was not a fleeting dream but a tangible reality. As Soren opened his eyes, Aurora was a vision of strength and vulnerability. His voice barely articulated his feelings. "I love you." His eyes searched hers before turning his attention to her hands, which still shook with power. "How?" He reached toward her.

Aurora's heart fluttered at those three little words, and anxiety crept up her throat. She had longed to hear those words, but they scared her just the same. *Did he really love her? Was it possible?* Just as her brain began to analyze the weight of those words, she shook her head, turning her attention to Soren's question.

"I don't know," she said. "Yesterday I just felt this vibrating energy growing inside of me, burning to get out. And when ... when Isolde told me what she did to you, it enraged me, and I just unleashed it somehow." Her eyes fell on Soren's face.

The gentle touch of his hand on her neck was both comforting and grounding. Soren met Aurora's confession, her admission of the powerful and uncontrollable force that had surged through her with awe.

Concern etched into every feature of Aurora's face as she surveyed Soren's injuries, her voice quivering with worry. Her gaze lingered on his motionless left leg, her heart aching at the thought of his suffering. The sight of his powerful form, now marred by wounds and immobilized, struck a chord of despair in her.

Soren, despite the pain, forced his attention away from the comforting presence of Aurora to assess his condition. He noted with a hint of relief that the gashes on his chest, while deep, were not life-threatening. But the reality of his fractured leg brought a grimace of pain to his face. A heavy weight settled on his heart as he realized that his identity as a sentinel, defined by his physical prowess and agility, was compromised.

The thought of sending Aurora alone to seek help made him scowl. He knew the mountain's treacherous paths were no place for her to traverse alone, and the creatures that loomed were enough of a threat. But as he contemplated their predicament, an idea ignited in his mind. The memory of Aurora transforming into a being of pure, radiant light offered a glimmer of hope. He was willing to take a chance on the possibility that Aurora's power could heal him.

With a mixture of hope and uncertainty, Soren's eyes met Aurora's. The ethereal glow that still clung to her hinted at untapped potential. It was a risk, but in their dire situation, even the slimmest chance was worth pursuing.

Soren took Aurora's hands in his. He placed one on his bloodied chest, watching her face as the warm stickiness of his blood darkened her fingertips. He lowered her other hand to the rocky ledge on which they sat. And then he placed his hands on top of hers and instructed her, "Close your eyes and call on the elements for healing."

Aurora searched his amber eyes, and he nodded in response. "You can do this," he whispered. "You summoned light from your body. Now call on the earth, the sky, and the sun for healing power." Soren waited for Aurora to close her eyes, and he watched her do so with hesitation.

His trust in her filled Aurora with courage. She could sense the urgency in his voice.

With a deep breath, Aurora surrendered to the moment, her eyelids fluttering closed. The world around her faded into a hush, leaving only the symphony of nature and the rhythm of two hearts in unison. The wind whispered secrets of ancient healing as it danced around them, and the sun bestowed its nurturing warmth upon her skin, infusing her with its life-giving energy.

As Aurora tapped into this primal force, a spark ignited deep within her core. It was a sensation both foreign and familiar, a convergence of the sun's heat, the earth's resilience, and the wind's agility. She channeled this power through her arms, directing it toward Soren. The elements obeyed, intertwining in a harmonious dance of restoration.

The moment her energy touched Soren, a luminous glow emanated from her hands, enveloping his chest in a blanket of healing light. The air around them crackled with electricity, a tangible manifestation of Aurora's power. Soren's breath gradually eased into a calm rhythm, signaling the mending of his wounds.

Aurora's eyes widened, still grappling with the reality of her ability to wield magic. The shock on her face was clear as she looked at her own hands, marveling at the miraculous healing she had just performed. Soren's chest, once marred by deep wounds, was now whole and unblemished, as if the invisible claws of the shadow weaver had never touched him.

Soren, with a deep and appreciative sigh, met Aurora's gaze, his eyes glowing with pride and gratitude. "I knew you could do it. Thank you for trusting me," he said.

"Now for the leg," Soren urged, capturing her hands once more. His eyes, brimming with encouragement and belief, locked onto hers. "Just do it again. One more time."

Aurora's breath hitched, fatigue and uncertainty clouding her features. "I'm just so tired. I don't know if I can do it," she confessed, her voice quivering with exhaustion. Her heavy eyes sought comfort in Soren's reassuring gaze.

"I do. I know you can do it. Just one more time and I can get you out of here. Take you somewhere safe." Soren spoke with gentle insistence, his voice a soft caress against her doubts.

Aurora's mind flashed to Isolde, the looming threat that had brought them to this precarious moment. "But Isolde. What ... what do you think happened to her? Is she ... dead?" The question escaped her lips, laden with a mix of hope and fear.

Soren's expression hardened, his voice gaining an edge of urgency. "I don't know. But it's best we get out of here as fast as we can," he said, acutely aware of the danger that might still be lurking. His words were a call to action, a reminder that their safety hung delicately in the balance.

The urgency of the situation, with the threat of Isolde's return, fueled Aurora with a fresh wave of bravery. She laid her hand upon Soren's strong, motionless thigh, feeling its inherent power even in stillness. Her other hand, guided by Soren, found its place on the rugged surface of the rocky ledge.

In the quietness that enveloped them, Aurora shut her eyes, reaching out to the swirling elements around her. Her muscles ached and there was a heaviness in her bones as she channeled the remnants of her power through her fingertips. A faint crackle of electricity jumped from her hand, seeping through the fabric of Soren's leather pants, reaching the broken bones with a healing touch.

Upon opening her eyes, Aurora saw the strained expression on Soren's face, his jaw set in a grim line as his leg mended under her healing power. She longed to ease his pain, to absorb it and release it far away from them both. She moved her hand to caress his clenched jaw, offering a soothing touch. Soren's pained focus drifted toward her, drawn in by her compassionate eyes, a tranquil blue mirroring the serene sky above.

As the warmth of healing receded, signaling the completion of the mend, Soren tested his leg. He pointed and flexed his foot, then cautiously bent his knee, placing his boot firmly on the ground. Aurora held his hand as he stood, ready to support his weight. But to her surprise, Soren rose with an ease that belied the ordeal he had just endured. She gazed up at him, her face a mixture of relief and admiration, marveling at the resilience and strength of her sentinel.

Soren's gaze, ablaze with a blend of pride and desire, turned Aurora's world into a dizzying whirlwind. He pressed her gently against the rugged wall, his presence a comforting barrier between her and the rest of the world. As he leaned in, his lips barely touching hers, he whispered, "You're incredible." His kiss ignited a fire within her.

Aurora, caught in the moment, allowed herself to melt into him, her mouth parting to welcome the depth of his passion. Their kiss, slow and profound, stirred a fear within her that she might once again become a glowing ball of light, so intense were the emotions swirling within her. As her legs betrayed her, Soren eased back, his eyes searching hers. "Thank you," he breathed, his gratitude palpable in the air.

***

Their descent from the mountain was swift, with Soren's one hand clasping Aurora's as if he was afraid that releasing it would mean losing her to the ether. He guided his borrowed horse down the slope in his other hand. The memory of his injuries was distant now, as he displayed no hint of the pain that had once wracked his body. Reaching Ash and Beacon, who were waiting restlessly at the base of the slope, Soren helped Aurora, wrapped in her shimmering white cloak, onto his horse before mounting himself. He pulled her close against him, his arms forming a cocoon of safety and comfort around her. He grabbed Beacon's reins, guiding the mare and the other horse beside them.

Aurora, feeling the steady beat of his heart against her back, tilted her head to meet his gaze. "Where are we going?" she asked softly.

Soren's amber eyes, reflecting the dawning light, met hers with a deep well of emotions. "Home," he purred.

Chapter 14

Despite the relentless speed at which Soren spurred Ash onward, Aurora had succumbed to exhaustion, her body finding comfort curled against the sentinel's sturdy form. The rhythmic cadence of the horse's gallop had lulled her into a deep sleep, even as they hastened toward their destination.

Upon waking, Aurora's eyes fluttered open to a scene vastly different from the expected woods of Whispering Glen, the gateway to her return. Instead, she found herself nestled in a plush leather chair situated beside a crackling fire in a modest hearth. Shadows cloaked the room, with the sporadic flicker of candles providing the only other illumination.

Her gaze drifted to a writing desk set beneath a window, its surface a chaotic landscape of scrolls and ink jars. Turning slightly, she eyed an imposing bed framed by four intricately carved posts that soared toward the lofty ceiling. The room was steeped in a sense of strength and raw power—unmistakably a warrior's sanctuary. This realization prompted Aurora to sit up straighter, her attention drawn to the door as it opened to reveal Soren entering with a tray of steaming food and drink.

He moved silently across the room, placing the wooden tray on a small table next to Aurora's chair. His gaze met hers, and a warm smile unfurled across his face, the flickering firelight casting a glimmer in his amber eyes. "I'm glad you got some rest," he said, his voice filling Aurora's ears, imbuing her with a sense of comfort and safety.

She cast a brief, exploratory glance around the room before her eyes settled back on Soren, finding solace in the depth of his comforting gaze. "This is your home," she said, a memory surfacing of him mentioning they were heading home just before she had drifted off as they fled the mountain.

"One of them, yes," he said. "My favorite, actually. It's quiet, secluded." His voice was a purr of contentment. "Eat." The command sent butterflies fluttering to Aurora's stomach and heat rushed to her cheeks.

Turning her attention to the tray, the aroma of the warm soup enveloped Aurora's senses, igniting a pang of hunger within her. Beside the bowl lay warm bread, a cup brimming with fresh fruit, and a steaming cup of tea—a simple spread. She exercised a moment of restraint before delicately tearing a piece of bread, dipping it into the stew with measured grace. The first taste sent a wave of warmth through her, so comforting that she moaned aloud.

Soren, leaning casually against the edge of the imposing bed with his arms braced on its wooden frame, chuckled softly. The movement accentuated the muscles in his forearms, a subtle display of strength. "I'm glad my cooking pleases you," he said in a light-hearted tone.

Aurora looked up, surprised. "You made this?" The realization dawned on her—never had a man prepared a meal for her. The thought stirred a warm fluttering sensation just below her stomach.

"Yes, I'm quite adept at cooking a modest meal," he said with a shrug, his amber eyes catching the firelight. "It's refreshing to have someone to cook for." His gaze held hers, a flicker of warmth passing between them in the shared glow of the hearth.

Aurora ate in a contemplative silence that spanned several minutes. She tried to focus solely on the food, acutely aware of the effort it took to divert her gaze from Soren's robust figure casually leaning against the bed.

She wanted to rush to him. To wrap her legs around his waist as they tumbled back onto the thick bedding. She'd kiss him passionately as her hands worked to free him. She'd strip her clothes slowly in front of him, holding his gaze as she removed each piece until she was completely bare for him.

Aurora bit her lip as she imagined Soren's wild eyes on her naked body, the firelight licking seductive shadows on her skin. She thought of his large, firm hands cupped around her breasts before he leaned toward them, pulling one into his mouth, gently tugging her nipple. She'd throw her head back in response to the pull between her thighs. He'd watch her as he moved from one breast to the other, his hand rolling her other nipple sensually between his fingers.

Aurora would return her fiery gaze to his wicked honey eyes as his hand slid down to the apex of her thighs. A grin would flicker on his face at the evidence of her arousal, before he circled his thumb on her skin, sending her reeling. He'd focus only on her pleasure.

Just when she thought she would shudder with release, she'd lower her hips onto his thick, hardened length. A primal moan would escape her lips, and she'd rock her hips back and forth at the pleasure it brought her. As her breath quickened, Soren's hands would match her pace, exploring every inch of her naked body. The passionate gaze between them would add to the intense pleasure, and as she climbed to the summit, she'd cry out, a violent shudder of bliss rocking through her body. At the mere sight of her release, Soren would allow himself the delight of his own.

The two would lay together, panting as the height of their embrace washed over them and pulled them into a dreamy sleep.

Soren cleared his throat, snapping Aurora back to the present. She blinked in surprise and saw her spoonful of stew suspended in mid-air. Its contents spilled over and formed small, wet droplets on her sweater.

She caught his gaze, piercing and knowing, as if he had stumbled upon a private, unspoken thought. A rush of embarrassment flushed her cheeks as she looked down at the unintended mess she had created, while her mind wandered through a haze of desire.

She swallowed her sensual thoughts. "I'm sorry. I must still be tired," she murmured. She rose, searching for something to clean the soup that had soaked into her shirt.

Soren's chuckle was light, but there was an underlying seriousness in his tone. "It's no matter. We may as well burn those clothes anyway," he said. Aurora blushed again, thinking of standing naked before him, her clothes burning in the bedroom hearth.

Soren crossed the room to a large armoire. He pulled open its heavy doors and returned to Aurora with fresh clothing. With an intense gaze, Soren extended a hand, offering her a neatly folded garment. She accepted it in silence. "I'm afraid I don't have women's attire, so this will have to suffice. I'll head into town tomorrow for proper clothes," he said.

Unfolding the garment, Aurora realized it was one of Soren's tunics. It was white, its fabric as soft as woven silk against her skin. The sleeves were overly long, and the hem reached mid-thigh, but it was suitable under the circumstances.

Her mind still clouded with the remnants of her vivid daydream, and she stayed wordlessly contemplative. Soren, sensing the need for privacy, said, "Well, I'll leave you to change." He placed the cup of tea and the bowl of fruit on the table, taking the tray with the spilled soup as he exited the room, leaving Aurora in a cocoon of silence and smoldering thoughts.

She quickly shed the garments Isolde had clothed her in, leaving them in a heap on the floor. Glancing at the fire, she contemplated whether Soren was serious about burning them, but she left them where they lay. As she slipped into the tunic, Soren's scent immediately shrouded her—a heady mix of smoky wood and the freshness of earth and sun, with a light kiss of jasmine.

The tunic's fabric was thin, bordering on sheer, prompting Aurora to wonder about Soren's intention of choosing it. But it was warm, draping over her form, subtly accentuating her feminine contours. Settled in the chair by the fire, she released her hair from its low bun, unraveling the braids that framed her face. Her golden curls tumbled over her shoulders in a cascade of waves.

As she watched the flames dance in the hearth, their hypnotic movement accompanied by a slender wisp of smoke rising from the chimney, a soft knock on the door interrupted her reverie. Her voice, slightly hoarse, said, "Come in."

Soren peered through the door, his eyes quickly finding Aurora seated in the chair by the fire. He entered, his gaze dropping to the floor as he made his way toward her. "I know it's late and you need your rest," he began softly, "but I wanted to express my gratitude for today. You saved both our lives."

As Aurora rose to meet him, Soren bowed his head in a gesture of deep reverence. "I am forever indebted to you," he said, his voice imbued with sincere emotion. Lifting his face, Soren laid bare his striking features in a display of vulnerability that took Aurora's breath away.

"And you need to know that the shadow weaver did not touch me," he added, his gaze strong and intent on Aurora. "It was a trick, a disgusting illusion she projected into my mind to use against you. It tortured me to watch it unfold, but I'm grateful that my body did not betray you. I could never live with myself if I hurt you like that." Sadness flickered across his eyes.

Aurora's heart raced, thankful for his words and that the shadow weaver had not crossed that physical boundary—though she was wicked for the twisted game she played.

Aurora caressed his cheek, her fingers tracing the angular line of his jaw and the light stubble that roughened his skin. "Thank you for telling me, but you owe me nothing," she whispered, her smile reaching her eyes, filled with affection for him.

Soren leaned into her touch, then stood, enveloping both her hands in his and bringing them to his lips for a kiss. "You are a marvel, Aurora, and Fate only knows what I did to deserve you," he murmured.

Aurora's knees weakened again as the powerful warrior stood before her, spilling his heart. She watched him as his eyes drifted from hers down the length of her body, taking in the view of the sheer smock illuminated by the firelight. She blushed as his gaze lingered on her breasts and then her hips before settling on her mouth.

"Stunningly beautiful," he purred. Her gaze flashed downward, afraid if she watched him any longer, she'd melt to the floor.

Aurora thought of the pained look on his face at the cave when he thought he had failed her—the look of a lost future. At the thought, she stepped into him, planting her forearms and palms on his expansive chest. She tipped her head up to meet his gaze and lifted her lips to his, returning his spoken compliment.

Soren responded with a gentle intensity, mirroring her affection. Aurora halted the kiss, her eyes searching his and finding embers. She crashed her lips into his again, and in one swift, delicate movement, Soren gripped the back of her thighs, gracing her rounded backside as he lifted her to him, Aurora's legs wrapping around his waist.

He steadily stepped backward until the back of his thighs nudged the wooden bed frame. He turned, holding Aurora's back while lowering her to the bed. Soren pulled back, watching her body rise and fall with each wanting breath in his sheer tunic. The fire threw an ephemeral glow on her glorious body, and the sight of her made him harden.

Aurora saw a tumultuous play of emotions dance across his face, a vivid display of unrestrained passion, before he wrapped his muscular arms around her thighs. With a decisive, careful motion, he drew her toward him, guiding her to the edge of the bed with an intensity that spoke of deep desire.

Her sheer tunic bunched above her waist, and with quick hands, she pulled it over her head, tossing it to the floor. Still watching her, his face lowered, and his warm breath heated the apex of her legs. She released her breath and arched her back as Soren's lips touched her warmth. He shifted his focus from her stormy eyes to the spread of her before him, using his tongue to press further into her.

Aurora couldn't help but writhe as Soren's mouth moved so intentionally between her legs and her hands reached down to entwine her fingers in his deep brown locks.

His mouth buried into her, his tongue slipping inside to taste her, and he growled at the sweetness. Every lick of his tongue burned deep into her, and when she thought she would come absolutely undone, Aurora breathed, "Soren. Please, I need you now." She pleaded, "Please."

He lingered for several moments on her warmth before standing, leaving her breathless and wanting. Aurora looked down the length of her naked body and watched him pull his weathered tunic off his defined torso. He hesitated a moment, as if teasing her before he undid the buttons restraining his length. He slid his pants down his powerful legs and let them fall to the rug with a relieved sigh.

Aurora's eyes hungered as she took in the full sight of his immaculate naked body. The body of a warrior. A protector.

Soren climbed onto the bed, his muscled arms bracing him over her naked and trembling body. He lowered his mouth to hers and slid himself inside her. She broke free from his kiss, arched her head, and released a rasped breath, relishing the glorious fill of him inside her.

Over and over, he slid himself back and forth inside her, his mouth dancing from her neck to her perky breasts, savoring every inch of her heated body. Her breath quickened, and his thrusts matched her pace until he was pounding into her body, unleashing a release that Aurora thought would shatter her body in a blinding light. She was grateful for the seclusion of Soren's home as her guttural roar rattled the windows.

Soren smiled softly before giving himself over to his own release, the sheets under his clenched fists twisting into a labyrinth of passionate desire. As he pulled out of Aurora, he was delighted to see her glowing, illuminated in a shimmering bath of brilliant white light.

Aurora smiled and reached for him, slowing her breaths and pulling him to her chest, embracing the warmth of his skin. She stroked his hair, drawing it back from his angelic face. Before she could close her eyes, he was breathing soundly on her, the faintest of smiles still lingering on his rosy lips.

***

Shade-filtered light drifted through the window, pulling Aurora from the deepest sleep she'd had since arriving in this realm. She squinted through lust-drunk eyes and glanced at the uncovered window, blushing at her gratitude for the seclusion of the forest and not the crowded town, which certainly would have gotten an earful last night.

Her arm slid across the empty space in the bed next to her, cool to the touch, telling Aurora that Soren had risen some time ago. A flash of panic fluttered in her chest, and she lurched forward, gripping the silken sheet that clung to her bare chest. Her eyes scanned the room, bathed in the soft glow of the morning's light. The room exhaled an air of both strength and vulnerability, a sacred space where the sentinel retreated to find solace, contemplating his duty.

"Soren?" Aurora called out, her voice displaying her concern.

A moment passed before her eyes glinted at the open door of the adjoined bathing room. A melodious voice poured out toward her. "I'm here." Soren's large form strode out of the room and into the streaming sunlight, casting glorious light onto his wet skin. A cloth barely concealed what lay below his waist.

Aurora's heart settled long enough for butterflies to fill her stomach as he moved toward her. She bit her lip as she eyed his dripping naked body, his dark hair slicked back from his striking face. There was a familiar pull between her legs, and she blushed at how hungry she was for his touch. Aurora couldn't get enough of him. Where she once feared someone would take him away from her, she now longed to be held by him.

Soren's gentle gaze sparked with desire as he registered Aurora's own on her face. Once next to the side of the bed, he let the cloth drop to the floor and a gasp escaped Aurora's lips. She pulled back the sheet, revealing her naked body and inviting him into bed. She relished his darkened gaze.

He crawled over her, intentionally letting his hardened length glide across her nude torso. Aurora shuddered at the sensitive, smooth skin. She could already feel her arousal pooling inside her, and Soren slipped a finger below her waist to feel for himself. He grinned at the acknowledgment.

In a swift movement, Aurora placed her hands on his broad shoulders, pinning him to the bed. He smiled up at her, eager to be the subject of her wicked plans. She straddled his waist, feeling him rise in anticipation. She placed a delicate kiss on his lips before her gaze met his and she trailed her mouth down his neck and chest, each sensitive touch igniting his skin.

Her mouth lingered on his nipples, circling them with her tongue before gently tugging them into her teeth. He moaned and his head fell back on the pillow while Aurora's name escaped his lips.

Soren's sounds of pleasure spurred her on, her mouth trailing down toward his waistline. She gripped his impressive length, hardened under her touch. She looked up devilishly at him through thick lashes before wrapping her wet, soft lips around him. He shivered in response, and his toes curled at the end of the bed.

She trailed her tongue under his length, enjoying the slow burn of his desire. Like he had done with her the night before, Aurora focused her attention on tasting him, filling her mouth.

Now it was his turn to beg. "Aurora, please."

With that command, she released him from her mouth and shifted her hips to lower onto him. A curse slipped from his lips.

She slid around him and gasped at how he delightfully filled her. She braced her hands on his chiseled chest, her fingers dancing at his nipples and tracing the lines of the serpentine tattoo. Her gaze tore through Soren's amber eyes, and her face twisted into carnal passion. Whatever bond she had formed with this powerful fae sentinel grew stronger as their bodies joined and moved as one.

The thought of his love, how her own heart swelled when she was with him, set fire to the apex of her thighs. Soren's hands slid to her hips, gripping them as she rocked back and forth. Encouraged by the view of her beautiful body on top of him, his thumb slid to where they joined.

Aurora moaned above him as his thumb circled her most sensitive spot. She moved faster, harder, surprised as even the mighty bed shuddered with her movement. Her release grew, and she kept her storming eyes on Soren. His lips opened in pleasure, his honey eyes burning with desire.

She thought the bed would crack in two. Light flickered in his eyes and his thumb continued to work its magic while his other hand lifted to her breast, tugging her hardened nipple between his fingers. With a long guttural gasp, she shattered into a million pieces around him. As her release came in waves, he hardened and spilled over, filling her as another curse escaped his beautiful mouth.

She fell forward onto his body, glistening with sweat. She was so fulfilled and free that she feared she would sob. Her voice hitched as she stifled her cry, her breathing slowing at the sound of Soren's heartbeat. He relaxed, wrapping his massive arms around her huddled body on top of him. He brushed back her damp golden locks before pulling her chin to look her in the eyes. "I love you, too."

She hadn't wanted to say it. Not like this. Not in the heat of passion where lust and love swirl and it's hard to know which is real. And he knew. He knew she loved him but couldn't say it. Not yet. And he didn't force her to.

He simply cradled her, stroking her back, as happy tears silently slid down her angelic face, falling into a tiny pool on his chest.

Chapter 15

Aurora was utterly famished after the morning's impassioned activity with Soren. To her delight, Soren had practically leaped out of bed when she mentioned her hunger, rushing to the kitchen to whip up fresh scrambled eggs, warm bread, and heavenly strips of bacon that she chased down with freshly squeezed orange juice.

No man had ever happily volunteered to prepare food for her before. He watched her take several bites, delighting at the gratitude on her face before turning to his own plate. After she ate, Soren said he would fulfill his promise and travel into town to get proper clothes for her. Someone had mysteriously made the pile of clothing she had shed the previous night disappear, and she wondered if Soren had turned it to ash. He also wanted to visit the town to see if anyone had seen any glimpse of the shadow weaver.

Aurora's blood turned to ice as she thought of Isolde lingering in town, waiting for them to make their move. He also mentioned he needed to see a healer to restock some supplies. When Aurora had fluttered with panic at being left alone and allowing Soren to stride in the open while they remained unsure of what had happened to Isolde on the mountain, he assured her she was safe in his house. An enchantment on the house kept out any uninvited guests and cloaked it in invisibility, leaving its location completely unknown.

She breathed a sigh of relief and Sorren jabbed, "Besides, your bursts of light are enough to banish away any darkness." A small smile crept onto her face at his effort to calm her.

Aurora watched from the frosty window as Soren strode toward town atop Ash. He gave her a final glance over his shoulder and a flash of a smile before he vanished into the thick forest.

The house was modest, an unassuming stone home nestled into the woods. Along with Soren's bedroom suite at the back of the house, a practical kitchen filled the space in the front of the house near the entrance. Aurora found a storeroom just off the kitchen and pulled it open to find an armory of sharpened blades, daggers, and heavy-plated armor. The metal glistened in the light, and the intricate beauty and deadly essence of the weapons mesmerized her. She traced her hand along the razor-sharp edge of a large sword, but stopped short, shivering at the thought of the metal on her skin.

Aurora backed out of the armory and retreated to Soren's bedroom, deciding to distract herself with a warm bath. The bathing room was larger than Aurora expected and drenched from floor to ceiling in a deep midnight blue. A small window on the southern wall allowed streams of sunlight to penetrate the walls, letting light shimmer across the blue paint like stars.

In the center of the room, Aurora found the most massive bathtub she'd ever seen. The shiny glint of copper shimmered in the sunlight and stood at her waist. If it was filled to the brim, she'd easily slip under the surface. She turned on the faucet to let the deliciously hot water rush in. When it reached a comfortable level, she slipped off Soren's sheer tunic and stepped into the warm water.

Left in silence, there was nothing that filled her mind except her own thoughts. Less than two weeks ago, she had been getting some much-needed R&R with her best friend. Aurora closed her eyes, thinking about the terror and panic her friend must have endured once she realized Aurora was missing.

A wash of realization rushed over Aurora as she admitted to herself that Camryn was the only person, the only thing she missed. She thought of her small apartment, where she shut herself into loneliness. She thought of her dead-end job with no flicker of excitement. Even the landscapes of her home were clouded, as if she was looking through a foggy mask.

At home, she was like a wheel on a track to nowhere, just endlessly rolling through life. But here. Here she was alive. Energy and light radiated from her body, no matter how much terror she had experienced in the past several weeks. At least she felt something.

And Soren. Her face brightened at the image of her stunning sentinel. A man strong and fierce, but soft and kind. Powerful but not commanding. Not with her.

She'd braced his quiet reserve and cracked open a shimmering pool so deep of feeling and desire. She understood why he had put up those walls and prevented himself from letting himself get hurt. What he did required it. And he'd taught her so much about herself as well.

Aurora could be strong and independent, but she craved the emotional and physical connection of another. Of a partner. At the word, she slipped her head beneath the water's surface.

What was he to her? And her to him? How could it be anything but what it was, two beings colliding at a predetermined point in time, only briefly? Two people from different worlds.

But she let herself think: *What if she stayed?* What if she kept a hold of this rein? Holding onto this bond was giving her life, filling her with brilliant light. *Could she sacrifice everything she'd ever known to stay in a world that wanted to rip her apart?*

Aurora's practical mind bubbled to the surface. But the risks. The risks were too great—to never return to her life back home. Never again see the faces of her friends or family. Stay vulnerable in a world where creatures with terrifying powers would hunt her? A sadness fell over her. She knew she needed to pull herself out of whatever delirium she had thrown herself into. She blew frustrated bubbles in the water before hearing the heavy thud of the front door.

Leaving her introspection to flow down the drain of the bathtub, Aurora quickly dried and dressed and found Soren at the small table in the kitchen, his brows furrowed in concern. He had quietly left a bundle of new clothing on the bed before Aurora emerged from the bathing room, leaving her in privacy.

The celestial blue tunic caught Aurora's attention, as the fabric shimmered like a night sky. She cinched the tunic at the waist with a supple leather belt. Aurora tucked the hem of the shirt into form-fitting mossy brown riding pants. She slid thick woolen socks into brown leather boots that hit just below her knees.

She had let her golden curls loose, falling in gentle waves around her shoulders. As she strode into the open room of the kitchen and saw Soren's concerned face, her heart ached. Despite being deep in thought, Soren turned to Aurora as the midday light illuminated her tunic, complimenting her sky-blue eyes.

"Thank you for the clothes," Aurora said as he turned to her.

"They suit you." The warmth radiated from Soren's eyes, and, for a moment, Aurora forgot his previously concerned demeanor.

She blushed at his compliment but met his gaze. "Did you learn anything in town of ..." Her voice trailed off, not wanting to speak of the shadow weaver.

Soren bristled. "Villagers told me the town has been quiet. Too quiet. But no sightings of her." His lips pursed together.

Grateful that Isolde hadn't appeared in town, Aurora let out a sigh. She placed a hand on Soren's stoic face, and the strain eased from his gaze. She moved into him, stepping into the cocoon of his powerful legs. He looked up at her and slid his hands around her waist to the small of her back. Soren sighed and leaned in to place his head against Aurora's warm chest. She wrapped her arms around him, stroking his hair. The two held each other in silence for several minutes, the chipper of songbirds and hum of a breeze the only sounds to seep into the house.

Aurora breathed deeply and then pulled away so she could investigate Soren's face. "So, what's the plan?" She knew he had done plenty of planning while she had enjoyed the warmth of the bath.

Soren's broad shoulders rose and fell. "Since we don't know exactly what happened to her, we need to assume that she fled alive. This means, no doubt, that she will make another play for the portal location. She is tracking us. While the isolation shield of this home will buy us some time, once we leave its boundaries, she will pick up our scents. We suspect the rift is just a few miles from here, in the northern woods near the Silverveil Mountains. She's likely to expect us to make a move in the morning, which is why I think we should leave tonight, using the cover of darkness." He looked warily at Aurora as if he wanted to say something else, but he swallowed down his thought.

Aurora's heart skipped a beat as she thought of them racing through the darkened forest, the shadow weaver hot on their trail. But she trusted Soren. She knew he would only suggest it if he thought it was the best plan. Then her heart fell as she thought she only had a few more hours with Soren before leaving him forever.

She shuddered but met Soren's hopeful eyes. "Okay. We leave tonight then."

For the next several hours, Aurora did her best to mask her nervous energy as she paced around the house while Soren took care to prepare for their brief journey, packing bottles of his recently purchased potions and laying out his chosen weapons from his stocked armory.

Aurora sat silently in the kitchen as Soren delicately placed his weapons on the table. A long sword was the first he had chosen, which she recognized as being the one usually sheathed on his back. But she had never seen it up close. Her eyes marveled at the exquisitely crafted blade, etched with symbols, and pulsated with magical energy. While the blade was a gleaming silver, its hilt was a darkened gold, swirls and curves molded into the metal, perfectly formed for his firm hand.

An elegant bow of curved dark wood sat next to the sword. A quiver of arrows shimmered in the afternoon sun flickering through the kitchen window, revealing tips made from cobalt-blue gemstones. Incredibly beautiful and just as lethal.

The last piece of the warrior's equipment was a broad shield made of the same darkened gold as the chosen sword's hilt. Intricate patterns adorned the metal, and its protective power radiated off its curved surface. The beauty of the deadly weapons mesmerized her, and her heart quickened as she thought of Soren wielding them to protect his charge.

Soren watched Aurora's eye behold the weapons before giving a soft command, "Come with me. I have something for you."

Aurora broke her gaze from the weapons that called to her and followed Soren's mighty form into the armory next to the kitchen. He strode to a wall and pulled off a small dagger. He turned to her, holding the weapon across both hands as if offering a prized jewel. Aurora beheld the sleek dagger, its silver blade shimmering as if it were a gentle stream filled with starlight. Its craftsmanship was simply elegant.

Without a word, she reached for it and gauged the weight of it in her hand. It was surprisingly light, but she couldn't deny its strength and lethal ability.

Soren's voice filled the small room. "It was my mother's. Crafted with Elvin steel under a full moon and cloudless sky."

Aurora tore her eyes from the beautiful instrument of death to look at Soren's gleaming eyes. "I can hear it. It's ... It's like it's singing." Her eyes were wide in surprise as she heard a harmonious melody erupt within her, a song so pure and captivating that it vibrated at the very core of her being.

A smile appeared on Soren's lips. "It calls for you. For the one that should wield it," he said.

Aurora looked at the blade in her hands and whispered, "Thank you. It's beautiful."

Soren grabbed a dark leather belt before following Aurora out of the storeroom.

At Soren's suggestion, Aurora retreated to the bedroom to rest before they would depart at midnight for the portal. Despite the comfort of Soren's bed and the darkness of the room with the curtain closed, she tossed and turned, uneasy about the journey and leaving Soren.

What would happen if she stayed here? What would become of her? The uncertainty sent ice through her veins. But she'd have Soren. He could guide her. Soren could protect her while she became what she was meant to be in this world. She thought of him riding next to her, striding over rolling, lush hills toward a blazing sunset. The wind whispered in their hair and their laughter drifted in the breeze.

It was so easy. Being with him was easy.

She fell asleep imagining the warmth of the sun and Soren's smile on her face.

***

Soren sat at the kitchen table, his senses tuned to the gentle rhythm of Aurora's breathing as she slumbered peacefully in his bed. Over the years, he had mastered the art of coping with his heightened sense of hearing. In his youth, the various sounds he encountered during travels with his parents often robbed him of sleep. As he matured, the constant barrage of noises often overwhelmed him, leaving him feeling as though his mind was as noisy and chaotic as a bustling tavern.

But, in the quiet of this moment, Soren found himself captivated by the sound of Aurora's breathing. It was like a soothing, rhythmic lullaby, a melody so hypnotic that he wished it could go on indefinitely.

For several minutes, he stayed utterly still, immersing himself in the gentle cadence of her breath. His life was typically marked by solitude, with only his thoughts for company and occasional barkeeper chatter, rarely graced by such tranquility.

And he, being a man of few words and reserved nature, wasn't the best at keeping company. But in the presence of Aurora's soft, peaceful breathing, Soren enjoyed a rare sense of ease and fulfillment.

When Aurora entered his life, it was a sudden and unexpected shift in his solitary existence. And he didn't want to go back.

The memory of their first encounter remained etched in Soren's mind like a vivid painting. He recalled finding her by the river, her appearance a striking juxtaposition of beauty and distress, her face marred by wounds but still radiantly captivating.

That morning had been an unusual one for Soren, marked by a sense of restlessness that had stirred him awake before dawn. Compelled by an inexplicable urge, he had ridden toward the river. It was there he found Aurora.

As he sat, lost in his thoughts, his heart stirred at the recollection of her smile, the depth in her stormy blue eyes. He thought of her laughter, a joyful resonance, and her constant, simmering curiosity. Aurora was braver than she gave herself credit for, her spirit of adventure rattling below the surface, often restrained but unmistakably present.

But when he was with her, he marveled at the way her wall came down and her lively spirit flickered to life.

Tangled together in the sanctuary of his bed, Aurora was the epitome of freedom. It was there, in their shared seclusion, that the world narrowed down to just the two of them, surrounded by an electric current of unspoken passion that crackled in the air around them.

Aurora had upended Soren's entire understanding of love and intimacy. Throughout his life, he had built walls to keep others at a distance, a protective measure to spare both himself and them from pain. But no woman had ever breached his defenses and captivated his mind and heart, as Aurora had. Her influence extended far beyond the visible strength of her inner fire; she possessed a power that challenged his long-held beliefs and awoke emotions he had never expected.

A profound understanding washed over Soren as he sat alone in his cabin. He yearned for Aurora to stay, to choose to remain in Silverveil. To choose him. A wave of guilt accompanied this admission, made in the silence of his own heart. His role as a sentinel had always been to prioritize the needs and safety of others over his own desires, to be the steadfast protector of both the people and his realm. His happiness came second to his oath.

But overriding his sense of duty was a deeper, more selfless longing—the desire for Aurora's happiness. If her heart truly belonged to her own world, then that was the path he wanted for her. The thought of her returning to where she came from, where she would be safe and content, was a bitter but comforting consolation. If she was happy, he could bear the pain of watching her disappear through the veil.

With these somber reflections echoing in his mind, Soren meticulously sharpened and polished his blades, each stroke a meditation on his internal conflict. Afterward, he turned his attention to the kitchen, determined to prepare a last meal, a heartfelt gesture for the love that he knew was as transient as it was complex.

***

It was the smell of roasted meat and boiled vegetables that roused Aurora from sleep. A peek outside the window told her it was well into the night, and she swallowed. She slipped quietly to the kitchen, where she found Soren plating the delicious food that tempted her senses. He smiled as if he could hear the growl of her stomach.

"Hello, beautiful." His honey voice made her blush, and she tucked a loose curl behind her ear. "Sit, please." She obeyed his soft command and took a seat at the set table.

After watching Aurora pile food onto her plate and take the first few bites, Soren joined in. Soren had placed a bottle of deep red wine on the table and Aurora happily filled her glass. She took a sip and lowered her glass, eyeing her companion. So many questions flooded her, the recollection of limited time to ask them.

She focused on the one biting at her cheek. "Do you have any magical abilities?" she asked.

Soren took a bite and thought deeply before wiping his mouth and meeting Aurora's curious gaze. "Not like what you've shown, no." He continued, "My mother was a powerful elemental mage. She could call on the elements to fuel and bend her magic."

"And your father. Did he have powers?"

Soren released a breath and focused on an imaginary spot on the table. "My father's power was in his strength and speed. He was one of the most successful sentinels our lands had ever known. I inherited his speed and strength, which serves me well as a sentinel. Powerful protective magic infuses my weapons, but I do not possess my mother's powers."

Aurora's voice quieted, almost to a whisper. "What happened to them that day? When you were a boy."

Soren took a deep breath and searched Aurora's eyes. "A traveler had come through a tear in the veil, similar to what happened to you. My parents were patrolling nearby and came across the young man. He was terrified. My father knew of a portal just north of Raven's Ridge, just a two-day ride. But it was risky. Many dark creatures roamed the mountains, each one with an insatiable hunger for torture or power. But we moved quickly, and we reached the portal in less than two days. Unfortunately, a frost wraith had picked up on our scent and arrived in the clearing moments after we did, taking us by surprise with its firedrake. The winged reptiles have scales as hard as obsidian and are fiercely protective of their masters. And the wraith was powerful. And crazed, desperate to feed off the life of the traveler and escape through the portal.

"My father battled the drake, looking for the soft spot of unshielded skin beneath its breastplate, while my mother worked to call on the elements to protect the traveler and clear a path to the portal. But the frost wraith was able to easily manipulate the wind and ice. And it was quick. The moment it touched the traveler, his body froze to ice, draining the life from him. I still remember the petrified look on his face beneath the ice. It was my scream that drew the wraith's attention to me, causing my parents to falter in their efforts. The drake struck my father against the rock with its powerful tail before the tip pierced through his heart. His last breath was my mother's name. While the drake turned on her, she used all her power to shield me in the warmth of glowing sunlight, keeping the wraith at bay. She told me to run, and as the wraith pounced on her, she said, "I love you." And then the wraith froze her and shattered her into a thousand shards of ice."

Soren's face mourned. A single tear slid down Aurora's cheek at his pain.

"I spent four days in the woods beneath the mountain, wandering toward home. Clara found me huddled under a fox's pelt that I had trapped a day earlier. I thrashed and snarled, and it took me a week before I could speak. She raised me from that day on, never forcing me to talk about what happened."

Aurora's words were hushed and raspy. "Oh Soren, I'm so sorry." She stood from her chair and walked around the edge of the table to his seat. He pushed back, allowing Aurora to slide her onto his lap.

"I've spent my life working to never feel that fear again. The fear of losing the people I love and being helpless to stop it." He gazed at Aurora with remorse. His throat bobbed. "What happened with the shadow weaver brought me back to that place. Seeing you in harm's way. I would never forgive myself if anything bad happened to you."

Aurora shushed quietly and lifted his chin to kiss him softly. "I'm okay. And I know everything will be okay." Her reassuring smile was as much for her as for him.

Soren cleared his throat and shifted his weight, standing as he lowered Aurora to her feet. "We should get ready to depart." He looked down at her body, causing a rush of heat in Aurora's cheeks. "I retrieved some more appropriate clothing for you for the journey. I've laid them on the bed."

Aurora reluctantly stepped away from the comfort of his grasp, lingering just a moment before turning toward the bedroom. There, she found clothing strategically placed on the expansive bed, mirroring how they would look on her body. One glance and she realized Soren had chosen warrior clothing for her as well.

At the core of the ensemble was a fitted leather bodice adorned with intricate patterns and reinforced with hardened leather plates, offering both protection and flexibility. Sturdy leather armor with engraved designs would protect her shoulders without hindering mobility. Straps criss-crossed over her chest, securing them in place.

Atop her woven tunic, Aurora tied on leather elbow guards with metal accents, offering added protection to her arms without sacrificing agility. She tucked form-fitting black leather pants into her dark riding boots before strapping on leather thigh guards.

Embossed patterns, subtle embroidery, and decorative accents adorned the garments, reflecting a magical language and culture that Aurora didn't understand. She braided her wild curls back into a single plait, letting it fall behind her back.

Feeling self-conscious about the foreign look and feel of the clothes, Aurora nervously returned to the front of the house. Soren was busy securing his weapons and his armor. Her entrance into the room claimed his attention, and he stood frozen as he eyed Aurora in her warrior gear.

Her voice hitched as she caught his burning gaze. She walked slowly to him before asking a shaky, "Well?"

"You look like a warrior queen," Soren said. Aurora's cheeks flushed as his gaze fell to her lips and then dragged slowly down the front of her body, her leathers clinging tight to her curves. Soren's gaze trailed back to her face, causing a ripple of shudders up her spine. "There's one more thing." He turned to the counter behind him and gripped a black leather utility belt that would sheath her dagger.

To Aurora's surprise, Soren kneeled before her, looking up at her with a devilish gaze. He held the belt open as Aurora placed her hands on his massive shoulders, stepping through each hole that would slide up her thighs and then secure around her waist. As he pulled the belt up the length of her body, Aurora gasped as Soren's hands graced her leathers, lingering around the roundness of her backside before tugging them up and fastening them to her body.

He stood slowly, watching her face flushed with heat and desire. His hands steadied on her hips and Aurora wanted him to take her right there in the kitchen. To throw her on the table and fuck her hard as the wood groaned beneath the weight of her body, getting passionately ravaged by Soren's powerful thrusts.

Only unfastening enough clothing to allow access for their tryst, Aurora's senses would explode with the sensation of skin, heat, and leather as Soren moved fast and rhythmically before shattering her in release.

Knowing she was wet with desire, Aurora looked up at Soren through thick lashes, eyes storming. Soren's eyes darkened as if he saw every lustful detail in Aurora's mind. And he moved to her, his lips crashing into hers. She opened for him, letting his tongue stroke hers with desire.

Soren quickly unfastened his pants, unleashing his hardened length, eager to be inside her. Aurora slid her hands to the front of her pants, feeling the smooth hardness of Soren pressed against her. She fumbled for her buttons and Soren's lips curled into a mischievous grin before his hands moved to the leather, helping her unbutton and slide them down just enough for him to enter her.

Aurora's face contorted with pleasure, and her voice hitched as he filled her. Soren growled in response, and she opened her eyes to see the fire in his gaze. His pouty lips moved from hers to her neck, licking small circles and sucking softly on her heated skin. His hands slid down the leather on her back and his powerful hands wrapped around her tight ass, lifting her. Aurora wrapped her legs around him, leather squeaking against leather.

Soren placed her on the edge of the table, but his hands stayed firm on her backside. Aurora moaned and his pace quickened. She braced herself, her fingers wrapped tightly around the edge of the table, her knuckles tight under her skin. She moaned louder and louder with each thrust, causing Soren to pound harder and harder until she exploded with pleasure. Her body shook, and she wasn't even sure if she was breathing. Soren took one look at the woman shuddering in front of him and allowed himself to roar with a release of his own.

He worked to control his breath, heaving in sync with Aurora before kissing her softly on the lips and sliding himself out of her. Aurora fell back onto the table, afraid she would faint if she tried to stand. Soren chuckled before filling a cup of water and reaching out his hand to Aurora, helping her sit up and drink the cool liquid.

He laughed softly. "Even dark sentinel leathers can't contain that glow." His eyes danced on the translucent shimmer radiating around Aurora's body.

She laughed softly before replying, "Only for you." Aurora didn't let herself dwell on the fact that it would be her last intimate encounter with her sentinel. It was poetic in a way—hard and fast, like how they had met.

Soren helped Aurora to her feet before pulling her cloak from a hook and handing it to her. The shimmering snow-white of the cloak was a stark contrast to the black leather of her warrior's uniform. Like a full moon encroaching on a night's sky. She wrapped herself in its warmth and pulled up the hood before turning to get one last glance at Soren's home, her retreat, before following him out the door.

The air bit at her cheeks. It was silent as they mounted Ash, leaving Beacon in the glow of the night. The moonlight that trickled through the trees illuminated the ground. Soren held Aurora tight as he pulled the reins and nudged Ash into a quick stride.

The moon hung low in the sky, casting an ethereal glow over the dense forest as Aurora and Soren raced through the ancient, moss-covered trees. Their breaths mingled with the whispers of the wind, and the shadows of the past lingered, chasing them like silent specters. With every heartbeat, the intensity of their trek grew, their connection deepening, knowing that time was both an ally and an adversary.

Aurora focused only on the path ahead, not allowing herself to glance at the dark scenery whipping past, like racing shadows. As the portal's rumored location drew near, the air itself pulsed with arcane energy. Aurora could feel the vibrations in the air and hear a subtle hum of electricity. A sacred clearing, bathed in a soft luminescence, unfolded before them—a place where worlds converged, and destinies entwined.

There, in the center of the clearing, suspended in air, was a tear, much like the gash on Aurora's hand in the cave. Even from a distance, Aurora could see the tear was only a few feet long and a couple of inches wide. She imagined that to pass through it, you would need to pull open the tear like a piece of fabric.

Being within sight of the portal, reality came screaming in Aurora's ears. *This is it. You're leaving him.* Tears stung her eyes as she tried to hold them back from falling, becoming real. Her heart pounded in her chest, and she looked up at her sentinel.

Soren gazed down at Aurora, his brow furrowed, and the heartache was clear in his eyes. "It's time. You must go now." His command was only half-hearted, and it broke Aurora's even more.

She lifted her hand to his face and stroked his cheek, illuminated in the moonlight. "Thank you. For everything." Aurora's voice was soft, and she stifled a cry. Soren hopped down from his horse before lifting Aurora and setting her on her feet.

"I am honored to have met you. For the rest of my days, I will be grateful for finding you that day on the river." His honeyed voice threatened the hold on her tears. There, just feet from the humming of the portal, Soren kissed her one last time. Aurora closed her eyes to relish the moment, letting everything else fall away. All the terror of being chased by Isolde. All the agony of having to choose between two worlds. She only wanted to remember him and how he made her feel.

Their respite was fleeting.

With an ominous rustle, the shadow weaver emerged from the shadows, a sinister silhouette against the moonlit glade. Eyes gleaming like a malevolent galaxy, Isolde bared her glistening teeth, thirsting for revenge. A red, jagged scar crossed Isolde's once smooth porcelain face, the consequence of Aurora's fiery outburst outside the cave. "Going somewhere?" she asked, her voice pouring out like poison.

CHAPTER 16

Aurora's eyes widened, and ice filled her veins. She turned to Soren, who was already calculating his attack.

"Go, Aurora. Now." Soren's determination remained unyielding.

Aurora hesitated, torn between the instinct to fight by Soren's side and the urgency to flee through the portal before Isolde could slip through and wreak havoc on her world. The veil shimmered before her, a flare of promise and uncertainty.

As she stepped to the portal's threshold, a shadowy tendril lashed out, ensnaring her in its insidious grip. Behind her, she heard the clash of blades as Soren confronted the shadow weaver in a dance of steel and shadow. A feared rasp escaped from Aurora as Isolde's shadowy grip pulled her back from the portal. Soren whipped his head in Aurora's direction, faltering for just a moment, allowing Isolde to bring an obsidian blade down on Soren's shoulder, a vibrating clang as it hit his armor.

"Soren!" Aurora's cry echoed through the glade, her heart pounding in a desperate rhythm.

Soren winced as a shudder of pain shot through his body. Isolde's wicked grin flashed in the lunar light. "Aurora, you have to go now." Soren's voice was thunderous as he gave her a steely gaze. He focused on the dark tendril of power Isolde had wrapped around Aurora, keeping her from pushing through the veil. Aurora watched as his glinting blade sliced through the air, severing the shadow of magic that bound her.

Isolde hissed in response and curled her fingers, holding them toward Soren as if she were wrapping her hand around his neck. Aurora watched in horror as Soren's feet lifted from the ground, kicking and thrashing against the invisible power that held him.

"You are such a nuisance. Like an unrelenting insect that refuses to die." Isolde's voice was full of frustration and fury, her angry scar slicing through her dark beauty.

Aurora's heart pounded in her chest as she watched Soren gasp for air, but his eyes met hers, urging her to go. Tears streamed down her cheeks as Aurora stumbled toward the portal, her fingers brushing the threshold. She felt the thrum of its power. And so did Isolde.

The shadow weaver, desperate and unflinching, lunged once more. A darkness descended on Aurora as her arm extended through the portal, enveloping her in darkness. Suddenly, something flung her backward in the clearing. She landed on the ground beneath Isolde and Soren with a thud, her back screaming from the impact.

Aurora looked up at the devious Isolde, her violet eyes wild with fury. "How inconsiderate of you. You can wait your turn." Isolde's voice tore through the clearing.

Soren still thrashed above Aurora, but his gaze was cast downward. Aurora saw a silent command flicker in his golden eyes, and she understood. She placed her palms on the ground, her fingers sinking into the cool earth beneath her. Keeping a watchful eye on Isolde, Aurora focused all her energy on the world around her. She heard the wind whisper a song, foreign to her ears. She smelled the earth as it churned below. And she felt the celestial energy of the moon and stars that blanketed the sky.

When Soren looked into Aurora's eyes, they reflected the midnight sky, specks of brilliant white and gold flickering in a deep blue. She saw Isolde's eyes widen as Aurora stood and threw both arms straight out in her direction, a beam of light shot toward her, spearing the dark figure and throwing her across the clearing. Aurora heard a crack as the shadow weaver hit a massive evergreen, falling to the ground with a thud.

The attack had severed Isolde's hold on Soren, and he landed on the ground next to Aurora, who rippled with a cosmic glow. He gasped for air, and as much as Aurora wanted to turn to him, she kept her fierce gaze on Isolde, who was slowly climbing to her feet.

"You need to get to the portal. I can hold her off and close it as soon as you're through," Soren choked.

Aurora burned with fury. Fiery rage filled her as she focused on Isolde. "No. I'm not leaving you." Her voice rang with crystalline clarity.

Soren looked up at her, his gaze wanting. "I'll be okay. If you don't go now, I don't know if you'll ever be able to get back home." His voice was breathless as he spoke the words that cut through him.

Tearing her gaze away from Isolde, who watched with curiosity from across the meadow, Aurora's gaze met Soren's, and it was as if someone set fire to the sky. "What if I am home? What if this is where I am meant to be? And Fate brought me here for a purpose. I love you. I'm in love with you, and I've never felt so alive as I do when I'm with you here."

"Aurora," his voice honeyed as he considered her words.

"There's nothing left for me there. It's not my home anymore—if it ever was." Aurora had never been so sure of a decision. Although the words scared her, her heart filled as she realized she was putting herself and her needs first, for once. This is what she wanted. This is where she needed to be, no matter how terrifying and foreign.

Soren stood, his eyes searching for confirmation. Aurora smiled at him and nodded once, sealing her decision.

"Oh, how lovely. You two truly deserve each other. Makes me sick." Isolde's voice was smooth as velvet. "What an interesting treasure she turned out to be, this meek human." Her violet eyes gleamed at Aurora. "Oh, the things he will do to her when he learns of what power she has. So much potential." Isolde's voice was thick with malice. She turned her gaze to Soren's watching eyes. "What is it like when you bring her to ecstasy? Does her glow explode through you as well?" Her wicked voice stirred a fire in Aurora, and she heard Soren snarl. Isolde only laughed in response. "I hope you ravish each other as this world burns to the ground."

Aurora's mind raced as she considered Isolde's words. *Who was the man she spoke of?* Her mouth parted as the question played on her lips. But it was the shadow weaver's swiftness that drew her attention. As quick as an afternoon thunderstorm rolling in, Isolde had moved to the portal that still shimmered. Her devilish grin reached the fresh scar across her cheek as she slipped a lanky arm through the veil.

Aurora was running before she realized it, Soren hot on her heels, yelling words she didn't hear as fire and rage stormed inside her body. Aurora pulled the steel dagger from her belt and raced toward Isolde, her face twisting in fury. As she closed in on the portal, her arm slashed through the thick air.

But instead of the blade meeting flesh, a grip landed on Aurora's wrist instead. Her gaze lashed forward, meeting Isolde's malicious eyes. "Better yet, I could use a pet." The sound in Isolde's voice made Aurora's stomach churn, and her eyes widened as her body fell toward the rift.

Aurora heard Soren's voice, but the words on his lips were foreign and hummed with magic. She turned her head to see him moving toward her, his powerful blade raised above his head. Fury raged on his face as he focused on the shadow weaver. Aurora turned back to Isolde, space and time slowing and gurgling as if something had disrupted its plane.

She knew this was it. She had one last chance to fight for her world. Aurora summoned every ounce of power that thrummed through her body as the echo of the portal threatened to swallow her. She heard Soren's sword pierce the portal, and it sparked with electricity. Isolde deflected the blade as she tightened her grip on Aurora's wrists.

Then there was fire. Aurora unleashed her full power, and her body transformed into a churning ball of flame. She heard Isolde scream in agony as fire licked up the fingers that held Aurora's wrist. She tried to recoil her hands in pain, but it was Aurora who now clung to the shadow weaver, her eyes blazing as flames licked up Isolde's body.

And then Soren's blade plunged through the shadow weaver's fiery chest, releasing an otherworldly shriek. Aurora kept her furious gaze fixed on the creature that now bled and burned in her hands. The portal was closing in on them and she prepared herself to fall through the shimmering hole that would deliver her back to the world she knew if she didn't turn to ash first.

As she closed her eyes, filling her mind with Soren's beautiful face and not of the horrifying one before her, a firm hand gripped her shoulder. She turned in response, opening her eyes to see Soren focused on her, his teeth gritting as flames circled his hand. He pulled with all his strength, dragging Aurora back through the rift. She kicked at the vortex of the portal and held tight to Isolde, who was still shrieking in agony.

With one last tug, Soren fell backward, landing on the cold ground. Aurora landed at his feet beneath the portal, and Isolde's smoldering body crackled beside her. She held on tight, afraid Isolde would slip back through the portal.

Armed with the incantation to close the portal, Soren's lips moved with fury. Aurora's gaze flickered between Soren' battered body and the shimmering veil.

With a final whisper, Soren sealed the tear, cutting off Isolde's escape and the path to the world Aurora used to know. The clearing trembled with the echoes of the spell as the rift between worlds closed.

The flames enveloping Isolde's entire body brightened to an unnatural illuminance before the shadow weaver burst into the night, pieces of spark and ash dissipating into the midnight breeze. An eerie stillness fell over the glade as Isolde's shrieking was silenced.

Aurora looked down at her blazing hands and imagined her body dipped in icy water, drenching the flames. Fire withdrew into her until only a smoky haze drifted from her. She whipped to Soren, remembering the hand he placed on her burning shoulder as he pulled her back through the portal.

He sat on the ground, holding his injured hand. Aurora looked at his red and blistered skin. Despite the pain that must be throbbing beneath his skin, there was a look of relief on his face. Aurora touched her fingertips to his heated skin, and he winced. She put a palm to the frigid ground, calling on the healing energy of the land.

As her other hand hovered over Soren's burned hand, a soft light drifted from her palm and Soren's gaze turned from the skin that was cooling and smoothing beneath the glow to Aurora's calm, concentrated face. A treasured grin played on his lips as the pain completely diminished. Serene blue eyes looked at him through heavy lashes. "Sorry," Aurora whispered.

Soren's response was light. "It was worth it." He grinned at her as a smile spread across her face. Aurora held his gaze. In that shared moment, a silent understanding passed between them—the sacrifice made for the sake of the other.

As the moonlight wove through the trees, Aurora and Soren stood together, their destinies forever entangled in the threads of a love forged in the crucible of otherworldly makings.

Soren moved into her, his amber eyes full of love and admiration. Of pride for this incredible woman who stood before him. He brushed back loose strands of golden curls and kissed her lips. Aurora sighed and let herself fall into him, savoring the feeling of victory and choice. Of being brave enough to fight for her heart.

One mighty arm swept behind Aurora's legs, lifting her to his chest in a delicate motion. Her wondered gaze danced over his gentle face, illuminated beneath the moonlight as he carried her to Ash, who waited in the clearing. He placed her atop the horse, before leaping over its back, pulling his body to hers and wrapping his arms around her as he commanded Ash forward.

They rode in silence the short distance to Soren's isolated cabin. As he carried her over the threshold, the full weight of the battle sunk into Aurora's bones, and she feared she'd slip into sleep from the gentle rocking of Soren's gait.

Her eyes clung to his, desperately wanting to fight off sleep and feel his warmth as they tangled in the sheets. A passionate gaze radiated from Soren's eyes as he strode toward the bedroom.

Once inside the darkened room, Aurora heard a fire roar to life in the hearth and chuckled at whatever magic Soren cast over his home. He placed her on the bed, and Aurora relished the softness of the sheets that curled around her. The threat of sleep again danced around her eyes, but she steeled them on Soren, who looked at her, amber eyes swirling.

He leaned over the edge of the bed, whispering into her ear like warm honey, "You should sleep." His soft eyes were on hers.

"I want you," was all that she could whisper, her voice pleading.

A mischievous grin spread across his lips. "We can enjoy ourselves later, after you rest." His voice crooned.

Aurora replied in a clear command. "No. I need you now." Her eyes insisted.

A low groan rumbled from Soren's lips as he placed his lips on hers, the desire thrumming from Aurora's mouth. Soren kissed her slowly and deeply, savoring her. As Aurora shivered beneath him, he stood to remove his battle clothes, leather and metal falling heavily to the floor. Aurora watched him, her breathing ragged and wanting.

When he stood wholly naked before her, her eyes drifted from his honey-eyed gaze down the bulging muscles of his chest and chiseled stomach until her voice hitched at the length of him, hardened and ready. She returned her gaze to his, and he moved in, steadying himself above her as he intentionally removed her clothing, piece by piece. He unfastened metal clasps, pulled away buttons, and tugged loose strings until she lay naked beneath him.

His eyes feasted on the sight of her, her full chest rising and falling with the quickness of her breath. Aurora waited with torturous anticipation while Soren considered where he would start on her writhing body. She gasped as he leaned forward, his warm lips kissing her breast and then wrapping around her hardened nipple. A shudder rippled deep in her stomach. He pulled away just long enough to shift his attention to her other breast and suck the other nipple into his warm mouth.

Aurora's voice hitched and her hands slid through Soren's tousled hair, "Soren ..."

His mouth released her nipple to grin up at her. She held his gaze as he lowered his mouth, soft kisses setting fire to the skin on her stomach. As his mouth hovered above the apex of her open thighs, she his wanting breath caressed her.

Aurora's back arched as Soren dipped his mouth to her. Her fists clenched the sheets as he feasted on her, every movement of his tongue heating her body. Soren moaned as he slipped two fingers inside her, feeling her arousal as his mouth continued to fill her body with pleasure.

Aurora cried out at the sensation and her hands once again found Soren's locks, her hands gripping his head as he worked beneath her. His fingers slid in and out while his mouth gently teased and sucked until she could no longer hold back her release. A powerful sensation tore through her body, and she shuddered at the ecstasy.

Breathlessly, Aurora looked down at Soren, who was kissing the inside of her thighs. He prowled up her body until he held himself over her shaking body. She looked at him with nothing but love and awe blazing in her eyes. He kissed her softly as he entered her, another gasp of pleasure escaping her lips.

Aurora's breath hitched as the size of him filled her. His arms resting next to her shoulders, he held her as he moved slowly and deeply, Aurora's hips moving in rhythm with his. Aurora didn't want it to end.

Soren listened as her breathing increased, and the shudder within her body grew. He quickened his pace, still burying every inch of himself deep within her. Her nails dug into his skin as he brought her to climax once again, sparking to life every nerve ending within her body and exploding in fiery bliss.

Soren watched her gaping mouth and allowed himself his own sweet release. As he slowed, his fingers caressed Aurora's flushed cheeks, and he kissed her again softly. He pulled away and curled around her trembling, glowing body. She wrapped her arms around his and the two silently settled into sleep, smiles lingering on their lips.

CHAPTER 17

Aurora and Soren spent several days tangled up together in the comfort of the isolated cabin. Love and lust simmered in Aurora's body, causing a welcomed distraction from facing the reality of her decision to stay.

Her fingertips lazily traced the lines of Soren's muscles as they bathed in the sunlight filtering through the bedroom window one morning, her finger tracing over the raised lines of his snake tattoo. "What now?" Aurora's voice softly questioned her partner.

A playful smile played on Soren's lips. "I have a few ideas of what I can do to you." His voice sent a shiver down Aurora's spine, imagining all the ways he could please her.

She laughed quietly, "No, I mean, what do I do now that I'm here? Now that I'm staying. Forever." She looked carefully up at him through her bedroom eyes, but the back of her mind considered the reality of her decision, never to return home.

Soren smiled warmly at her. "I suppose we will return to Riverholm. Clara can help you strengthen your ability as an elemental, and we can train."

Aurora searched his eyes. "You want to train me to be a sentinel like you?"

His smile disappeared, but his eyes stayed soft. "Only if you want to. You have a natural talent for battle."

Aurora considered the idea—how she would spend her time riding through the realm with Soren, laughing and spending days protecting the lands. Although something in her stomach churned, she met his gaze. "Okay. I want to train and learn about the fae and the other creatures in this realm. If it means a lifetime with you, then yes."

Soren kissed her softly, and the two fell into a lover's embrace that threatened to hold them captive forever in that cabin.

***

The chill of the northern mountains warmed as Soren and Aurora made their way back south toward Riverholm. With obsidian peaks on her back, Aurora watched the landscape roll into lush, sprawling glens dotted with bright, tiny blooms. The pair took their time, stopping at inns along the way, rushing to bed early, and staying entangled in sheets until the afternoon sun loomed.

Aurora laughed and listened as Soren told her tales of his world and the people and creatures that lived within. She couldn't help but notice a restored balance that hung in the air, the lack of portal energy disturbing the enchanted landscape.

Clara had appeared in the doorway of her cottage as Soren and Aurora posted the horses outside when they returned to Riverholm. Her hazel eyes sparkled as she beheld the pair, and she pulled Aurora into a long hug without a single word. Aurora sunk into the comfort Clara offered.

That night, Soren invited Thorn, Olin, and Clara to dinner at his impressive stone house just outside the village. Aurora spent hours drifting through the halls and rooms of the fortress. Unlike the quiet comfort of Soren's mountain cabin, this home, which Soren called Stonesmoor, loomed over the village, offering security between the people that lived there, and the vastness of what lies beyond.

Aurora had laughed when Soren told her the name of his Riverholm home. "You name your houses? What do you call your mountain cabin?"

Soren's amber eyes flickered, and he replied, "Windflower."

The dinner guests moved between moments of laughter and pure silence as Soren and Aurora regaled them with their journey. And in that simple gathering of friends, Aurora knew, without a doubt, that she was home. A smile brushed the corner of her eyes that sparkled with hope and happiness, and she caught Soren's gaze watching her. He beamed at her as only a knowing lover would do.

***

As seasons cycled through Silverveil, Aurora trained in the ways of an elemental sentinel, and her and Soren's love deepened, growing like the roots of the ancient trees that cradled their secrets.

As Aurora grappled with the enigma of her recently discovered powers, questioning how a mere mortal from the human realm could have such abilities, Thorn had vanished into the labyrinth of his library, intent on uncovering answers. Meanwhile, Clara offered a different perspective, proposing that Aurora's powers were a blessing, perhaps a gift bestowed by the veil itself during her tumultuous journey through it. Soren, however, held a view unburdened by the need for explanations. To him, the origins of her powers were inconsequential. Powers or not, his love for Aurora was unconditional, rooted firmly in the essence of who she was.

Dedicated to her new purpose, Aurora devoted herself to training. Day after day, she and Soren engaged in rigorous sessions, honing her combat skills and delving into the knowledge of the various creatures that posed a threat to the realm's tranquility. Her strength grew with every passing day, thanks to Soren's steadfast love and support.

In the heart of Riverholm, Soren and Aurora created a haven—a sanctuary that symbolized their eternal love and triumph over darkness.

But unknown to the lovers, tendrils of darkness swirled deep within the Silverveil Mountains in the north. There, the dark lord—cursed to rule the bitter lands that only the most dangerous creatures dared to tread—seethed at having lost Isolde, one of his most prized subjects.

Time was slipping through his fingers like grains of sand, each moment bringing him closer to the inevitable, sinister twist his curse would take—a twist that threatened to ripple across the entire realm. The news that reached him was both startling and urgent—a mortal woman, wielding magic potent enough to vanquish Isolde, had appeared. It was a sign he couldn't ignore, a call to action that burned deep within his cursed soul.

He understood, with a clarity that pierced the centuries-old fog of his existence, that everything hinged on this traveler, this unexpected variable in his long, tormented wait. She was the key, the pivot on which the fate of himself and Silverveil precariously balanced. For nearly 500 years, he had endured the curse, and now, finally, the moment he had been waiting for had arrived, brimming with potential.

As Aurora slid into bed next to Soren that night, she remained restless for hours after her lover had drifted off to sleep. Her energy sparked to life within her bones. But not like the ethereal glow that radiated from her after her intimate moment with Soren. This droned and jolted as if it were a warning sound. It unsettled Aurora, but as Soren shifted in his sleep, his arm reached for her, pulling her tight to his chest. There in her lover's arms, Aurora was grateful for the gift of choice and the courage she had to make it.

Epilogue

The news of Isolde's demise at the hands of the traveler tormented him more than he cared to admit. They'd spent centuries together within his mountain palace and although their relationship had soured, he always remained in awe of her raw power and unflinching spirit.

But the promise of the traveler—the human woman from another realm who wielded such power overshadowed his grief. Could she be the one he'd been waiting for? Was she the key to unlocking the chains of his curse? Pacing the halls of his fortress, he tried not to dwell on the notion that she could be the one. He knew he needed to get her to the Northern Shadows to know for sure.

Even then, the rules of his curse were clear. There was only so much he could do. The rest would be in her hands.

That night, he crept down the quiet halls outside Isolde's room. He hadn't been here in years. Hadn't allowed himself.

But as he entered her bedroom, everything was just as he remembered—dark and cold but missing the alluring draw of Isolde's icy magic.

His mind flashed to the day Isolde had arrived at the mountain. She was so young, so inexperienced, and eager to please. He could feel her potential, the power she kept locked inside. She was desperate for attention and approval. For love.

But over time, as he withdrew farther away from her, denying the very thing she wanted most, he'd watched her heart turn to ice, like the magic coursing through her veins. In that, he knew she'd become more powerful, but he'd lose her loyalty to her own desire—an escape. A promise of another chance with someone else, somewhere else.

As the dark lord slid between the plush covers of Isolde's bed, desperately clinging to her scent, the balcony doors drifted open, sending an icy breeze across his pained face. It was the goodbye he needed. He looked at the chandelier hanging low over the bed, adorned with the silk shackles that haunted his dreams. It swayed in the breeze, and he knew that wherever Isolde was, she was free.

***

Camryn's thoughts drifted to Aurora and how scared she must be alone in the woods. *Why did I insist on taking her camping? I know she hates it.* Guilt had been consuming her for weeks, and she could barely keep food down.

She sat on the small bed in the dim room and took deep breaths. Camryn had replayed that night in the woods in her mind over and over, trying to make sense of what happened—she had left the tent to pee and followed the trail to the designated bathroom spot. Only she must have veered from the path because the next thing she knew, she stumbled, and her body was hurled through the air. When she landed, it was in the valley of dark, ominous mountains. Camryn knew at once something was wrong.

She must have fainted, because the next thing she knew, Camryn was being cradled in the arms of a muscular male creature with bright red feathered wings that carried them through a grey sky. As she stirred, he looked down at her with amber eyes, dark wavy locks falling to his chin. His black hair was streaked with strands of red and orange, like fire burning in a night sky. He smiled at her, a brilliant white grin that made her heart flutter before she realized the absurdity of the situation.

Camryn looked down at the ground rushing beneath them and screamed, wrapping her arms around the man's chiseled waist. He chuckled, and she felt the rumble in his chest.

"Where the fuck am I?" she asked.

"You're in Silverveil, darling."

What the hell? Did I die?

Camryn's mind raced as the winged male flew her to a mountain, where they descended deep inside. There, she'd met Lord Arcturus, a powerful fae who ruled the Northern Shadows. She audibly gasped when she laid eyes on his striking figure. His ice-blue eyes, fair skin, and platinum hair were a dizzying mix of harshness and ethereal beauty. He told her she could not return home—she belonged here. Then he locked her away in this room, where she could only leave for dinner and occasional walks in the gardens.

Camryn was sure she was dead and stuck in purgatory, or she was in a medically induced coma, someone having found her body in the woods. She learned that the male who flew her to the mountain was named Caelum, and she wished she could see more of him. Something about him made her more at ease.

She sat cross-legged on the bed. She had to do something—figure out a way to get back to Aurora. To make it home. She was a fighter.

Hot, angry tears rolled down her cheeks when she heard footsteps in the hall. She wiped the wetness from her face and straightened herself, leaping from the bed.

Lord Arcturus strode in, his eyes a burning intensity. "Your friend who was in the woods with you, what was her name?" When Camryn first arrived at the mountain, she told her story to him, hoping he would help her find a way home. But he'd only been interested in keeping her here.

"Aurora, why?" Camryn replied, tilting her chin up.

A sly smile curled on his lips. "It seems she came after you," he said. Camryn's eyes widened. "We better prepare for another guest." With that, Lord Arcturus exited the room, leaving Camryn's mind whirling.

Aurora came after me. She's here. Camryn shivered at the powerful fae's plans to capture her friend, but her heart lunged at the prospect of seeing Aurora again and making plans to get back home. Whatever it takes.

Acknowledgments

I am eternally grateful to everyone who helped birth this book into the universe. I am fortunate to be a part of a wonderful community of book lovers who enjoy escaping to other worlds.

To my husband, I want to express my gratitude for being a constant source of support and security in my life. Your unwavering love has allowed me to be true to myself and pursue my dreams without hesitation. You mean more to me than anything I can put into words. Thank you for keeping hold of me while my head floats to the clouds.

Thank you to my sister, Nikki, who loves books even more than I do. Your guidance and unfiltered insight on how to make this story worth reading was greatly appreciated. I hope you find room on your many bookshelves for it.

Finally, thank you, dear reader, for joining me on this journey. My debut novel was a labor of love and a dream come true. I appreciate you. You can stay connected by following me on TiktTok https://www.tiktok.com/@klpauthor and Instagram https://www.instagram.com/klperleyauthor/.

www.ingramcontent.com/pod-product-compliance
Lightning Source LLC
Chambersburg PA
CBHW031449160726
47994CB00005B/1951